MAKEUP AND MOCHAS
BOOK 3

The Dance For You

NIKKI GRANT

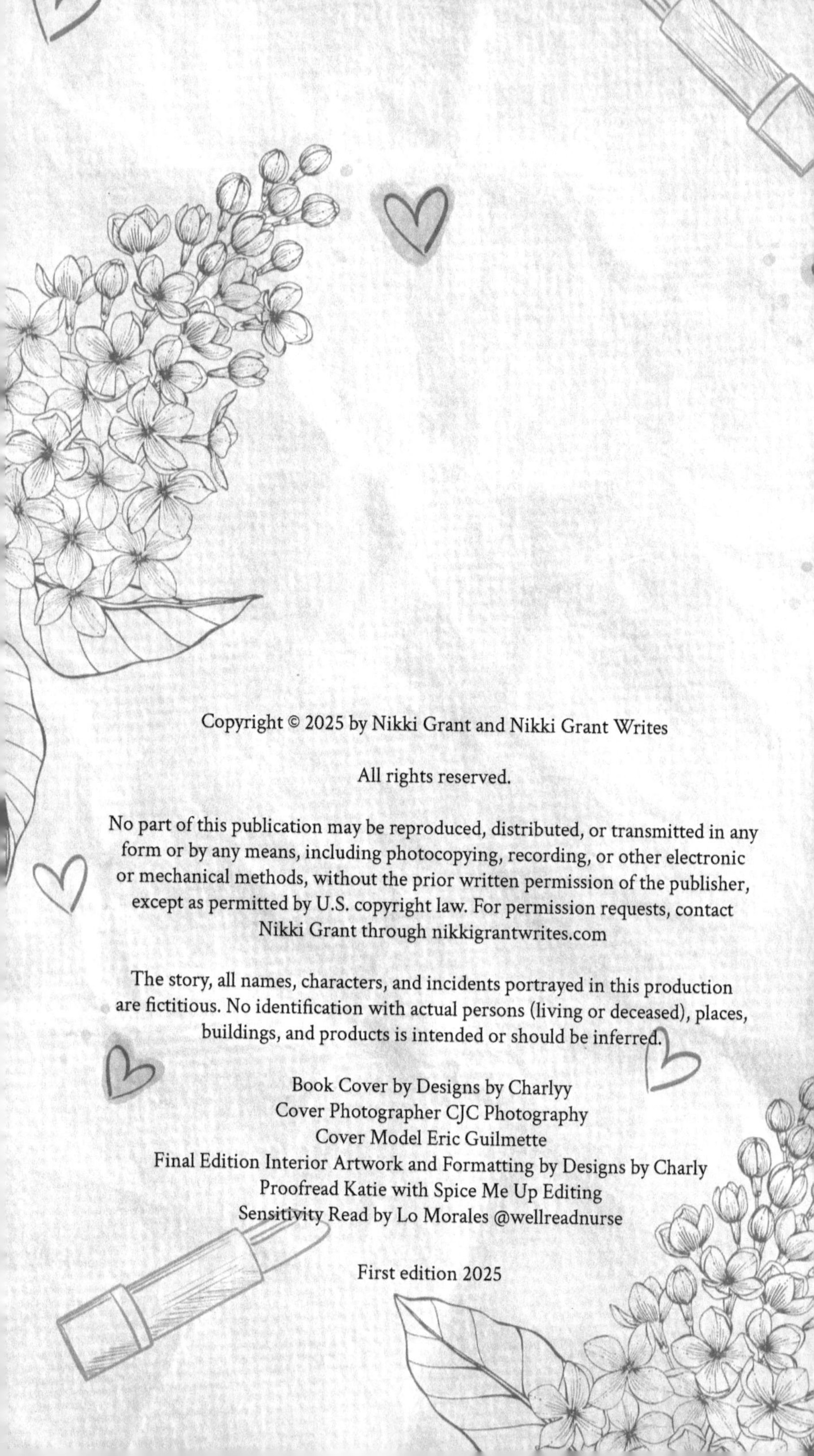

Book Cover by Designs by Charlyy
Cover Photographer CJC Photography
Cover Model Eric Guilmette
Final Edition Interior Artwork and Formatting by Designs by Charly
Proofread Katie with Spice Me Up Editing
Sensitivity Read by Lo Morales @wellreadnurse

First edition 2025

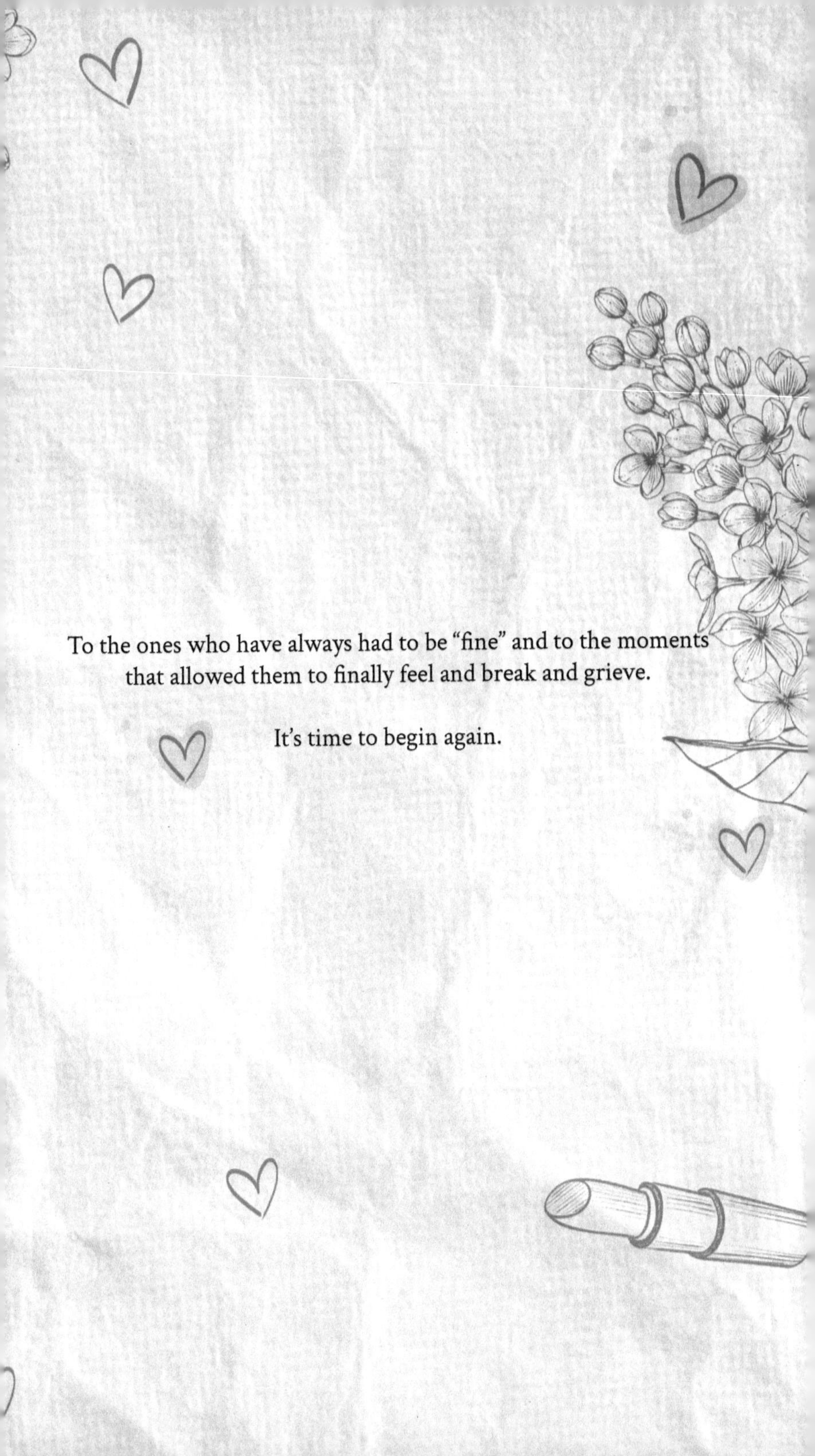

To the ones who have always had to be "fine" and to the moments that allowed them to finally feel and break and grieve.

It's time to begin again.

LETTER FROM THE AUTHOR

Welcome to book three in the Makeup and Mochas series. This book brought out a lot more emotion and vulnerability than I thought would happen, but I am thankful for every moment. Kylie's story of PCOS is very similar to my own. This medical diagnosis looks so different for each person that deals with it, and you will probably find some things you have seen before and maybe something you didn't know could be a byproduct of a PCOS diagnosis. I am thankful for my two PCOS babies, but I know that isn't the case for everyone. Kylie goes through the full range of emotions with her infertility journey and that is shown heavily on page. Take your time going through this if needed and know that your journey, no matter how you got there or where you ended up, is valid and beautiful. You are seen and you are loved.

There are also a lot of very personal moments for me in this story. I had originally mapped out this book two years ago (surprise!) and was hoping to make this a final goodbye to a family member I wasn't allowed to fully grieve. Last summer a lot of that was completely upended. I decided to still include those moments in this book as they are still so precious to me. Authors tend to pour a lot of themselves in their work, and this book is no different. Whereas this was supposed to be a final goodbye, now it's an acknowledgment and another step in my own healing process.

Thank you for taking the time to read.

Love and sparkles,
Nikki

CHAPTER BREAKDOWN (WHERE TW AND CW HAPPEN)

Feel free to skip this page if you want to go in completely blind. This list is here for you to use as you see fit. The chapters are also listed so you can skip certain things if you want or need to.

Cheating (not between MMC or FMC)
*FMCs partner at the beginning of the book
Ch 13, 21, 38/39

Gaslighting, Manipulation
Ch 7, 9, 12, 15, 17, 25, 27, 32, 36, 38

PCOS (including hospital and doctor visits)
Ch 3, 15, 23, 29, 37

Infertility
Ch 4, 23, 25, 27, 37, 39

OW Drama
Ch 13, 20, 21, 25, 27, 39 (resolution)

Coercion into sexual activity (inability to consent/consent denial)
Ch 5

Sexually Explicit Scenes (all - everything from make out sessions to intercourse)
Ch 5, 30/31, 33, 34, 35

Sexually Explicit Scenes between other partners besides final FMC/MMC
Ch 5, 21

Physical Altercation
Ch 23/24

Pregnancy as a result of cheating (not FMC)
Ch 38, 39

**Adult Language and Alcoholic Beverages used throughout
but sparingly**

**Excessive coffee/tea, social media references, and social
media content throughout**

Kylie experiences anxiety, depression, grief, internal doubt, and
mourning throughout the book. It is a raw expression of her
PCOS, infertility, and relationship journey.

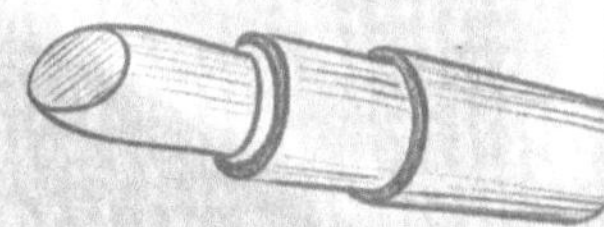

PLAYLIST

Full playlist can be found on Spotify - here's the highlights.
Love Myself by Hailee Steinfeld
it's time to go by Taylor Swift
tolerate it by Taylor Swift
Lego Blocks by Neriah
To the Moon by Meghan Trainor
you broke me first by Tate McRae
You're Losing Me by Taylor Swift
Second Choice by Audriix
I Forgot That you Existed by Taylor Swift
Middle Fingers by Aston
Lips are Movin by Meghan Trainor
Me Too by Meghan Trainor
Dance the Night by Dua Lipa
I Can Do It With a Broken Heart by Taylor Swift
Vigilante Shit by Taylor Swift
Ghost Town by Benson Boone
W.I.T.C.H. by Devon Cole
Karma by Taylor Swift
Bad Blood (Taylor's Version) by Taylor Swift
I Shot Cupid by Stela Cole
You Problem by emlyn, Cloudy June
We are Never Ever Getting Back Together (Taylor's Version) by
Taylor Swift
Really Don't Care by Demi Lovato, Cher Lloyd
Happier than Ever by Billie Eilish
SexyBack by Justin Timberlake, Timbaland
Whoops by Meghan Trainor
Burning Down by Alex Warren
Forever by Chris Brown
Honey Bee by Blake Shelton

VLOG POST NUMBER ONE

I have a hard time writing things on paper. And with everything that has happened in the last year, my therapist recommended I start a journal.

I've bought so many lovely books to write in, and my best friend even gave me a few to try too. And none of them felt right.

So, I decided to create a private video channel. Just for me. Somewhere to process my thoughts and emotions.

All the hurt and betrayal.

All the promises broken.

Those I know about and those I haven't yet discovered.

Maybe I will be able to understand what went wrong.

What did I do wrong?

And do I even want to fix it?

I don't understand.

Hopefully, this will help.

So anyway, thanks for being the space where I can pour my heart out to.

I guess, here is my story.

Signing off for now,
Kylie

Chapter One

EIGHT YEARS AGO, 22

KYLIE

STRAWBERRY LEMON DROP VODKA MARTINI
Social Post: It's girls' night out with my bestie!! #justus #coloradogirls #collegegrads
Image Description: My red lipstick sitting open on the bathroom counter.

There's something absolutely mesmerizing about a bartender who knows what they are doing. I'm sitting at the bar, sipping on something with vodka in it with my best friend, Sasha. I'm two drinks in, and both times, we've asked the bartender to make us something yummy and fruity, and he has done an excellent job at doing just that each time. Hence me not knowing what I'm drinking. Watching him be so at ease in conversation with every patron, seamlessly handle every interaction, and tossing glasses and bottles around like it's his job—well, I guess, it is his job—is sexier than it should be. I must be staring because the next thing I know, he's looking at me with a knowing smirk and shooting a wink in my direction. I quickly turn my head to look at Sasha, my cheeks heating in embarrassment, but she just laughs.

"What did you think was going to happen? You've been undressing him with your eyes for the last hour," she whispers to me, and I playfully smack her leg to subtly tell her to be quiet. Not subtle, though, because the motion causes my heel to slip from the bar stool and I not so graciously fall off it. I'm able to catch myself before I face-plant the floor, but I do manage to knock both of our drinks over. It's a sticky mess and wasted money.

I reach for the napkins only to have the handsome bartender's hands collide with mine as he wipes down the bar top with a dry towel.

"Note to self, ask you to go dancing before we hit the bar, good to know."

And with another wink and a fresh glass of water, I am absolutely smitten.

SIX YEARS AGO, 24

Did I envision myself as a waitress at a restaurant when I enrolled in college? Absolutely not. Do I absolutely love it now that I'm doing it? Absolutely yes! And being able to work alongside Carter is definitely a perk. We've been dating for two years, and being with him is just easy. We've fallen into a routine together. Work, hang out after work, and date night once a week. I graduated just weeks before we met at the bar he was working at, and then we were both able to get jobs at a new restaurant opening up in town. They're closed on Mondays and Tuesdays, so our schedules are pretty consistent.

I'm sitting at the end of the bar enjoying a very large plate of ziti and meatballs, waiting for Carter to get done with his shift so we can spend some time together before we head home. I love watching him work. The skill and ease with which he does his job was what first caught my eye two years ago, and it still fascinates me. I've tried learning how to do what he does, but I ended up with more broken glasses than liquid in glasses, so I leave the mixology to him. I chuckle at the memory and shake my head. Graceful, I am not.

"What's so funny over there?" Carter asks as he sets a new glass of water in front of me. I am horrible about remembering to drink enough water, so it's normal for him to hand me a fresh glass whenever he has a moment to chat.

"Just remembering my first attempt at being a bartender." He muffles his own laugh as he tosses a bar towel on his shoulder.

"You sure looked cute though." His smile is bright, and I can't help but return my own. "I get off in about ten minutes, and then I need to clean up here. Max should be in the back clocking in now, so once he's out here, I'm good to go. Do you want to do anything in particular tonight?"

"Can we go watch the line dancing? They're practicing next door and have some spots open for spectators." I'm hopeful with my ask. I may not be graceful and cannot keep a rhythm or beat to save my life, but I love watching. And being in Northern Colorado, you'd be surprised how many opportunities to watch different dance troupes there are.

"Just watching?" Carter is as apprehensive as I am about participation, but he puts up with my fascination.

"Just watching," I confirm what he already knows.

"Why don't you let me put your leftovers in the fridge so you can eat this later and go grab us some seats? I'll be over there soon." I squeal in excitement before I hop off the stool and take my plate to him. After a quick kiss, he is still on the clock after all, I shrug on my jacket and make my way to the dance studio next door.

FOUR YEARS AGO, 26

"To one big happy family!" I raise my champagne glass and clink it with Sasha's and Carter's. We are at a fancy dinner—okay, well, it's real plates and linen napkins, so fancy enough—to celebrate our new apartment. It was time for us to be full-on adults, so we've been going around town for the last six months looking at places. We went as far as an hour away but finally found a place in Windsor. Parking is going to be fun with three of us and only two designated spots. But it's two bedrooms, two bathrooms, and plenty of living space for us. And Sasha has her required big window so she can film makeup content. And I have a space in our bedroom that Carter is going to help me turn into a reading nook.

"It's only the three of us, babe." Carter presses a soft kiss to my temple as he sets his champagne glass down on the table.

"I know that. But it's ours. And we have our own place. It's so perfect, and we're finding out what our paths are going to be now that we're adults. It's exciting. And I'm going to celebrate it. Even if it's small and something we are supposed to be doing anyway. I love you both so much. I can't imagine doing life with anyone else." I've had too much to drink already tonight because I'm getting teary-eyed.

Alcohol makes me sad, so I don't drink much. Carter has gotten really creative with the mocktails for me. I love what he's come up with. But I figured tonight called for champagne. And I might have done a bit of pre-gaming at the house, trying my hand at mixology again so I could surprise Carter later. After a quarter of a bottle of vodka being poured out because I kept messing it up, I resigned myself to the fact that this is his specialty and not mine. I'll find mine eventually.

"Okay, time to eat our weight in calamari!" Carter pats my leg lightly underneath the table, a subtle reminder to keep my voice down. I don't realize how loud I get sometimes, so I asked him to help me. This isn't a sports bar on a Friday night close to the college campus. And my overexcited tipsy self needs to remember that.

TWO YEARS AGO, 28

"Sasha, can you let me know the next time you are heading up to Ulta? I need to get some more setting spray and maybe some new things for my hair. I don't want to cut it yet, but I'm dying at the restaurant." I let my purse fall to the floor next to the little table by the front door. I'm exhausted. I tend to feel less tired when I have more customers. On nights like tonight, where there aren't many tables to tend to, it's harder to stay busy. I'm so ready for bed. Sasha is sitting on the couch editing videos, and the exhaustion is clear on her face, too.

"How was your walk? Do you feel better now?" I push my own tiredness to the back—she needs someone listening to her right now. I have Carter to vent to. She's got me. She had texted me to say that she was frustrated and needed to take a walk, but I know she needs to talk something out. I go to the couch and settle in the seat next to her, twisting my torso to face her.

"A little. I lost an entire thirty-minute makeup tutorial and had a panic attack over it. Being outside helped, but I need to map some things out so I can turn this into more than a hobby. I'm giving myself until the beginning of December to be bringing money in with this, or I'm hitting that Pivot button."

"We have a Pivot button?!" I smile wide with as much sarcasm as I can muster and have to stifle the laughter at the deadpan look she gives me in response.

"You know what I mean, babe. I can't keep killing myself trying to do everything. I'm exhausted and can't fully appreciate the makeup content or focus on my job because I'm thinking about engagement or who to reach out to next. I don't even remember the last time I was able to go out and just enjoy myself—or go out on a date."

"I get it. Let me know if you need to talk anything out. I'm always happy to be used as a product model. You do magic on my face." I pat the couch next to me before standing to head to the room I share with Carter at the end of the hall. "I'm going to go shower before Carter gets home. He's off in like ten minutes and is bringing dinner home."

I stop at the door to my room and make sure Sasha is looking at me. I may not know everything, but I know what she needs to hear when she's spiraling. We've been friends for a long time.

"You're gonna do this, Sasha, and we are here to celebrate you every step of the way. Don't stress about all the details tonight. You've got to work in the morning, and you need your beauty rest if you are going to be able to treat Frank with all the grace and kindness you want tomorrow." Her boss is a total (insert derogatory word of choice here). Seriously though, I change how I refer to him regularly, so I've just come to associate his name with a derogatory term.

I take a quick shower but don't rush too much. I need to do a deep condition on my hair tonight. Having my hair up in a ponytail most days of the week takes its toll on my long brown hair. Add in the grease and the sweat—it's not a pretty picture. The products do their job and they make my hair smell good, too. Carter picked out this strawberry shampoo and conditioner a few years ago, and I haven't switched since then. It works well and isn't fifty dollars a bottle.

The rest of the night goes pretty normally for us. Carter comes home with dinner, and we spend over an hour going through options with Sasha. The three of us work well together. And I love being here to support my best friend as she takes ownership of what she loves. As Carter and I get ready for bed, the silence between us is comfortable. I'm in our bathroom going through my nighttime skincare routine—thank you, Sasha—when Carter comes in and stands behind me. He just smiles at me softly in the mirror as I finish applying my eye cream and lip mask.

"What's that little smile for?" I ask as I put my containers into the drawer.

"I love seeing you support Sasha in her goals. I know it's not your passion, too, but you're always there to listen and offer help where you can."

"And you don't mind the discounted skincare and makeup she gets sent on occasion, which I get to take advantage of either, do you?" I tilt my head to the side so he can rest his chin on my shoulder and wrap his arms around my waist. He places a gentle kiss where my neck meets my shoulder and then up to just below my ear.

"I'm not complaining about that. I do hate that you goop up your face right before bed, though. Kissing all of that off you is not an enjoyable experience." He chuckles into my neck, and I playfully bat his hand away.

"We both have to be at work early tomorrow. But I have no problem taking it off if you want to do something about it," I tease back, leaning against the counter facing him.

"Let's head to bed. I just need to hold you tonight, if you're okay with that. We can plan something fun on our next day off together when Sasha is working. I have a meeting with Shaun tomorrow to go over some things about the restaurant—he's talking about some expansions and wanted to chat through potential job opportunities with me."

"Does that mean a promotion?" I'm hopeful with my words. Bartending is an art to Carter, and he does it so well. But he wants a bit more responsibility and ownership compared to what he does at the restaurant. He's been there for almost six years.

"Don't get too excited; it hasn't happened yet." He places a soft kiss on my forehead and then turns on the fan on his side of the bed so we can have some white noise. And it isn't long at all before I'm snuggled into his side, falling to sleep with the comfort of the normalcy of it all.

Chapter Two

KYLIE

STRAWBERRY BASIL LEMONADE

Social Post: One perk of being roommates with a makeup/beauty influencer? I get a bunch of new stuff to try! Look at the new lip glosses that just came in from Natalie's summer collection. Now to pick which one to wear to work tonight. #natalie #sashaloveslipstick #lippies #sparkles Image Description: Flat lay of four lip gloss containers on my bathroom counter.

The summer goes by with a new excitement. Sasha is actively growing her platform, and I've been able to help her with some behind-the-scenes things when I'm not working. It gives me something to do with Carter's added hours at the restaurant. And I love getting to see her light up with her finding her passion. She generally has to be pulled out of her shell gently, and Matt does that beautifully for her, even in the few short weeks he's known her. His younger sister, Ashley, has also been around. She's being mentored by Sasha, and the two of them are working together.

Sasha asked me last week if I wanted to be more involved in their campaigns and what they are growing on social media, but I declined. Makeup and skincare are definitely her and Ashley's passions, but they're not mine. If I start something like that, having a social media presence and a growing brand, I want it to be something I can fully stand behind. And that doesn't feel authentic to me. Sure, I love makeup and getting dressed up, but teaching others about products or techniques isn't my strong suit. I'd much rather get cozy in a corner under a blanket with a book and a cup of tea.

Fall quickly approaches, which means college kids coming back to the area. Therefore, nights at the restaurant get busier with those legally able to drink, and during the days are busier with diners taking advantage of the free Wi-Fi. We are about twenty minutes from most college campuses; yes, there are multiple close by. But there are plenty of students who come here to work. There are coffee shops close by and smaller libraries, plenty of places to hang out and get work done without being on campus.

It's not unusual for me to get to the restaurant around ten a.m. to help with lunch prep and see students waiting in their cars for us to open the doors at eleven. There's a coffee shop right down the road. I will never understand why they prefer to sit in their cars scrolling on social media instead enjoying the fresh air and sunshine. One major perk of Colorado? It's sunny over three hundred days every year. So, the seasonal depression really only hits in January and February. Luckily, we are still firmly in summer.

I'm working an opposite shift from Carter today. With him taking over more bar responsibilities, it's becoming our normal. It took a bit to get used to the new schedules, but it's working for us. Right now, I work most days from ten to eight, with Mondays and Tuesdays off. And sometimes Thursday too, depending on how the week is going. Sundays, I only work until six, so those are my easy days where I get to help Carter with bar inventory when I'm done with my tables.

Carter is working from three in the afternoon until after midnight every day except Sunday. He gets off around ten on those nights, usually. At least we still have some overlap in our shifts and can sometimes take a break together. Both the restaurant and bar are fully staffed, which means we have a little bit of flexibility there. It's a Thursday, which means it's generally pretty slow. I'm able to work ahead on my tasks so that when it's time, I'll be able to head out pretty quickly. By the looks of things, I may be able to be out of here before it gets dark.

I tighten my ponytail and head over to the bar to touch base with Carter once he gets in. I give him a quick kiss on the cheek while he preps fruit for drinks.

"Hey, beautiful. How's your shift been so far?" He smiles at me before returning his attention to the cutting board in front of him. I pull the container of strawberries out of the sink and set them on the towel next to him so he can have easy access to them when he's ready.

"It's been pretty good. Slow. I've only had a few tables since the lunch rush cleared out. I'm guessing it's going to be a slow afternoon, but it's hard to tell. Is there anything happening downtown tonight?"

"I'm not sure. I forgot to check the community calendar before setting the schedule this week. Do you want to look real quick while you're still here and let me know?" Windsor is a fairly standard small town, which means that there are periodically different events happening in the evenings during the summer. We have a pretty large farmers' market every weekend, but the nightly events in August are a fun transition from summer to fall.

"It looks like there's a kids' event with a local author tonight at the library. Nothing else that should impact our foot traffic." I pocket my phone again and take a look at my tables across the room. I only have a table of two businessmen who are enjoying a lengthy business meeting. I'm not sure how much business is being discussed at this point, though. I cleared their plates an hour ago and have just been walking by to refill glasses and see if they want anything to snack on.

"Who is working behind the bar with you tonight?" I ask Carter as I swap out the full container for an empty one as he keeps slicing the fruit in front of him.

"I think I just have Max with me tonight. And then I have Chelsea on the floor tonight who I can call back here if things get crazy."

"How has she been doing with picking things up?" Chelsea started working here this summer as a waitress and then quickly started learning skills behind the bar. She's getting good at juggling all the craziness between restaurant orders and those who sit at the bar wanting to talk and nurse a drink for hours while watching a game. More of her shifts are being scheduled as a bartender and not just backup, and she seems to be enjoying it. You could tell that being on the floor wasn't her happy place, or maybe it was just working alongside other women. I'm honestly not sure.

"She's doing well. She likes it a lot and has been asking about adding in some more elaborate or seasonal cocktails. Every bar around here has the same local beers. So she wants to see what we can do to get people in for something new besides the consistency of the food and the chill atmosphere." Carter closes the last container and begins cleaning his space as a group of ladies come in—probably a late lunch after a downtown shopping trip by the looks of their bags. I squeeze his arm before grabbing a handful of menus and going to greet the women.

By the end of my shift, I am completely worn out. I don't know if I'm fighting off being sick or if there's some weird pressure changes happening, but I am beat. I clean off my last table and then head to the back to clock out before I go see Carter. Some nights, I stay until he's done, but I don't have it in me tonight. He's chatting with a regular at the bar when I get there, so I wait for a break in the conversation before I let him know I'm heading home.

"Are you all right? You look a little off." Carter picks up on my state very quickly.

"Yeah, just tired. I need a hot shower and some comfy jammies, and I'm sure I'll be fine. I might be getting sick, or my body is just being problematic. I'm set to start in the next day or so. Sometimes my body gets weird before that happens." Carter sets a soft kiss to my forehead, examining my face to make sure I'm not downplaying things.

"Okay, are you good to drive home, or do you need to call Sasha?"

"I should be fine. I'll text you when I get home. Will you be off at midnight tonight, or will it be later?"

"Probably close to midnight. I have some things to go over with Max and Chelsea as we start preparing for a new college semester. We need to make sure we are ready for the increased traffic and potential fake IDs. Text me if you need me to grab anything on the way home." I shoot him a quick smile and make my way outside.

The cramping starts before I even get to my car. I seriously hate my body sometimes. I've had bad periods since I was a teenager, and they haven't gotten any better. They were manageable for several years, thanks to birth control, but two months ago, my doctor needed to switch me to something else. So now the cramping and moodiness are back with a vengeance. I may need to call out tomorrow or Saturday if I don't get on top of this, which I hate doing. I don't want it to reflect badly on Carter.

I make it home fairly quickly and then make quick work of prepping the shower, my aromatherapy steamer on the floor and my diffuser going in my room for after. I've found a few things that help with some symptoms, but I need to buckle down and be ready to spend most of tomorrow in bed. Yay me.

The next morning, I'm woken when Carter closes the bedroom door, holding my heating pad and a cup of tea. And a book. I smile as I try to sit up and quickly have to roll to my side.

"My uterus feels like it's going to explode," I groan into my pillow as Carter plugs in the heating pad and sets it under the blanket.

"How long do we need to keep doing this before your doctor puts you on something that works? I know they just switched things a couple of months ago, but how long do we need to wait this out?" Carter hates seeing me like this. And I hate that I'm causing him this much worry.

"Six months."

"I don't know if I can watch this happen for another four months, babe. This isn't normal. Is there seriously nothing they can do for this?" Carter smooths my hair back from my face and then hands me a couple of pills. I don't usually take anything on an empty stomach, but I can't wait until I feel well enough for food today. There are a few crackers on my nightstand that I can munch on when I'm ready.

I down the pills and take a sip of water before I answer him. "Welcome to being a woman, Carter. Symptoms are dismissed and put into wide-spread categories. The only thing that might help is if I were to get pregnant. And I don't really love the idea of getting pregnant just for the possibility of feeling better for a year or so. I want to have babies with you when we are both ready, not just as a fix for the pain."

Carter sits for a minute, thinking things over before he answers.

"We've talked about it. You're twenty-eight, Ky, we can start trying. Sasha is getting established with her role. It may be time for us to start looking for that next chapter." He has a smile in his voice with his suggestion. We have talked about it. I want to be a mom before I turn thirty. And I want to raise little ones with Carter.

"Can we talk about it when I'm not dying?" I laugh in response. Now is not the time to decide to procreate.

Carter chuckles and places another kiss on my temple. "For sure, love. Get some rest. I already told the restaurant that you won't be in today. Take the day and do what you need. I'll be here until two, and Sasha should be home just after that. I'm going to go work on stuff in the main room, but I'll come check on you in a bit. Text me if you need me, okay? And after this cycle is over, let's look at that baby option." He winks at me and then heads out.

I don't even bother to hide the obnoxious smile on my face. I may not be preparing to grow a makeup empire like Sasha and Ashley, but I am so ready to be a momma. And it may be just around the corner.

Kylie

Chapter Three

KYLIE

CARAMEL BRÛLÉE FRAP

Social Post: I think there needs to start being a "waitress approved" tag on makeup products when shopping online. #waitressthings #motd #makeuplook
Image Description: Variety of makeup products on my bathroom counter.

We ended up deciding to "stop preventing" instead of full-on trying to get pregnant. At least for a little bit. The relief of stopping birth control was bigger than I was expecting. My hormones have been all over the place since I stopped. It's only been four weeks, but I'm hopeful that things will even out soon. And if I get pregnant, great. The doctor said it might take a while for my body to get back to its baseline, so we can start tracking things and actively try to conceive. But for now, we get to enjoy being together. No pressure, no ovulation tests, just us. And it's kind of nice.

The big downside—I have absolutely no idea when my next period is going to be. So, my bag is always ready with an extra pair of underwear and a variety of feminine products. Seriously, why do we call tampons and pads 'feminine care'? How are those things feminine? Oh yeah, my attention span is completely shot. My doctor said it's my hormones regulating. Which would also explain my fatigue and bloating.

The hardest part is not having someone to talk to about this. Carter asked that we keep this between us for now. Not telling Sasha is killing me, but I don't want her getting her hopes up for this before it's time. And she's doing so much with her social media with Ashley right now. They are preparing for a massive campaign next month for local women-owned businesses and charities. I don't need to split her focus.

I get ready for my shift at the restaurant, checking to see if Sasha has left me any notes on new products I need to try out this week. She gives me new things most weeks now and asks me to check the wear with working at the restaurant. Restaurant-proof makeup is surprisingly hard to find. So, I get to be the guinea pig. Today, she has a new primer and setting spray for me to test out—normal makeup routine outside of that. Easy enough.

Ten minutes later, I've taken some photos for her to see the before. All those selfies in high school are really proving to be beneficial now. I chuckle to myself before sending her the pictures.

Me: Thanks so much for the new goodies. The primer took a while to dry down, and I didn't love how it laid over my SPF. Definitely curious to see how it holds up today. The setting spray went on well. It's definitely a shake before applying type of product though.

Sasha: Perfect. Thanks for letting me know. I'm so glad you went with the pink eyeshadow look today! Your eyes look incredible today! Kisses!

Me: LOL, thanks, Sash. Have a good day, and I'll see you tonight.

It turns out this primer and setting spray are not sweat-proof. I take a picture for Sasha four hours later, and half my makeup has melted off. And I'm super blotchy. Which is just really odd for me. I have a makeup remover cloth in my bag, and I end up just removing everything. Going makeup-free will impact my tips, but looking like I just stood in the oven for an hour with blotchy makeup is worse. I put on a bit of moisturizer and touch up my perfume and hair before leaving the bathroom. I practically run into Carter on my way back to the dining room.

"Oh, hey, babe. How's Chelsea doing at the bar tonight?" I take advantage of the quick moment with him in the middle of the crazy of tonight.

"She's doing well. First night with her taking the lead. Max is assisting, and neither have had to call me out there to handle anything. How are you? You feeling okay?" He looks me over like something is wrong, and then I realize my face is probably a little red still.

"Yeah, I'm good. I just needed to take my makeup off. Sasha had me testing some new products, and they weren't holding up well." I pop up onto my tiptoes to give him a kiss, but someone drops a glass or something in the kitchen, and something shatters. Carter turns his head, and I stumble as I startle from the noise.

"I'm okay!" someone shouts from the kitchen, and laughter

follows. Carter looks down at me and smiles before he takes my hand and gives it a gentle squeeze.

"Let me know if you need anything. I'm going to be in the office tonight, but I'll come check on things when dinner rush starts."

"Okay, don't have too much fun without me." I do my best to act playful, but I am not feeling it. It's too hot back here. I squeeze his hand back and head to the dining room. My one table of diners has packed up and left while I was in the back, and I don't have a new group yet, so I go grab some water from the bar while I wait. A few minutes later, a group of college-aged guys comes in and moves right for the bar. I quickly scoot out of the way. I am not a bartender, and being behind the bar with a group of people talking all at once is a recipe for disaster if I'm involved.

Chelsea and Max are busy at work behind the bar, and I have new diners to take care of. Three more hours to go, and then I can put my feet up and read in Carter's office until he gets off work. I can do this. The dinner rush ends up being a little late tonight, and so I don't end up stopping until nearly nine. My ankles are swollen, and my lower back is killing me. I probably haven't had enough water tonight. I head to the bar to get a drink before I go close out my last table.

"You feeling okay, babe?" Chelsea asks, and I know I must look like absolute trash if she's asking me that. I wouldn't say that we are friends, but I try to establish a relationship with others in the restaurant. We spend so much time together. I've just never quite hit it off with her for some reason.

"Yeah, just a little warm and sore. I was not prepared for that level of busy-ness tonight. Can I get a glass of water? Then I need to go close out that last table. How was it over here tonight?" Chelsea fills a glass for me before passing it over the bar. There's a stack of empty containers in the sink that were full of fruit at the beginning of the shift, so it looks like they were fairly busy, too.

"Nothing too crazy. Max was out here with me the whole time. Carter had to come out twice to help get the new keg going and more glasses. I can move the half kegs on my own, but the full ones are a bit much for me."

"That's what we have these big strong men for though, right?"

I make sure to say it loud enough for Max to hear me, and he plays into it perfectly, flexing his muscles and picking up the case of beer from the floor to show off said muscles. We laugh, along with the two girls that are sitting at the bar, obviously enjoying the eye candy. "Thanks for the drink, Chelsea. I'll check in once I finish up. Is Carter in the office?"

"Yeah. He had a few purchase receipts to input, and then I think he was going to come out and help us finish out the cleanup for the night."

"Perfect." The next thirty minutes is a blur of cleaning rags, receipts, and splitting tips before I'm finally able to head to Carter's office. Luckily, there's a couch in his office, and I am desperately ready to use it. Carter still has a couple of hours before he is going to be able to leave. I make a quick stop to the kitchen to get a mug of hot water. It's definitely a tea night, and I have a stash of my favorites in the office. We don't serve hot tea at the restaurant, but I'm hooked on it. Coffee in the morning to get me going and then tea for the rest of the day, and always when I'm reading. I decide on a mint green tea for tonight. The smell instantly settles me as I bundle up under a lap blanket on the couch. There are definitely a few perks to Carter's promotion.

I'm woken up by a kiss on my forehead. I must have dozed off. "What time is it?" I ask before I fully open my eyes. I know it's late. The last check I remember on my phone was quarter to midnight.

"It's a little after one. Are you ready to go home?" Carter's voice is quiet as he walks across the room to set some papers on his desk.

"Yeah, what happened out there? It wasn't that busy when I came back before ten." I stand and fold my blanket as I straighten up the space I had taken over while I waited for Carter.

"I had to go over some of those new fall drink specials with Max. Chelsea came up with a few things, and we are adding two new drinks to the menu this fall. We had some practice time with those and had to decide how prep was going to work. And then I had to order a few new items too. I should be able to leave on time tomorrow since we got so much done tonight, though."

"Oh, good. Yes, let's go home. I need a shower."

"I think you may want to check with Sasha on that makeup again, too. I think you may be having a reaction to one of those new things." Carter looks me over with concern in his voice.

"Reaction? What do you mean?"

"It just looks like a bit of acne by your chin. Nothing major, but I'm not sure whether it was one of the new products she gave you or not. I know you take good care of your skin, so that's not normal for you." He takes my hand, and we begin heading to the car. The restaurant is quiet and only has the bar lights on. We are the only ones still here.

"I haven't had a breakout in years. I wonder if it may have something to do with coming off the birth control."

"Hormones are weird." We both laugh at that statement, and Carter places a soft kiss on my forehead as we get to the car.

"That they are. But hopefully, things even out in a few months." I smile up at him. He's not too much taller than me, but enough that I have to tilt my head a bit to meet his eyes. I love the way he looks at me. Like I'm his.

"Crossing all the fingers and wishing on all the stars, my love. And maybe we can start looking at houses this winter—one step closer to our happily ever after."

"That sounds perfect."

"You're perfect."

"Okay, that was cheesy, even for you." I laugh again as I sit in the passenger's seat, and Carter walks around to the driver's side.

"Yeah, but you liked it." The smirk in his eyes is knowing. We still find joy in the cheesy things together, and I love that he still makes me smile.

"Very much. Okay, take me home, Prince Charming."

"As you wish."

Kylie

Chapter Four

KYLIE

CHAMOMILE TEA MOCKTAIL

Social Post: In my feels today and thankful for the little things that bring a smile to my face. #cozyday #giftsfromhim
Image description: New book, hair ties, and candy from Carter.

A week later, I'm in the bathroom, trying to figure out what I can possibly do to cover up this acne. It has gotten so bad in the last week, and I know it has to do with my hormones. I can barely put any makeup on it, but I cannot go to work like this. I had a full breakdown last night when I got home from work. A customer made a comment about my face not being very attractive, "with all that red mess all over it," and, "aren't you a bit old for acne?" Apparently not, sir. I appreciate the feedback, though. Have a nice day. Ugh. I hate this. I ended up sending a message to my doctor to see if we can rerun my hormone tests a bit early.

A soft knock on the door gives me a quick minute to take a breath before I crack it open. Carter is on the other side, a soft smile on his face. "So, I went out and grabbed you a few things. I hate seeing you this upset, and I want to try to help where I can." He passes me the bag and then steps into the bathroom with me. Inside are a candy bar, a pack of gum, a new romance novel, a new pack of scrunchies, and a pregnancy test. I jerk my head up to look at him when I see the box.

"What is this for?"

"With you being off birth control, we don't know when you are ovulating. This may be the cause of the acne and bloating. Timing-wise, it's a possibility. You don't have to take the test if you don't want to. But if we know for sure, we can make a plan from there."

I take a few deep breaths. It's just a test. I can do this.

"How are you going to feel if it's positive?" I can't help but ask the question.

"I'll be excited about this new chapter with you. And I think you are going to make a stunning pregnant woman." He places a kiss on my temple and then steps out of the bathroom.

"Okay, let's pee on a stick," I mumble to myself and then take everything out of the package. Turns out, it's harder to do than you would think. But I finally figured out the best way to angle myself to make it happen. I leave the test on the counter and head into the bedroom to pick out my jewelry for the day. At least my outfit is pretty easy since it's the same thing every day—jeans or khaki pants and a black polo shirt.

"Did you do it?" Carter asks as he sets a cup of coffee on my vanity.

"Yep, it should be done in about two minutes. I couldn't sit in there and wait for it to tell me."

"I get it. And no matter what, I'm happy. I love you. We'll figure this out. I just hate seeing you hurting and not feeling good. You are beautiful, and I hate that someone told you otherwise last night."

"Can I keep you?" I tilt my head to look up at him, and he smiles back at me.

"Forever and always."

Nothing prepares you for that first negative pregnancy test. Or the second. Or the third. Even when you aren't "trying to get pregnant," seeing that negative brings on a wild mix of emotions. The bit of relief in knowing that you have a little more time, the questioning if you are doing something wrong or if your body isn't doing what it's supposed to, and then the sadness because you dared to get your hopes up. I let myself feel relief the first time. I wasn't really ready to be a mom. There was so much up in the air with Carter's new position, Sasha with all her stuff, and then my body figuring out how to do things normally after coming off medications.

The second test was a mix of emotions. I let myself cry that time. And Carter sat and held me while I cried. I could tell he was disappointed too, but he didn't tell me he was. He wants to be a dad just as much as I want to be a mom. The doctor told me that it could be up to a year before we conceived. They don't do further testing until we hit that mark. I can't see me going through this range of emotions for a full year, but hopefully it doesn't take that long.

The third test was defeat. I know it's only been three months. I know that. For some women it takes years and they're able to conceive. Three months isn't that long. But for some reason, I had it in my head that it wouldn't take me that long. I take care of my body. I'm in good shape. I eat well. I sleep well. I'm in a long-term relationship. Why isn't this working? I took the third test while Carter was in the shower. I needed a moment where he wasn't looking and I could let myself have my own response before I told him.

"Do you think I should go to the doctor again? I know it's only been a few months, but I'm having these awful symptoms that look like pregnancy, but I'm not pregnant. I'm gaining weight, and I feel so gross. I don't know what to do." I take a moment to collect my thoughts as I wait for Carter to respond. He pulls back the shower curtain enough so I can see his face peeking out.

"Let's give it some time. Call if you would be more comfortable with that. But she said it could be a year. Maybe let's stop testing for a while. Your body needs to figure stuff out. Maybe we can start using condoms for a few months so we aren't stressing about a baby for a few months. Take the pressure off and let you have some time to regulate."

"We haven't used condoms since we first got together. Are you seriously going to be okay with that?"

"I think it's the best option right now, Kylie. I don't like seeing you depressed and disappointed over this. Let's give it a few months and then go from there." He offers a small smile and closes the curtain again. I'm not sure why the thought of him using a condom makes me so sad. It's not like he's saying 'no' to sex or intimacy or me. Why does it bother me so much? And this is one of those moments that I wish I had told Sasha that we were going to stop preventing pregnancy because I could really use someone to talk to about this.

That night, I asked Chelsea to make me something fruity at the bar. I would have asked Max, but he's busy flirting with some college girls at the other end. I had to repeat my question a couple of times before she registered that I was asking as a patron and not as a waitress.

"I'll make it for you if you'd like, but I thought you weren't drinking right now." She has a soft question in her voice, like she knows I don't really drink. But I never told her that.

"What do you mean?" I have been melancholy all day. That's the best way to describe it. I am just sad. And I know my tables realized that I was off today, especially my regulars. But I need to move past this. I won't have to see that negative test result for a few months at least, so I'm allowed to have a drink after my shift if I want to.

I'm not pregnant. I'm not driving. And I'm not on the clock. I am allowed to do this.

"I just thought that with you coming off your meds and talking about getting pregnant that you were avoiding the alcohol. But I might have misunderstood what was happening." She tries to brush it off, but I'm almost positive I never told her this.

"Did I tell you about this? Because I don't remember. I know I've been out of it a bit some days, but Carter and I specifically talked about keeping this between us for now." She's flustered and trying to figure out how to respond, and I'm getting irrationally angry.

"He mentioned something when you fell asleep in his office a few months ago. He was excited about the possibility of becoming a dad. But he hasn't brought it up again. I didn't mean to overstep. Let me get you that drink." She busies herself behind the counter. All I can think while watching her is the fact that I wasn't allowed to talk to my best friend about this, but Carter was totally okay with talking to his female employee about this. Carter is with Shaun, the restaurant owner, at a community meeting today, so I can't even go storming into his office and demand answers.

Chelsea mutters an apology as she passes me my drink. I plop a ten-dollar bill on the counter, not even asking if it covers the total. I need to not be in front of her anymore because I'm about to start crying. And she does not get to see me like that. She already knows more about me than I would prefer. After locking the door, I make myself comfortable on the couch in Carter's office. I turned on the small floor lamp instead of the big overhead one. I want to sulk today. Tomorrow, I'll go back to being in control and happy and fine, but right now, I am not fine. I turn off my phone, finish my drink, and lie down to take a nap. The sound of giggling wakes me up. I'm already annoyed before I even open my eyes. I lie there listening for a minute before I decide to actually get up. I can't hear words through the door, but I can tell it's Carter, Shaun, Max, and Chelsea talking in the hallway. I give myself another moment to pout by myself before I fold my blanket, put my things away in their proper place, and then open the door to see what everyone is laughing about.

"Hey, babe. Did you have a good nap?" Carter is obviously

amused, and I hate that I'm annoyed by that. I'm sure I look like I just took a nap after drinking something that was more vodka than fruit juice.

"Yeah. I needed that. Are we good to head home, or do you need to get some stuff done first? Is everything closed up?" I try to tone down my bad mood. No one needs to be made aware of my pity party.

"All good here. I was just coming back to get you." Carter takes my jacket, which was draped over my arm, and helps me put it on.

"See you all tomorrow," he calls over his shoulder and then we make our way outside. Once the fresh air hits my face, I close my eyes and breathe in the cool air for a moment. It feels good out here. It's quiet except for the occasional car on the road and the door closing behind us. All the other businesses in the plaza are closed, so there are only a few vehicles parked out here.

"How much did you have to drink tonight, Kylie?" Carter's voice isn't angry, but it's also not gentle.

"Just one. Chelsea made it for me, and then I went and took a nap. I needed to relax a bit so I could sleep. I was too worked up, and I had finished everything."

"You weren't answering your phone. I was worried."

"Yeah, it sounded like you were." I can't clip the tone fast enough, and I know that came across as snarky. I wince at myself and immediately apologize, "I am so sorry. That was completely unnecessary. I am not handling this well." The tears start coming, and I can't hold back the sobs. Carter pulls me into his arms and holds me, stroking my upper back, letting me get it all out.

"We are going to be okay. *You* are going to be okay. We will have a baby when the time is right. And maybe deciding to wait will be good. Let's focus on you getting better and having some answers. And we have the Estes trip with Sasha and Matt this weekend. But please, if you do decide to have a drink, keep your phone on. You don't handle alcohol well, and I need to be able to get in touch with you."

"Okay, and I am sorry for snapping at you. That's why I don't drink. My body doesn't handle it well. I either get weepy or bitchy. There's no in-between." Carter just chuckles.

"You're not wrong there. Let's get home and into bed."

"I like the sound of that."

Chapter Five

KYLIE

ICED CHERRY CHAI

Social Post: I have always loved short road trips. Bigger ones where you have to plan excursions, hotel stays, and restaurant reservations can get a bit overwhelming, but this level of visit is perfect. Now, if only I could get the motivation to actually finish packing. #roadtrip #packing #noco #estespark #weekendtrip

Image Description: Photo of my open suitcase on my bed—empty obviously.

I love Colorado in the fall! There's something amazing about the crisp morning and the leaves changing. The golden colors of the aspen trees contrast so beautifully with the snow on the distant mountains. It's still fairly warm, light cardigan weather, but the tops of the mountains have started getting their dusting of snow. This is the time of year that I wish I could take good photos or put into words the beauty around me, but I would much rather curl up under a blanket and stay in bed reading.

"How much are you taking up with you this weekend?" Sasha calls across the hall. I'm supposed to be packing for our drive up to Estes this weekend, but I'm too busy staring out the window and not going through my closet.

"Um, probably just one outfit for each day, an extra sweater in case we go to dinner one night, and comfy jammies. I have no idea how cold it's going to be in the cabin, and I don't want to risk it if I only bring something lacy with me."

She pops her head into my room and sees that I'm sitting on the bed instead of sorting through clothes. "We leave tomorrow morning," she prompts.

"Fully aware. You're the one who should be stressing because it's your first overnight trip with your man—me, on the other hand, Carter has seen me from full glam to puking my guts out from the flu. I know the outfits I feel good in and the ones he appreciates. You still need to learn what you feel good in and what makes Matt forget how to use his words." I smile at her. Seeing the start of their relationship has been amazing. The nervousness paired with the excitement between the two of them has had me reminiscing with Carter a few times about those awkward first dates and encounters.

"Okay, fine. But you can still push those expectations a bit with Carter. Didn't you get a new outfit the last time we were out? Maybe a new location would be fun to push your normal a bit. I got you a new red lipstick, too." She pulls the tube out from behind her back and drops it on the bed next to my empty duffel bag.

"You know I can't say no to a new lipstick. But Carter hates it when I wear a bold lip. He won't even *try* to kiss me."

"It's been over a year since you wore red lipstick, Kylie. I know this color is going to look incredible on you. Give it a try and see how you feel. I learned that new trick to set lipstick since the last time you tried it." I hesitate before I respond to her. I do love wearing a bold lip color, and red used to be my preferred color, but she's right. I have stopped wearing bright and bold colors. Carter never asked me to stop wearing them, but he wouldn't kiss me when there was a chance of transfer. And he wasn't as generous with the compliments on those days, either.

"Okay, fine." Sasha lets out a little squeal at my willingness to try. "Maybe I will try something new this weekend."

The next morning, I am confident with what I've packed in my bag. Mildly nervous, but confident. Working in a place where I have to wear a uniform means I have gotten very comfortable with a few options on workdays, and then comfy leggings and oversized sweaters when I'm home. It's just going to be the four of us for a few days, so I'm trying something new. I head out into the main room just in time to see Matt hand a travel coffee mug to Sasha and then place a kiss on her cheek.

"You two are beyond adorable." I have to stifle a laugh at their utter cuteness as I set my duffel bag by the front door next to Sasha's. Carter isn't far behind me with his own bag. He is planning to be fully 'off the clock' this weekend. I can't wait to have his undivided attention, without the possibility of him being called in to help cover the bar.

Carter and Matt bring things out to the car, Sasha and I top off the sunscreen and water bottles, and we are on our way. We make a quick stop at our road trip staple whenever we head up to Estes—the Colorado Cherry Company. Seriously, if you are ever in the area, make sure you stop there. I pick up a soda and a muffin for myself and one for Carter, and we are back on the road. It's only an hour's drive, but we still get enough snacks to classify this as a full road trip. It's an easy ride, and the boys talk comfortably. I love that Carter and Matt get along. It definitely is going to make any future double dates a lot easier.

The cabin is beautiful! Sasha and I had fun going through websites to find a place that would work. I'm so glad this one was available. It's close to the river, and we will have to drive a bit to get to downtown Estes if we decide to go out for dinner one night. But it's quiet and absolutely beautiful out here! Matt goes to the main building to get us checked in, and then we are on our way to our cabin.

We head inside, and Carter immediately motions toward the door down the hallway. "Why don't we take that one so they can have the window looking out at the river?" he asks as we start walking to the door.

"Perfect." I pop up on my tiptoes to give him a kiss and head to the back bedroom. It is just as beautiful as I was expecting. There's a huge picture window facing the woods so you can see all the trees and birds hopping around looking for food. Maybe we'll be able to see a moose or elk while we are up here. We have a king-sized bed in this room as well as a huge soaker tub.

"Do you want to start out the weekend with a bath? I stopped and got the bath stuff you like." Carter pulls a small box out of his duffel.

"Oh, my goodness, thank you so much!" I practically squeal as I run over to him and grab the box. It smells perfect! Like champagne and strawberries.

"I know these last few months have been busy with work and heavy with everything as you come off the meds, but I love you. I need you to know that you are amazing just as you are—I am so incredibly glad that I get to do life with you." I have to fight back the tears at his words. I was not expecting sweet Carter on this trip, but I love when he says stuff like that.

"Any chance of you joining me in there?" I ask as I start unbuttoning my shirt in front of him, slowly backing up toward the bathroom.

"I have two emails I need to answer that came in once I connected to the Wi-Fi. I know I said no work, but this will be super-fast. I forgot to give Max access to something before I left. Go get naked. I'll be in there soon."

"Promise?" I stand in the doorway to the bathroom, trying not to sound disappointed.

"I promise." He smiles at me and then sits on the edge of the bed, unbuttoning his shirt and toeing off his shoes. His emails should be pretty quick. I head into the bathroom to get the tub ready, adding in the bath bomb once it's mostly filled up and making sure towels and soaps are within easy reach. I peek my head out of the bathroom to see if he's done. Only to find him on the phone, sounding frustrated. I wait until he makes eye contact with me, and with a subtle shake of his head, I know I'll be taking the bath alone.

After dinner that night, the four of us are sitting on the porch, enjoying the stars and cool air. I'm snuggled into Carter's side under a flannel blanket that was in our room. I had found him out here after my bath and hoped we would be able to have some alone time in the hot tub. Apparently, Matt is freaked out by hot tubs, but I plan on getting buzzed enough on the wine I brought up that I won't be thinking about who else might have had some "alone time" in that thing.

Matt and Sasha head inside to watch a movie, and Carter goes to grab the wine while I get the hot tub uncovered. At least it looks clean and well-maintained. That's a plus.

"Don't stay up too late!" Sasha calls to me as I walk back inside the house to grab some towels for when we get out. I'm already wearing my black one-piece under my clothes in case we had the chance to do this. It may be a one-piece, but I look hot in it. And I'm not afraid to say it. It hugs my curves beautifully and shows off enough of my shoulders and upper back that I know Carter is going to have a hard time keeping his hands to himself. I pin my hair up into a messy bun before stepping into the tub, my clothes piled on the floor of the deck.

"Didn't want to wait for me?" Carter asks playfully as he steps outside with a small plate of snacks and the wine. He sets it down on the ledge of the railing that butts up against the hot tub. They really planned out this area for easy use, with numerous places to put drinks and cute areas to sit outside.

"I took off my jeans, and it was just too cold to stand outside half-naked." I smirk back at him. "I wasn't sure if you had left your phone in the bedroom and didn't want to be waiting for a while if you were going to get another call. I knew you'd be out as soon as you could."

Carter steps out of his sweats and pulls his T-shirt off in a way that guys always seem to do, which is so effortlessly hot. He's just in his boxer briefs. I love the way he looks, standing in the soft light of the porch lights.

"Don't do that, Ky. You know I can't help it right now." He steps into the tub and gets settled across from me. He closes his eyes and tilts his head back as he adjusts to the temperature. I take a sip of my wine.

"I'm sorry, babe. Not gonna lie though, I was disappointed earlier when you couldn't join me."

"I know you were. I got that bath stuff for you, though. Can I make it up to you now?"

"What did you have in mind?" I make my way over until I'm standing directly in front of him, letting him take in my body. My body is bracketed between his legs, his hands coming up to rest on my hips, his eyes taking in the water dripping off my suit, and gently stroking his thumbs back and forth.

"Come here, Kylie," he softly directs as he helps me maneuver so I'm straddling his lap, my breasts pressed up against his chest. I lean closer so he can reach the space where my neck meets my shoulder, an area he loves to kiss and one that drives me wild. His lips caress my skin, the warmth a contrast to the cooling water on my shoulder. His hands hold me exactly where he wants me, and I can't help but run my hands up to play with his hair. It's shorter than it was when we first got together, but there's still enough for me to grab onto when he gives me a reason to.

"I love feeling your hands on me, Carter," I breathe out, trying not to be too loud, knowing that there are other cabins not too far away and that Sasha and Matt are just inside. Probably not watching a movie like they were planning, at least that's my hope. That girl needs some attention. I have to force myself not to squeal when I feel a sharp pinch on my shoulder. "Did you just bite me?" I whisper-shout at him and look down to see him smiling mischievously at me.

"Stop letting your mind wander. Be here with me right now. Close your eyes and feel what I'm doing, okay? Can you do that for me?" He maintains eye contact, and I am breathless. He's always been a little on the "let me direct things" in the bedroom, but this feels entirely different. And I think I like it.

"Yes. I can do that," I finally respond as I settle my legs further down, my knees now touching the seat on either side of his thighs, spreading myself wide over him. I can feel how hard he is, and I desperately want to touch him. I begin dragging one hand down his chest so I can do just that.

"Eyes closed, hands on my shoulders or behind my neck, Kylie. Let me make you feel good," he whispers in my ear as he stops my hand from advancing further. I let myself surrender to his words, feeling the sensations of his lips, his hands, the water, the breeze cooling the droplets on my skin. Before long, his lips travel from my shoulder to my collarbone, sliding his fingers under the straps of my bathing suit to touch the skin of my breasts, playing with my nipple through the fabric on the other side. I fall into the sensations, just enjoying the way he is playing with me, working me up, and I can't help but glide my center across his length.

"I need you, Carter. Please." I grip his hair harder as he continues to pull on my nipple and massage my breast. I can come just by nipple stimulation, and he knows it. And he loves to see how much he can get me worked up this way.

"Give me one like this, Ky, and then I'll see how needy you are for me." I can't stop the moan that comes out now. I love when he talks like this. I've missed this. I keep my eyes shut like he asked, but I don't miss the small adjustment as he brings his mouth to my ear and nips lightly at the skin just below my lobe. He pinches my nipples hard at that same moment, and I lose it. I just hope I was able to keep it kind of quiet because I know we aren't fully alone.

"You are so beautiful when you let go for me, Kylie. Are you ready for me now?" His whisper is soft and sultry, but still so strong, he already knows the answer.

"Yes, please, Carter." I push my hands into the water again, trying to free his cock from his briefs. He's so hard. I need him inside me.

"I think that since you were sassy with me earlier, I should make you work for it a bit. What do you think?" His tone is clipped, almost like a flip has been switched internally. It catches me off guard and I'm not sure how to respond.

"What?". We've never done the whole punishment thing, and I don't know what he means by his mentioning of 'working for it.'

"I think you need to show me that you're sorry for not responding the way you should have earlier. I know you said you're sorry, but I think you should show me." I open my eyes so I can meet his gaze, he's serious about this.

"Um, how can I show you that I'm sorry? I'm not sure what you want, Carter," I know my voice sounds unsure, because I am right now. But if he wants to try something new, I'm not opposed to it.

"Can you kneel without the water covering your face?" His voice is gentler now than it was earlier in the conversation, so I have no problem following his directions. I slide off his lap and onto my knees. I have to prop myself up a bit to keep my head above the water, but I'm able to do as he asked. His smile is approving, if not a tad condescending, but I'm probably looking into his facial expression a bit too heavily. This is why I don't drink. Who thought wine was a good idea? Why can't I just enjoy the fact that I have attention right now instead of reading into what his look means?

I feel the trace of his finger along the subtle V-neck of my suit, leaving goosebumps in its wake before he props up, so he is practically standing directly in front of me. "Eyes up here, Ky," he softly speaks and I don't hesitate. He's not going to have me give him a blow job out on the deck, is he? "Stop thinking and just look at me, Kylie. I'm not going to make you do that out here. Maybe once we are inside and warmed up though." He smiles down at me, and I love the look of adoration he gives me.

"So, how can I make it up to you?" I ask him again. Wanting to do what he needs, but not sure what he's asking for.

"Just stay where you are and let me look at you." He speaks in an almost reverential tone, showing his love for me, as he brings his hand down and starts stroking his cock over his briefs before sliding his hand under the fabric. I have to force myself to keep my hands at my side, but I let my eyes drift to his length as he pulls it free. This man really does have a pretty cock. I know that's a weird thing to say, but he does. He was self-conscious about being "smaller" when we first got together, but he knows how to work it, so I am never left unsatisfied. He's a magician with his fingers too.

I watch as he drags his hand up and down his length, squeezing gently and then a bit harder once he starts leaking from the tip.

His other hand comes up and grabs my hair, keeping me steady, not letting me move to take him in my mouth like I so desperately want to.

"Are you going to stay still for me? While I finish all over your gorgeous chest, Kylie?" His words are harsh, but I do my best to lighten my tone in response. I want to do this for him. And if this is what he needs, I can do this for him.

"Is that what you need from me right now, Carter?" He tilts my head back in response, a little harder than was needed, but not too much. I'm okay. He's enjoying this. I can do this for him.

"Don't move, fuck, Kylie, you look so good like this for me," he breathes out the end as he releases all over my neck and chest. My eyes are fixed on his, so I couldn't even see him finding his release. But I can feel it all over me, dripping down into my suit, covering my skin. Now, what?

"Are you going to be a little more aware with how you respond to me now, Kylie?" His words are soft and so out of the blue. I don't know what that even means.

"I told you I'm sorry, Carter. It wasn't on purpose. I know you don't have much choice in working right now." I feel used and dirty, instead of the sexy woman on her knees for her man—giving him what he needs and wants.

"I know you are. Thank you for understanding my frustration. Let's get to bed." And then he climbs out of the hot tub. With me still on my knees, covered in him. I stare at the house, trying to figure out how to respond. Should I be feeling upset about this or am I'm overreacting?

I finally stand up and step out, and Carter wraps me in the towel he had been holding for me. He places a kiss to my forehead. "I love you, Kylie. Thank you for doing that for me. Can you grab the dishes, and I'll get the shower started for you?" And then he starts toward the back door of the house.

What the actual fuck was that?

Chapter Six

KYLIE

ICED PUMPKIN SPICE LATTE WITH SWEET VANILLA COLD FOAM

Social Post: There's nothing like the sounds of the morning in the mountains. #estespark #roadtrip #weekendtrip #morningviews

Image Description: Photo of the woods behind the house through the window. A few squirrels and birds are visible in the trees and the sky is still a little pink from the sunrise.

I wake up before Carter does the next morning. I needed some space and quiet. And I hate that I feel I need space from him, and I don't even fully know why. I'm still feeling hurt about last night. He's never acted that way while we were having sex or fooling around. And I don't know how to tell him I didn't like it because I don't know what I didn't like. Was it the way he talked to me or the way he just left abruptly afterward? He did make me come, so that wasn't the problem. Once I hear him up and moving around in the bedroom, I get the coffee going. Sasha will probably be ready for more coffee soon. I top off my mug and grab a fresh one for Sasha and head out to the porch to sit with her for a few minutes. She's been out there for a while, and I need some company. And the boys are going for a run today, because they're crazy.

The air outside is as cool as last night, but the morning light is welcoming. "Figured you would be ready for a second cup pretty soon." I hand Sasha the mug and sit next to her. She jumps right into telling me about what she has been working on, and I allow myself to slip into the role of supportive best friend. Pushing my own concerns to the back of my mind is where I am most comfortable, and I've gotten good at it. I need to focus on her right now. She is so incredibly happy, and I just want to see her succeed.

And I have to give her a bit of a hard time about her first sleepover with Matt last night. She might have gotten a bit more attention than I did, from the sounds of it. Sasha is so effortlessly comfortable around Matt.

"I'm just enjoying where we are right now. He is taking this whole dating me thing very seriously. I'm not mad about it." I laugh at her statement. They really are so perfectly matched.

"And he's someone you don't wear makeup in front of, which isn't normal for you. I mean, how long was I dating Carter before you came out of your room without a full face on?" It was a long time.

"I don't feel like I have to 'get ready' to see him. I'm ready just as I am. He looks at me like I'm the most beautiful thing he's ever seen, whether I'm all done up or not. He saw me in my coffee jammies last night and this morning, and I still got a reaction out of him." A slight pang of jealousy hits me, and I immediately dismiss it. What the heck was that?

"With the way you are blushing, that reaction was a good one." I stand and grab my mug. "Why don't we head inside so we can start getting ready? The guys should be back from their run soon, and I want to braid your hair today."

A little while later, I look at myself in the mirror in my bedroom.

I definitely went outside of my comfort zone today, but after last night, I'm glad I took the chance in packing this. I look hot. My hair is braided out of my face, letting my facial features really shine. I found a pair of leather pants that aren't insanely hard to get on and paired them with a cherry-colored oversized tank top and a gray blazer. Black booties complete my outfit, along with that bright red lipstick that Sasha gave me a few days ago. I can own this style. It's way outside of my normal, but I like it.

"Going for biker chic today?" Sasha asks as I start working on her hair.

"Trying something different today. I wore these pants a few weeks ago, and Carter about choked on his drink. I wanted to see what happens when I push it a bit. Plus, I feel amazing in this slouchy blazer. Definitely think I need more of these—or at least an excuse to wear it more often. It's not exactly waitress-approved." I top off my lipstick, and Sasha smiles at me.

The guys are talking as we head into the main area. My eyes immediately go to Carter, needing his approval or at least something positive from him. His eyes lock with mine and then travel from my eyes to my feet before coming back up again, taking in everything. Is he picturing me on my knees again? With his release all over the skin below my collarbone like it was last night? Carter walks up to me and runs his fingers over the fabric of the blazer.

"This needs to be a date night outfit at some point when we aren't doubling with those two," Carter says softly to me. Apparently not soft enough because Sasha pipes up.

"Those two have names, Carter."

"Don't care at the moment." His gaze never leaves mine, and he begins to lean in to kiss me.

"Do not mess up my lipstick, Carter," I warn him. I look good, and I don't want the color smeared all over my face. At least, not this early in the day.

"Oh, babe, let's go set the lipstick so you don't have that problem." Sasha runs around Carter and grabs my wrist so she can drag me back to her makeup kit. The lipstick thing is something we've talked about before. Carter is one of those guys who hates lipstick stains on his skin or clothes. Which is a big reason why I don't wear it very often. Setting this so it doesn't come off later is fairly essential. I want to be able to do this again without him giving me a hard time.

Going back to work and normal after our few days away is weird. Carter told me he loved the lipstick, but mentioned that he was hesitant to kiss me because the setting method might wear down, and it made my lips feel weird. There was no transfer all day, and I ended up buying the same lipstick in other shades because I love it so much. But I don't want to wear it if Carter is going to be using it as an excuse not to kiss me with it on. The restaurant is busy as we prep for Halloween and some theme nights in the last week of October. At least I'll have an excuse to be out of dress code that week. And I plan on taking full advantage.

Except my body had other plans, and my cycle started on Monday night, which meant I was home on Tuesday. The cramping leading up to the start was practically unbearable, and I was moments away from asking Carter to bring me to the Emergency Room. I finally decided to try taking a bath and then took some Melatonin. I was able to relax enough that I could go to sleep. By the morning, the bleeding had started, and the cramping wasn't as bad as the night before. But I was so worn out that I knew I would be no good at the restaurant. Especially dealing with a bunch of drunk college kids in costumes.

The plan for Wednesday was "Badass Barbie" night at the bar—normally our Ladies' Night, but we're adding a spin to it for the holiday. I decide to give my leather pants another try, but the bloating was so bad when I pulled them on that I couldn't wear them comfortably. "Leggings it is, I guess." I have fun with a shiny emerald-green silk top and some edgy makeup—including black lipstick. I added a bit of eyeshadow to the top of the lip, and it created a gorgeous chrome effect that matched the color of my top beautifully. I put some curls in my hair and pin it back from my face. Some extra eyeliner and some falsies, and I'm ready to go. After enough setting spray to make even a drag queen proud, I feel ready to handle a shift at the restaurant.

"What do you think?" I ask Sasha as I come out of my room. She's going to drop me off at the restaurant for my shift, so we can limit cars in the parking lot. Apparently, last night, there were too many cars parked outside, and someone got towed for parking in a no-parking zone.

"Ma'am! Please let me take some pictures for my blog!" Sasha practically squeals at me as I do a little spin for her in the living room.

"Have at it. It's products from the last collection you shared with me, too."

"How did you get this lip color, though? Is it a metallic one?"

"Eyeshadow." Not gonna lie, I'm pretty proud of myself that I did something new that Sasha couldn't figure out without asking how it was done.

"You are going to have to show me the next time you give that a try. I love this! I'm going to ask you again, why don't you want to jump in on the beauty stuff that Ashley and I are doing?" Sasha moves my head a bit so she can get the right angle for some photos. I swear she minored in selfie and product taking in college—except that wasn't an option. It could have been, though.

"Makeup isn't my passion. I have zero desire to film tutorials or reviews. I'm happy being in my cozy corner. I'm so happy for you and Ashley, and I can't wait to see where this goes for you. Just know that when you go on your first brand trip out of the country, I want to be your plus one. Matt can stay with Carter."

"Deal." Sasha laughs before showing me the photo she took.

"Send me that one!" I must have been right in the sunshine because my highlight is a stark contrast to the deep green on my shirt and the metallic black on my lips. "I look like a model," I joke with Sasha. We head down to the car and start making our way to the restaurant as we continue our conversation.

"You know, you could be. Or it looks like those really pretty editorial photos of the professional dancers we watch on YouTube.

Do you want me to send it to Carter, too?" I hesitate for a beat before I respond.

"No. Let him be surprised when he sees me. Let me surprise him when he gets to work. By the way, I can't remember if I already told you, Carter and I will both be there for the Halloween party this weekend."

"I can do that. This week is going to be so fun! I can't wait to see what Matt comes up with for the party."

"Is he doing it on his own?"

"No, he has some of his friends coming over. Ashley and her friend from college, Tilly, will be there, too. I think cleanup is just going to be the two of us, but it's a small group. Max is coming too, isn't he?"

"Yeah, that's the plan anyway. I think Chelsea was going to try coming too, but she has a friend coming in from out of town, so she can't now."

"That stinks. It'd be nice to see her outside the restaurant at some point. She seems pretty cool."

"She's been working a lot. I'm glad she is able to get a few days off this weekend. Hopefully, the staff will be able to start rotating weekends off soon. They're all way too overworked, and even I'm over it."

"You'll have to let me know the next time Carter has a weekend off so we can make plans." I give her a look that communicates my disapproval of that.

"Or make sure I am out of the apartment with Matt so the two of you can have a night to yourselves." She laughs with me.

"That's more like it."

Kylie

Chapter Seven

KYLIE

PASSION FRUIT ICED TEA THREE PUMPS MELON THREE PUMPS RASPBERRY

Social Post: Take every opportunity to show off the diva that you are. How amazing is this lip combo though? #badassbarbie #workoutfit #ootd #motd #boldlippie #halloween

Image Description: Selfie of me in front of my window. Showing off my black ankle boots, leggings, and emerald tank top. My makeup is bold with a black base and an eyeshadow shimmer top to add to the effect.

I walk into the restaurant so incredibly confident. There are only a few patrons inside, so I'll be able to ease my way into the day a bit. Chelsea is behind the bar, and there's only one other waitress on the floor. Carter must be in his office.

"Is Carter in the back?" I ask Chelsea as I walk past the bar. She's been a bit distant since the conversation we had about Carter and me trying to get pregnant, and I haven't pushed her on it. I am starting to wonder if I did something to upset her, but I'm not sure what that might have been.

"Um, I think so. He had to pop out for a bit to grab some things for tonight. He might not be back yet." She takes a moment to look me over. She's wearing something very similar to what I wanted to—shiny black leather skirt, a tight white tank top, and a red leather bomber jacket that matches her lipstick perfectly. It looks amazing against her blonde hair. "You look incredible, by the way." She lets me know as I turn to head toward Carter's office.

"You, too! Red is so very your color. I think that lipstick needs to become your signature color."

I knock on the door to Carter's office before I turn the knob to see if he's inside. He is, and he's on the phone, looking over some papers. I step inside and close the door and wait for him to see me. Finally, he glances up and does an immediate double-take. Yes! But the look in his eyes isn't hot and excited. It's confusion and then disappointment. Did I do something wrong? Carter doesn't wrap up the phone call, and after fifteen minutes of him talking about ingredients, suppliers, and how to get the younger crowd here during the day, I slip out of the office to start my shift.

Tonight, for the first time in a long time, I don't ignore the compliments I get from those in the restaurant. I look absolutely gorgeous tonight. If my boyfriend isn't going to appreciate me and the work I put into tonight, there are others who will. Everyone knows I'm happily taken, and that isn't even a doubt in my mind, but having some attention, a few lingering eyes, and a nod in my direction as I pass the bar carrying a tray of dishes—it's not a bad feeling.

"Ma'am, you went all out with the theme tonight! I am loving this!" A group of college girls at a table in the corner is quick with their compliments, and I feel like I'm a part of the group with the way they are talking to me. And it's such a good feeling. There's four of them—all dressed in black and hot pink—hair in high ponytails and lips painted traditional Barbie pink. Somehow, it works on each of them!

"Why, thank you. You all look pretty spectacular, too. Any plans after tonight?" I pull out my notepad to take their orders while they do their final look of the menu.

"We are going to go line dancing next door," one of them offers.

"We're going to try to, at least," another one pipes up, prompting laughter from the entire group, and I easily join in.

"I get that. I love going over to watch the different classes and dance nights, but I have two left feet and no rhythm whatsoever." The girls give me their orders, and I collect the menus from the table.

"Well, if you get off and want to embarrass yourself with others in the same boat—we'd love to have you join us. It is girls' night, after all."

"Thank you, I'll think about it." I smile to myself as I walk away. Maybe it's time for me to find a few more friends outside of my circle, or at least do something outside of the restaurant that I enjoy. I immediately feel guilty for entertaining the thought. Carter is working crazy-long hours, and I already don't get much time with him. Adding something outside of our set schedules right now is selfish and not necessary. I'll politely turn them down when I bring them their meals. And then I'll see if Carter and I can do a dance class together on our next day off together.

The shift goes smoothly. It's so incredibly busy, but the vibes are perfect. Everyone is having an amazing time. The bar stays packed all night, and I see Carter working alongside Chelsea and Max several times. They work together like a dance, and I don't miss the way Chelsea looks at Carter when he picks up a new keg and places it behind the bar. He is handsome, I'll give her that, but she needs to keep her eyes off my man.

My section stays seated until eight, and then it starts tapering off. Everyone has been great about the increased wait times and noise levels in here, though. I hope the rest of the week is like this. We need to do more theme nights. I'm clearing my last table and heading to the bar to drop off the tip split with Chelsea and Max when I see that Carter is the only one behind the bar.

"Hey, you. Tonight was crazy. Did you enjoy having some bar time again? I prop myself up on a stool at the end of the bar so patrons can sit and get a drink if they come in.

Carter sets down the glass he was drying before he looks over at me, a smug grin on his face. "It was a good shift. Tips are always good on nights like this, and I've said 'Hey, Barbie' more times than I can count. What about you? It looks like you had a fun night, too."

"Yeah, it was fun. My customers were all great and super kind. We should see about doing more theme nights or dress-up nights. I feel like it's a much better atmosphere in here, which I wouldn't mind seeing more of that. Maybe I can help with some of the planning and brainstorming for future events." Maybe event planning could be something I start doing, especially if it overlaps with something I'm already doing. And it's something I can do alongside Carter, which is an added benefit.

"Maybe. I'm working with Shaun and Chelsea on that right now. So, I think we have that covered. Why don't you wrap up and head to my office to wait while I finish my shift? It's going to get busy again, and I've got a new book for you on the couch." His tone isn't condescending, but it's close.

"Um, okay. Do you not want me to help out with things? I know I don't have any experience in event planning, but I've been here for a while and know the area and demographics. And I think it would be fun to do that with you, you know?" I can't hold back the hopefulness in my voice; I suddenly want to do this desperately.

"Kylie, I don't think this is going to be your thing. Chelsea has taken several event planning courses at college and even interned with a local venue last summer. Too many cooks in the kitchen and all that. You do a great job at being a waitress and supporting Sasha and me in our new chapters. Don't put pressure on yourself that isn't needed." He reaches over the bar and gently squeezes my hand before he walks over to greet the new group of ladies at the end of the line.

"Okay. That makes sense. You'll let me know if I can help with anything?" I slide off the seat and make my way the length of the bar so I can finish this conversation before he gets distracted.

"Yes, Kylie. I'll let you know." He offers me a small smile and then shifts his focus to the ladies in pink and leather in front of him. "Hey there, Barbie, what are we drinking tonight?" The giggles that immediately ensue tell me that they've probably already been to a few places tonight or decided to do some pre-gaming. It's nights like these that I wish I could drink without getting super weepy and emotional. I'd like to be able to turn off all the noise in my head and just enjoy, well, being.

I wipe down my tables and make sure I have everything ready for my shift tomorrow, and then I get settled into my spot. A place I now feel relegated to instead of a place that's been created for me to be comfortable while my man works. At least this book should be good. It's short and promises a good time without much plot, and honestly, I need that tonight.

Halloween comes quickly, and at least I am far enough into my cycle that I can wear something cute without feeling bloated and yucky. I had wanted to dress up like bikers again with Carter, but he didn't have anything that fit the vibe, and he didn't go shopping like he said he would, so we had to pivot at the last minute. So, we are Princess Kate and Prince William—if they were to dress casually and not the soft elegance we've come to expect from the royal couple. It's fine, though. We are adorable together. And I get to go out with him and several of our friends tonight. He'll be mixing drinks alongside Max tonight, but that shouldn't take up much time.

We get to Matt's house at the same time as Ashley and her friend, Tilly. They are dressed as Influencer Barbie and Makeup Barbie, and it's so perfectly them. Barbie pink looks so good on them. Sasha is Spider-Gwen, black lipstick and all. And I'm dressed in dark-wash skinny jeans, a cute floral top, and a baby blue cardigan. And the subtlest, barely there, nude lipstick that ever existed. But it's fine. Everything is fine. Oh good, Matt already put some of the drinks on ice.

"Can you make me something yummy once you set up at the bar?" I ask Carter after we have a mini-tour of Matt's house. This place is nice! Matt is younger than us, not by much, but enough, and is already pretty settled. I guess what he does with algorithms and business consulting pays well.

"Will do. Are you trying to get me working already?" he jokes and pinches my side as he pulls me in under his arm. I love it when he holds me like this. He smells so good, like whiskey and cinnamon.

"No. Never. I like spending time with you. But everyone else will be here soon, and you like getting set up and knowing what's happening before you start taking orders." I look over the bar at all the bottles and fruit that's already been prepped.

"We are only doing two cocktails tonight. The rest is just cans and bottles. Easy prep, easy service, easy cleanup. And Max will be here in a minute. But I'll make you something." He places a soft kiss on my temple and then washes his hands at the sink before checking that everything is where he needs it to be. Within a few minutes, I'm holding something red, sparkly, and yummy.

"What is it?" I ask as I take another sip. There's only the smallest burn at the end, so I know there isn't much alcohol in here. Which is probably a good thing.

"Just a dirty Shirley Temple, light on the vodka, heavy on the grenadine. What do you think?"

"It's perfect." I blow him a kiss before pulling the cherry out of the glass and popping it in my mouth, pulling the stem free from my teeth as I bite into the fruit. Carter chuckles and shakes his head. My cheeks heat a bit. I love this man so much.

It doesn't take long for everyone to get here and get settled. Max and Carter are playing behind the bar. That's the best way I can describe it. They're having a good time and trying different concoctions. Matt's friends are sampling things and chatting. I got to meet Luca and Jonathan when they got here. Luca is quiet like Matt is. His hands were rough as he shook mine when Matt introduced us. I must have held on for a beat too long because he immediately explained, "I'm a woodworker, so my hands are pretty rough from my tools and materials."

"Ooh, that sounds so interesting. I'd love to see some of the pieces you've made. Do you have any pictures?" I get so excited when I hear someone doing something crafty. These types of jobs are passion vocations. And it's almost always the case that their work holds a piece of their heart.

"Kylie, let the man not have to talk about work for a bit. He literally just walked in the door," Carter whispers in my ear as he extends his hand to greet the guys.

He falls into easy conversation with Jonathan. Jonathan is a talker and a joker. You can tell he's one of those easy-going types that just enjoys being around people. I go find Sasha, and we start passing out candy. The doorbell rings for hours! There are so many kids that come to the door, including the cutest little baby pumpkin I've ever seen. I love seeing the parents coming out with their kids. It's a fun night in a quiet neighborhood. As I look around the room, taking in all my friends and the people in their lives, I'm so incredibly thankful that this is my life.

We settle into the living room area to chill for a bit in between groups when Sasha starts up the conversation with something I've been wondering too: "I am honestly surprised at how many kids we have had come here tonight."

Matt heads to the candy bowl to refill the chocolate mix before answering the implied question, "Yeah, a couple of years ago, I met with a bunch of the other neighborhood homeowners. We planned a few events for the kids on the block throughout the year. Halloween became another one of those nights, and now a lot of the kids bring their friends. It's a quiet street, and most of us know each other, so parents feel safe. The kids recognize us, so it helps with the younger ones not being nervous."

I'm not sure where it comes from, but Carter is the next one to join the conversation. "So, even though you weren't a parent, you jumped in?" I give him a look, like 'what the heck are you getting at?' And then say a silent prayer that nobody else saw it. I don't need those questions right now.

Matt makes eye contact with Carter from across the room before he responds.

"Yes, sir." Matt is serious with his tone and facial expression. "My sister and I had that growing up, and it was important to me to be one of the adults that kids and parents could rely on if needed. And when the time comes that I have kids in this neighborhood, or wherever that may be, I want to be able to have that same relationship. I can't expect them to treat my kids well in five years if I am not doing the same today." A soft quiet settles over the group for a moment until I can't help but ask a question. Call it curiosity for my bestie.

"So, you've thought about having kids?"

"I think most of us in this age group have, haven't we? I'm not in a huge rush, but I'd like to be a dad someday. Again, I had a great childhood and would like to have the chance to be a dad." I don't miss the eye contact between him and Sasha, and I internally start giggling and kicking my feet in excitement for them. I need someone else to experience baby fever with because it is hard! I'm about to get up to join Sasha in the kitchen to get a water when Carter pipes up again, and I have to try hard to school my expression.

"I haven't thought about kids. I enjoy the flexibility of my job and being able to choose when we do a weekend away. Adding kids into the mix is going to create a whole new set of challenges." So, we are straight-up lying to our friends now? If I stay here, I'm going to say something, and it won't be kind. I get up then; I need some space.

"Do you not want kids ever or just not right now?" Ashley asks him. I haven't gotten to spend much time with Matt's younger sister, but I see her as a friend. And I appreciate her asking the question that popped into my mind at Carter's last statement.

"Not right now, for sure, maybe never." My heart drops, but he doesn't stop there. "I'm not thirty yet, not married, and don't want to add that into where we are in life right now. You're with me on that, right, Kylie?" Sasha lets out a small scoff next to me, but I ignore it, sipping my water and adding a subtle nod. I can't get any words out. I turn so I'm facing the wall of kitchen cabinets and not my boyfriend.

Sasha knows I'm upset, but she doesn't know why. And I need to keep it that way. When the doorbell rings again, I let her get it. I slip into the backyard to get some air. And to let the tears fall where no one will ask me questions I don't want to answer.

Chapter Eight

LUCA

BEES KNEES MOCKTAIL WITH LEMON BALM

Social Post: Finding new pieces to work with is almost as hard as deciding what to turn them into. Good thing I have friends who pull pieces from walks or the back woods by their houses so there's always plenty to choose from. #woodworking #woodworker #rawmaterials

Image Description: Pile of wood and sticks in a dimly lit backyard.
Thanks, Matt

I'm approaching my limit of dealing with people today. I was already frustrated with how the bench I was working on was coming together. I had two gorgeous pieces of aspen boards that I was gluing together, but they just weren't cooperating. I was thankful for the excuse to put the project on pause to come to Matt's house tonight. Jonathan picked me up on his way over, and I'm excited to meet Matt's girlfriend as well as some of the other people that have started joining the friendship group.

For the longest time, it was just the three of us. And now it looks like the first one of us is going to be settling down. I know it's early, but Matt doesn't do anything he isn't sure about. I wouldn't be surprised if he isn't already moving heaven and earth for this girl. I was barely able to change my shirt into something not covered in sawdust when Jonathan let me know he was outside. Most people find a hobby that helps them relax. My hobby turned into my career. While I still love it and do relax as a project comes together, there are still those projects that I do because I'm getting paid for them and nothing more. I need this night off.

And then I got to the house and met everyone, I quickly found a comfy stool at the end of the bar so I could watch the room. I'm a people-watcher. I like trying to figure out who they are, what's important to them, and how they relate to what's happening around them. Tonight is going to be a challenge because I only know a few of them already. But I'm happy to be off to the side. This way, I can watch the path leading up to the house and make sure we are ready for each group coming for candy.

"Okay, but I need to know how you came up with all of the design stuff for the décor for tonight," one of the girls asks Matt while she waits for her drink. Her name is Corinne, and she's Tilly's roommate. Tall but petite, wearing another Barbie-inspired outfit like Ashley and Tilly. Shy when she was checking everyone out, but she's getting more comfortable around everyone.

"A lot of it was Ashley and Tilly." There's a loud cough behind Matt and I can't help but smile at Jonathan's interruption. "And Jonathan and Luca came over to help too. We had to move some furniture around. Luca created the mock graveyard with left-over pieces of wood and metal from his last project." I don't need the recognition, but I appreciate being able to have something to do. Matt paid us in pizza last night, so I'm thankful that I didn't have to worry about lunch today.

"Project? What do you do, Luca?" Corinne directs her attention to me and starts sipping on her sparkling red concoction that Max has made for her. Is this girl even twenty-one yet? It must have been a mocktail. I don't drink, so I asked Carter to make me a mocktail. It looks like the one he made me, too.

"I'm a woodworker. I make custom furniture and décor, everything from picture frames to bookshelves to dining room sets. I'm working on a mixed-media dining set right now, hence the extra metal and wood. It's a lot of puzzle pieces to get together, but it's going to be a stunning piece when I finish it." I love getting to share what I'm working on. After this commission, I don't have another booking until early December, so I'll get to do some fun pieces in the coming weeks. That's if I can actually finish this set.

"Can I see some of your work?" Corinne starts walking over to me, and I don't miss the way Max looks at her as she walks in front of him. He likes her. Or at least thinks she's pretty. He's not wrong, but she is definitely too young for any of us in here right now.

"Yeah, here's my Instagram." I get out my phone to show her my account. "It's a mix of the fun pieces I do when I'm trying out a new technique and the commissioned pieces I've done."

"Is this the coffee shop up the road?" She points out a series of photos in the first few rows of my feed.

"Yep, I got to work on a few art pieces for them when they remodeled last year. I had fun with those. I stained the wood with different coffee grounds and syrups. It was a new medium for me. I enjoyed seeing how the elements interacted with each other. And then I got to do some of the fine work, carving and engraving for the shop logo and coffee bean shapes."

"And that's all wood?" Max pipes up as he walks over to us to look.

"These ones are, yeah. Some of my other work uses other materials, but this is all reclaimed wood."

"Speaking of reclaimed wood, if you have the time and remember, there's a new pile for you to look through by the shed outside. I found some pieces by the river on my run this morning and went back to get them this afternoon," Matt calls out from across the room, and I nod in acknowledgment. He always finds me the coolest pieces. Sometimes, I can use them for a full piece, but usually, they get added into a bigger project. Each piece of wood has a story, and they come together to create a brand-new chapter with each completed work I'm able to leave my mark on.

About an hour later, I head outside to look through the woodpile. I haven't been out here long at all when I hear the back door close a little harder than necessary. It's dark out here right now, which probably isn't the best time to look through this pile, but I'll blame Matt for that one. He shouldn't have told me about this when it was already dark. My phone flashlight isn't awful, though, so I can see most of what's in front of me. But I can't see who just came outside. I can hear soft mumbling and a foot stomping on the deck. Is someone throwing a temper tantrum right now? I pick up the piece that I know I want and then make my way back to the deck.

I'm greeted by a small squeal, and I realize that I must have scared Kylie. She thought she was alone out here. "Are you good?" I ask as I come up onto the porch, standing under the light so she sees who I am.

"Um, yeah," she takes a deep breath, and it's obvious she's trying to hold back some tears. "It's Luca, right?" Why is she deflecting the conversation? She knows my name. We talked earlier.

"Yep, did something happen? Are you feeling okay?" I don't know what's wrong, but she's obviously upset.

"Stupid hormones, nothing more. I'm fine." She closes her eyes for the briefest moment, composes herself, and then shutters the hurt I saw behind a shield. She's back in control, she's fine, nothing's wrong. Except I know something is bothering her. But I don't know her nearly well enough to push her on that. I'll play along for now, but I'm already making a mental note to check on her before the end of the night.

"Just needed some air?" I offer her an excuse for being out here. "It can get a little stuffy in there, especially with the door opening a lot and the heat turning on."

"You're not wrong there. I didn't realize how warm it would get in there. Why are you out here?" I hold up the piece of wood in response. "What's that for?"

"I'm not sure yet. I'll have to see what it tells me when I get it to the workshop."

"What it tells you? Does the wood usually speak to you?" She's holding back a chuckle now, and her eyes are glistening in amusement. There's some actual happiness in there, not just the pretend type she's showing me. Good.

"No, that would be ridiculous," I whisper to her behind my hand, like I'm sharing a secret that I don't want the wood to hear. And I'm rewarded with an actual laugh. Not a polite giggle. A laugh. And it is the most amazing thing I've ever heard.

"But I do like seeing the full piece in my space to see what it would work well for. It's hard to see where the knots are and how this piece was originally cut."

"What do you want it to be?"

"Something that reminds me of your laugh." I can't help myself. The statement is out before I can hold it back. That was so corny. I can't believe I said it. But the blush on her cheeks shows me she thought it was cute. Okay, maybe not the worst thing I could have said.

"And what would that be?"

I take a moment to think about what her laugh reminds me of before I respond, "A honeybee."

"My laugh reminds you of a bee? I don't know how I feel about that." She scoffs a little, but her smile is still there. It's in her eyes. That sparkle is making itself known, and it's stunning.

"It's a good thing. I promise. You ready to head back in?" I position myself to point toward the back door.

"Do I get to know what the reason you thought of honeybees when I laughed is?" She walks next to me and waits at the threshold for me to respond.

"Not yet. I want to create this piece for you first."

"You're going to make it for me?"

"I think you need something beautiful that is just for you." Her smile falters for just a moment, and I see a hint of hurt cross her eyes. Whatever is bothering her, she's not ready to talk about it. And certainly not with me. But maybe I can give her something to make her smile again.

"Thank you, Luca." She offers me a smile of acknowledgment, nothing more. And then we head back inside.

I don't miss the way that Max and Carter's eyes both snap up to meet mine when I shut the door. Carter's follow Kylie's for a moment before coming back to mine. A question is in them, an angry one. Does he seriously not trust his girl to be outside for five minutes with someone else? Under a porch light? With fifteen people inside the house? Someone is feeling insecure and threatened. I'll have to talk to Matt about how I should proceed here. I don't want to step on any toes, but that whole interaction was just off.

Luca

Chapter Nine

KYLIE

CHAI, DOUBLE SHOT ESPRESSO, 4 PUMPS ZERO SUGAR DULCE DE LECHE SYRUP, AND OAT MILK

Social Post: Can it be spring yet? #fallincolorado
Image Description: Throwback photo to the lilacs in a local garden from last spring.

While I was outside, Ashley had left with Tilly and Corinne, so now it's just the older ones of the group here. I think I may actually be the oldest one in here now. We are all in the twenty-four to twenty-eight age group, so we are all pretty close. We're all hanging out in the living room now. No kids have come in the last thirty minutes, so most of us are sipping on tea that I brought over just in case. And I'm so glad I did.

The conversation is simple, and it's very easy to see the possibility of this group getting together again. We've chatted through so much. Sasha is sharing more about her not celebrating Halloween growing up. She grew up in a very strict religious household, so she didn't get to experience Halloween until we were in college. That first year was an experience for her. I know we are probably going to dive into talks of either childhood trauma or religion. I smile to myself when Max surprises us with his input.

"It's definitely interesting to see how each family and religion handles things like Halloween. I took a few comparative religion classes in college and had roommates that were part of different backgrounds, so I was exposed to a lot over the years. How are you feeling about things now?" Max asks Sasha as he sets his empty mug on the table next to him. I should see if anyone wants more.

"You mean your degree isn't in bartending?" Carter jokes with him. I don't know why I'm bothered by everything he is saying tonight. It's got to be the hormone changes.

"No, it's actually in Creative Writing and Journalism. I focused on modern religions and organizations for most of my assignments. I was always fascinated. Hence, I would love to hear what Sasha has to say about my earlier question." Max is teasing in his tone, but his eyes and body language say he is picking up on Carter's weird vibe, too. I'm glad it's not just me.

Sasha answers Max, and I get up to see if anyone wants more tea, setting the kettle on the stove. A few minutes later, everyone else is up and getting things cleaned up. I turn off the burner and put the tea back in the small container I have for my favorites. I'm glad I brought this. It isn't long before I'm wishing Sasha a good night and mouthing to her to "call me" in the morning. I'm so glad she's spending the night with him tonight. She needs this. I'm excited to have a night alone with my man.

"Did you have a good time?" I ask Carter on the way back to the apartment. I really hope he isn't too tired. I need some attention.

Especially after the weird conversations earlier.

"Yeah. It was fine. It looked like you were enjoying yourself." His tone is off.

"Are you mad at me?" I try to keep my reaction soft, but I don't know what he's talking about.

"I'm a little frustrated, Ky. You were all over that friend of Matt's. I would have appreciated a little support with the whole baby conversation. That was so awkward. You just left the room instead of supporting me. I thought we were doing this together." I take a second to process what he just said.

"Okay, first, I was not all over anyone. What are you talking about?"

"Luca. You absolutely lit up talking to him. And then you were outside together for God knows how long. And you expect me to believe this is the first time the two of you have met."

I am beyond shocked at his accusation.

"Do you really trust me that little?"

"You're not denying it."

"Because it's ridiculous. I didn't 'light up' talking to him. He said something about his interests, and I continued a conversation like a kind, considerate human being. I went outside in the first place because what you said about kids and being parents really hurt, Carter. I know we aren't telling our friends about any baby plans right now, but it's something we had talked about wanting. Sooner rather than later. And then you just turned around and said you may not ever want kids. You lied so effortlessly—to my best friend. I didn't know what to do. So, I went outside to get some air. Luca was outside looking for wood or something. That's it. I can't believe you would even think I would be thinking of another man. You're it for me, Carter."

My face is soaked in tears by the time I finish my mini-tirade. I can't believe we are having this discussion right now. Tonight was supposed to be fun. There were some amazing moments, but some pretty awful ones, too. We pull up to the apartment, and Carter parks, turns off the car, and steps out. I take another moment to compose myself and then head out, too. I grab my box of tea and purse and follow Carter into the building. Neither of us says anything until we are in the apartment. I don't even know what else to say. I feel like I need to apologize, but I don't know why.

Carter drops his keys in the small bowl by the front door and then toes off his shoes. I just stand there, waiting for him to say something.

"I wasn't lying." He's not even looking at me; he's hanging up his jacket in the front closet.

"What?" I didn't hear him right. There's no way.

"I wasn't lying when I was talking earlier." He turns and looks at me. He's upset, but he's also standing in a way that says he's made up his mind about something. Decision has been made. And that's that. I normally love how sure he is. But this, what?

"What part weren't you lying about, Carter? I'm going to need you to say what I think you're saying." I put everything into the effort to keep my voice steady.

"I don't know if I want kids, Kylie. Not now. Not ever. I wasn't lying. And like I said before, it hurts that you didn't back me up over there. I felt like an idiot when you walked off."

"How did you think I would feel? You have known since we met that I wanted kids. We have talked about this extensively. You've been with me at the appointments. You held me as I've cried. You made baby name lists with me. Where the heck is this coming from? I'm feeling all kinds of blindsided right now."

"You're upset, and I get that. Let's talk about this when you've calmed down." He starts walking to the bedroom, and I don't hesitate to follow.

"We are not done talking about this. We have been together for six years, Carter. You did not just change your mind on this tonight. If you weren't lying tonight—when did you start lying to *me?*" He turns , and the rage in his eyes is something I have never seen. And I don't like it.

His entire body is rigid, and he spins around so fast that I ran into him. He reaches out and places his hands on my shoulders, holding me steady. Maybe a little harder than necessary, but not too hard that it hurts. Much anyway.

"We are done talking about this tonight. Take a shower and get ready for bed. You need to calm down, and so do I." He lets me go and steps away before heading into the closet to grab a pair of sleep pants. He continues talking while he changes in front of me, never meeting my gaze. "I'm going to sleep on the couch tonight. I have to be at the restaurant to open tomorrow morning to prepare for brunch. I'll see you when you get in."

"I don't think I can drop this, Carter. Are you serious?" I am holding my arms around myself. Trying to keep some composure. I still don't even know what just happened.

"Yes, Kylie. I'm serious. And you're going to need to drop it. Because I'm done talking about it tonight." He walks to the bedroom door and closes it behind him as he steps into the hallway. "Goodnight." I close my eyes and let the tears fall as I hear the click of the door, followed by the soft thuds of his footfalls as he heads to the living room couch. Where he's going to sleep away from me for the first time in years. And I'm left wondering what I did wrong and how I can possibly fix it.

Chapter Ten

KYLIE

ICED CARAMEL MACCHIATO WITH PUMPKIN SAUCE

Social Post: Comfort reads and cozy clothes. #weekendvibes #onamonday #cozyvibes

Image Description: Small stack of books on the coffee table next to my oversized chair.

The only time I see Carter in the next week is at work. And he's always busy. I'm lucky if I get a wave or "hello" from across the room. I'm trying to give him the space he asked for, but I really don't know what to do. I focus on work as best the I can and start helping Sasha with some stuff behind the scenes. She got an invite to a pretty big event next month in New York. So, there's a lot of prep already happening there. I'm happy to stay busy; it helps me forget a little bit.

It feels like months later by the time Carter and I have a day off together. In reality, it's eight days. He's been sleeping on the couch, going to sleep after Sasha is in bed or once he knows that she is spending the night with Matt, and then he's awake and out of the apartment before anyone is up. I'm wearing comfy joggers and an oversized sweater today, and I carefully select a book from my shelves that I've been wanting to read. It's a new release from my favorite author, and I finally have a cozy day off to enjoy it. It's days like this that I really wish I had a reading corner, but my big chair in the living room will be perfect. It's not the reading nook I was promised, but it's enough.

I make quick work of starting a pot of coffee by the time I realize that Carter is still on the couch. It's past nine. What time did he get home last night? I stay as quiet as I can with what I'm doing in the kitchen so he can stay asleep. He must have pulled over seventy hours this last week and definitely needs the rest. Maybe he'll be up for talking when he wakes up. I find his favorite black mug from the cabinet, which has the restaurant logo on it, fill a cup for him, and set it on the coffee table in front of him. I debate what to do next. Part of me really wants to wake him up and see if he wants to get breakfast or if I can make something for him. The other part is enjoying the peace of the moment. He's not angry at me right now. He isn't breaking my heart and dreams right now. And I immediately can't believe I've just thought that.

Maybe I should change my plans for today and see if Sasha wants to hang out instead of staying home. No. I need an at-home day. I need some time for me. And right now, that means curling up in my oversized chair with some fuzzy socks, my favorite throw blanket, a cup of coffee, and this new romantasy book that has been calling my name for the last month. I can take some time for me. It's okay. I can be selfish.

It's not until I get a good twenty percent into the book that I realize Carter is awake. He's lying on the couch, phone in hand, and has obviously been awake for a little bit because he's answering emails or something. He chuckles quietly at something before sitting up and taking the mug of coffee in his hands.

"I can warm that up for you if you would like," I offer quietly. I don't know if he knows I'm sitting here, and I don't want to startle him.

"Oh, hey. No, this is fine. How long have you been up?" He turns his body a bit so he can see me. He at least looks like he's in a better mood this morning, well-rested.

"About an hour. Figured I'd spend the morning reading and taking it easy. How was work last night? What time did you finish up?"

"Can we not start the morning with a million questions, Kylie? It was a busy Saturday night. And I'm glad it's over. I have to head in for a bit today to go over inventory so I can place the orders for the week." He stands and brings his coffee mug to the sink, pouring out the leftover liquid, before he starts walking to our bedroom. I quickly place my things down before trailing after him.

"Do you not get a day off this week?" I try to approach the question with concern without any accusation in my words. He won't handle that well.

"This is what management looks like, Ky. You knew this when I got the promotion. I shouldn't have to be in for long, but then Shaun wants to take me to a meeting with a potential investor. I don't know when I'll be home tonight." He grabs a few things and heads to the bathroom. I stand in the doorway, watching him shave.

"Okay, Sasha has a meeting coming up that she may need some help prepping for. I'll see if I can do anything to help her out this week outside of my work hours..." I trail off, seeing if he is going to show any sort of interest in our conversation.

"Sounds good. You having something to do outside of work or reading your fluffy romance will probably be good." It's an accusation.

"I read maybe a total of two hours a week on a good week, babe. You've never had a problem with it." I can't mask the hurt in my voice. I don't want to.

He sets his razor down and turns to look at me. "It's fine, Kylie. You need something that you enjoy. Sasha is building an entire brand pretty quickly. You need something to do outside of your friendship with her. I wouldn't be surprised if this turns into a full company or 'boss babe empire' for her at some point. And you just waitressing is not going to be enough."

"Well, I have you, too…" I trail off again. Was he trying to talk down to me? It felt that way.

"Of course, you have me." He leans over to place a kiss on my forehead. "Think about what you want to do. I need to get ready now." He starts closing the door, and I put my hand out to stop the door from latching shut.

"Can I join you? I miss you." I just want to be in his arms for a few minutes.

"Not today, Ky. I have to be quick. I need to be at the bar in thirty minutes. Maybe when I get home if you are still up."

"Oh, okay. I'll go put some coffee in a travel mug for you, then." I turn and start walking to the kitchen, praying the tears don't start falling until I'm out of his line of sight. The door clicks as the lock is engaged before I even leave the room. And I can't help the sobs that take over my body.

I feel like I'm living alone. Sasha is at Matt's more than she is home now. And I don't even know the last time I shared a meal with Carter. I miss him. I miss us. I deserve better than this. But it's a season, and then things will even out. Sasha is actively building things into a new stage and has been able to give more responsibility to Ashley and Tilly. They are talking like they will be starting an actual company next year. I couldn't be happier for them. I've always been the supportive friend. The one cheering on the others from the background. I never gave myself the chance to think what I wanted to do. I guess I just figured I'd be married and pregnant by now. But now, I don't know.

I am interrupted from my self-reflection by my phone buzzing next to me on the couch. It's Carter with a text. Oh, he actually does remember I exist, nice.

Carter: Matt keeps calling me, and I'm at work. What is going on?

Me: I'm not sure. Let me see what's happening.

I'm barely able to put my phone back down when my phone starts buzzing with a call from Ashley. What the heck is going on? I'm in the middle of texting Sasha to see if everything is okay when I realize I should see if she's home first. I knock lightly on her door and then gradually open it. She's on her bed, just staring at the wall in front of her.

"What happened? Matt is blowing up Carter's phone, and Ashley is calling me. We haven't answered, but I'm starting to get the idea that something has happened." I sit next to her and wait for her to share what she's comfortable telling me. This is something I know how to do—listen, process, encourage. I can put my stresses on the back burner for a while.

"I don't even know where to start, Kylie. I turned my phone off when I got home. I feel so overwhelmed right now. My entire existence is a lie. Nothing was real." Okay, I was not expecting that. I'm going to need more details here.

"What are you talking about? Just start at where it makes sense. I'm here to listen. My phone is in the other room, and yours is off. I'm here, babe. Let me in."

Then she starts telling me what she discovered this morning. Through tears and a few follow-up questions, it seems like Matt was helping out with a lot more than what she was paying him for. Manipulating algorithms, tracking certain company demographics to place her in a position to get seen easier, and a whole lot more. And it started before she ever reached out to him. I get why she is spiraling right now. It's a lot to take in all at once.

I hold her while she cries, and we wait for Ashley to get to the apartment before we make a game plan.

"Okay, babe. You have an important virtual meeting soon. Go take a shower and get in the right headspace. We will set up the laptop and webcam for the meeting. Take the reset you need and focus on what you know. You're good at this. And you are going to absolutely kill it in this meeting. You're about to get your first collection collaboration with a major makeup brand. You did this. Not him. Not his algorithms and systems. You did." She nods at me and gives me another hug before going to get ready.

The meeting goes off without a hitch. Like we knew it would. This is her passion, and it shows so incredibly clearly. She is so good at this, and she deserves the world. Once she logs off and I get the kettle on for tea, the three of us sit down to debrief.

"I'm pretty sure he has a few alerts on my phone to make sure I'm safe, but not to the level he had for you, Sasha. I'm so sorry that I didn't realize what was happening and say something sooner," Ashley tells Sasha, and it's obvious that she is just as blindsided by this as Sasha was.

"Girl, this isn't on you. I'm just having a hard time wrapping my mind around everything he did. How much of this success was because of the work I did? Or was it all because of the manipulation he was doing on his side?"

Ashley let us know that she saw Matt before she came over here and made him unlink everything. He's not tracking any of her socials or her devices anymore. Yeah, that was a fun one to learn.

Sasha takes a deep breath before she continues sharing more about her morning with Matt. "Did he tell you that he told me he loves me?" I immediately spin around and can't stop the words before they're already out.

"He did what?!"

"Yeah. I told him he wasn't allowed to tell me that right now. I don't even remember what else before I left. It was all just too much. I wish I had recorded the conversation."

"That probably wouldn't have helped anything, Sasha. And he didn't tell me that, but honestly, I'm not surprised. My brother has been in love with you since our first meeting. That was obvious even to me. He just took his time to start pursuing you in that way." Ashley is gentle with her tone, and it seems to ease Sasha a little bit. She's a really good friend, and I'm glad the two of them found each other through Matt.

"Was any of the business stuff even something he wanted to do, or was this just some massive ploy to get me to be his? To sleep with him? What was he trying to do here? I don't know what to do with this, and I'm second second-guessing my entire life for the last two years now. It's been two years. Two years of him watching and doing things behind the scenes. Do you understand how violated I feel?" Sasha is crying again, and it breaks me to see her like this. She deserves the world, and I hate that Matt's choices are causing her to doubt herself.

"I get it. You need to let this sit for a bit. Focus on the collaboration. If he says anything, ask for the space you need." I take a beat before continuing, remembering that Carter has asked for space too, and even though it's hard, I am giving it to him. That's what partners do for each other. "What he did wasn't okay, but I genuinely think he had a plan for making sure you were comfortable with connections and gradually helping you to step out of your comfort zone. I'm not condoning what he did at all, but I get his thought process."

Sasha squeezes my hand in acknowledgment before she looks to Ashley. "Can you ask your brother to please give me some space for a bit? I haven't turned my phone back on yet, and I don't want to deal with it tonight. I need to focus on this trip next month and what that means for us going forward."

The two of them make plans for what their next steps are for the collaboration and the trip next month. I sit and listen. This isn't an area I can really help with. But I can be here for my best friend. As they are wrapping up the conversation, I stand up. "I'm going to run you a bath. Have a good night, Ashley." I wave goodbye to her as I make my way to Sasha's bathroom—after grabbing some of her favorite bath stuff from my own.

I'm just turning off the water when Sasha steps into the room. "Okay, love, have some quiet time and holler if you need me, but otherwise, I will see you in the morning." I am so incredibly drained, and I know it's a mix of providing emotional support and the fact that I'm about to start ovulating. Yay, hormones.

"Thank you so much," she pauses and I stop, knowing she has something else she wants to say. "Can I ask you something about the Halloween party?"

"Sure, what's up?" I think I know what she is going to ask, but I hope she didn't pick up on the tension that night.

"It felt a little off when Carter brought up the whole marriage and baby thing. Did something happen?" I knew she was going to ask, but I don't mask my emotions. I know she saw my hurt for a moment before I could rein it back in. How can I downplay this before she asks more questions and potentially talks to Carter? I can't have this escalate.

"We had a pregnancy scare a few months ago. I was just coming to terms with the fact that I might be ready to be a mom. He was so excited when it was negative when I finally was able to test. He then went off a little bit on how he may never want kids, and now I think I may want them. So, I'm just processing things and trying to figure that out. Especially with his promotion, things are a little weird right now. I'm hoping that we can give it some time and then talk again." I say a silent prayer that she drops it.

"I'm sorry, hon, I can't even imagine. Why didn't you say something?"

"I didn't want to bother you about something that wasn't actually happening. But it's going to be okay. Now we have to focus on getting you reset and ready for New York, so go enjoy that bath and wine. I will chat with you later, okay?" I turn my head so she can't see the tears starting to form in my eyes. It's the first time I've talked about this with anyone, besides Carter, that is. And it hurts so much all over again.

"Okay. Thanks, Kylie. Love you, babe."

"Love you, too."

The tears wait until I close the door, and I immediately climb into my bed. To fall asleep after crying out all my own questions and hurt. And to wake up to a cold and empty side of the bed all over again.

Kylie

Chapter Eleven

LUCA

CHAI TEA COOLER MOCKTAIL

Social Post: Talking to woodworkers, especially those that create more of the artisan pieces and not just standard furniture, many will say that the individual pieces will speak to them – on what they want to be made into. It doesn't happen often, but when it does, I listen. #currentproject #rawmaterials #workbench

Image Description: Sawdust covered workbench with smaller pieces of discarded wood left behind from my current project.

People are unpredictable. Sometimes, they do exactly what you expect of them, what they say they will do. They follow through on commitments and are there for you when you need them. That's how Matt and Jonathan have always been for me. I've known these guys since high school. Even with each of us taking different routes and careers, we've remained close. I've known Matt to be a very even-keeled guy since we met. I didn't, however, realize he was low-key stalking his girl—for years! Okay, not exactly stalking. It was just some light algorithm manipulation, but still. Unpredictable.

Sasha and Ashley are in New York, and I'm in my workshop, trying to finish this piece that has been waiting for me. I finally finished that big dining set, and now I get to work on the honeybee piece for Kylie. I still don't know why, but I know it's meant for her. Sawdust coats every solid surface, and the smell is comforting. To me, at least. Matt is having a slight nervous breakdown next to my workbench. I have to hide the chuckle when he pulls his phone out for the twentieth time in five minutes to see if Sasha has called or texted.

"Dude, she asked for some space. You need to respect that. You crossed some major boundaries with Sasha. She needs to know she can do this on her own." I examine the wood in my hands again and finally decide how I'm going to turn this raw piece into a finished work of art that will make me proud.

Matt lets out a deep sigh and pockets his phone again. "I know. I know I messed up, and it's killing me. I just want to be there for her. This presentation tomorrow night is going to be huge for her and the brand she's building. And I want to support her and cheer her on."

"I get that, but you've done all you can from here. Maybe when she gets back, she'll be ready to talk it over and see how things look for the two of you—business and relationship wise. Don't push it. Or you're going to totally waste this time away."

"When did you get so smart?" Matt chuckles and takes a sip from his water bottle. The condensation leaves marks on my workbench, and I try to discreetly place a coaster next to him. Water is fine, but not when I'm trying to work with pieces that need to stay dry. And tools that will be ruined if they get wet.

"I read things. I like to pay attention to what's happening around me. It's really not that deep, Matt." I finish sketching out the rough design of the honeybee and then pull out the tools that I'll need.

"What are you making, anyway? You didn't take much from the pile I set aside for you."

"Something for Sasha's roommate. Not sure why, but I think this needs to be hers. And I didn't take much because it was dark outside, and Kylie was crying. But that's beside the point. I know where to go if I need more. This should be sufficient for what I'm doing."

"You do know that Kylie is in a long-term relationship, right?" Matt suggests, and I know he's trying to make sure I don't get myself in any trouble. I just look at him like, 'no duh, Sherlock,' and continue working.

"It's just a piece I want to make. It's a few new techniques I've been wanting to try. I think they'll do well next spring when we start having the local faires and markets. It's a good chance to try something new."

"So, what is it?"

"Don't give me any grief about this, but it's going to be a pair of bookends."

"I was expecting more than that with the way you've been analyzing that chunk of wood for the last week." Matt chuckles, and I level a glare at him.

"I wasn't done. I'm going to stain them with some honey and lemon tea, continuing my series on natural stains. And they're going to be carved into a coordinating set. Not a matching one like I've done before." I start sanding the edges so I can determine where to make the first cuts.

"What kind of coordinating set?" The electric saw whirrs to life to split the piece in half. Once the buzzing stops, I respond.

"This is going to be a honeybee, and the other is going to be a honeycomb." I'm happy with these pieces. They're going to work out really well.

"I didn't know Kylie liked bees."

"I don't know if she does. Like I said, it's weird. I just know this is the project for her." We get lost in the silence again until Matt decides he needs to head out. He's got the coffee cabinet I made for him to stain and set up. It was originally going to be Sasha's Christmas gift from him. I hope he still gets to give it to her.

Absolutely no one is surprised that Matt's grand gesture to get his girl back was nothing short of spectacular. I mean, the guy flew to New York to surprise her. It wasn't long before they were getting back into their version of normal. With a whole lot more conversations about social media boundaries and how he was able to help her in the future. He still tracks things on her phone and the algorithms that she needs to be a part of in order to grow her brand, but she knows about it now.

Christmas means my books are filled with custom orders, and my honeybee set gets shelved for a little while. I see it every day while I'm in my workshop. I can't wait to see the finished pieces come together. I hope she likes them. I still need to figure out how I'm going to give them to Kylie without coming across as a creeper. She has a boyfriend. A live-in boyfriend. And they've been together for six years. I don't want to come between that.

The next time I have the chance to hang out with Matt, I'll see if he can subtly ask Sasha what she thinks. Or maybe we can all do a movie night or something. That would be a good chance to talk to her myself. Should I make something for the boyfriend, too? No, that would definitely be weird. I put a note in my phone, so I don't forget to bring it up later. I really need to find something else that gets me out of this space a few hours a week. Don't get me wrong, I absolutely love what I do. I get to create things and bring new stories to worn and outdated pieces. But, more and more of this feels like work and instead of fun. I need a hobby. I add that to my master to-do list, and then start shutting down my space for the night.

After parts are oiled and the floor is swept, I take another look around. I take a quick panoramic video of my shop to post on social media once I get settled inside my house. And then I lock up and head inside for another night of Friends re-runs and leftover lasagna from Mrs. Carter, Matt's mom.

Several weeks later, when I'm over Matt's house with him and Jonathan, I'm given an idea for a hobby to try out. Kylie's project is finished. I just don't know when I'm going to give it to her yet. But I fell in love with creating my own stains with tea, and I'm working on a new collection that I will launch this spring. I can't wait to see what pieces will come together with this inspiration. We are finishing up with dinner—a special treat after the guys helped me move a few larger pieces to a new coffee shop. Yes, I pay them in food. They don't complain.

"Have you guys seen any of these videos?" Jonathan slides his phone over so it's on the island counter between us. There's a couple dancing at what looks like a competition. But it's not like anything I've seen before. They are having an absolute blast. The laughs and smiles are genuine. The music is newer and the vibe is definitely one of fun. The group watching ranges in age from early twenties into their sixties, probably.

"What is it?" Matt asks. I don't move my eyes from the screen. You can tell these two absolutely love what they are doing. They move seamlessly together.

"West Coast Swing—it's a dance style. There are a bunch of these videos online. I'm hooked." Jonathan takes his phone back and scrolls to another one to show us.

"Have you tried it out?" I ask, still transfixed by the dancers. The joy on their face is contagious. I can't help but smile as the male dancer guides his partner in a series of steps across the floor. It's sensual and graceful, and the connection between them is indescribable.

"No. I wish I had the time, though. It's a really cool dance style. This competition is fully improv, too."

"There's no way that isn't rehearsed," Matt pipes up, and I nod in agreement.

"Totally blind. They don't know their partner or the song until it's their turn on the floor. Like I said, it's addicting to watch."

I have never danced a day in my life. But I think I just found something I want to try. I add another reminder in my phone to see if there are any dance classes for beginners. This could be fun.

The first class has me seriously questioning my choices. I am not a dancer. And this all looks way too complicated. I was filling up my water bottle before debating a gym membership or a yoga class—maybe both, when the instructor came up to check-in.

"Hey, thanks so much for trying out the class today. I appreciate you giving it a go. I know it can be a little overwhelming. I'm Stacey, by the way." She offers her hand, and I take it after moving my bottle to the other hand.

"Luca. Thanks so much for the class. It's definitely a lot. I saw some videos online and was mesmerized by how much fun everyone was having. I had to check it out. I think I may need to take up yoga to work on my flexibility if I'm going to keep this up." Stacey laughs with me and nods in agreement.

"It might not be a bad idea if you can make it work, just remember it's not required. You'll find that it gets easier the more you do it. It's a fluid dance form; finding the right partners and learning to work with the music more than a memorized set of steps is going to be your biggest hurdle. We have classes every Friday night. I'd love to see you back if we didn't scare you away."

I take a moment to look over the space. Most of those here tonight were single, just enjoying the company of other adults in the area. Turning off work for a little while. Some are parents and married, and this is date night for them. It's casual but still exciting. This is what I need right now.

"I definitely won't be ready for any kind of competition any time soon, but I think I'd like to come back. Any suggestions for helping what I know will be insanely sore quads tomorrow?" Stacey chuckles and gives me her contact info so she can email me some recovery yoga videos for tomorrow.

"You'll find a flow that works for you between classes. And if you decide you want to do more than casual fun dances on Friday nights, we can chat about those options, too. Don't be afraid to just have fun with it with no extra expectations for a while, though.

You're allowed to have a hobby that isn't connected to a career or competition. That's the biggest thing I tell my millennial students. The drive you all have is incredible, but you are allowed to enjoy something. For you."

"I think I needed to hear that. Thanks, Stacey. I'll see you next week." Stepping out into the cold after sweating in a studio for the last hour is quite the shock to my system. If I wasn't so sweaty, I would probably pop over to the restaurant a few doors down to grab something light to eat. Maybe next week I'll bring a change of clothes and a book and go there first.

Chapter Twelve

KYLIE

MANGO GREEN MILK TEA

Social Post: Authors need to put a warning before the chapters that are going to make me cry while I'm ovulating...not really. #readerthings #readingcorner #whatimreading #romantasyreads
Image Description: Book stack under my lamp on the coffee table.

Have you ever just existed with someone else? Carter and I live and work together, but it's almost like we don't interact much at all. He works every day. When he's home, he's on his laptop, a phone call, or preparing for meetings. My shifts haven't changed, so I have more hours by myself than I am happy with. Reading has become my escape again. I can't wait for the weather to warm up a bit so I can go to the park to read before my shift. I have to keep reminding myself that I don't actually need a full reading space. And that the elaborate reading rooms I see online are a 'want' and not a 'need.' It would be nice, though.

I must have fallen asleep reading on the couch last night, because I woke up being carried. I can smell the familiarity of Carter's arms around me, and I revel in his closeness for a moment. It's been weeks since he's touched me. I don't want to ruin this by letting him know I'm awake. I've missed this so much. He sets me in the bed and slips off my slippers, laying the throw blanket that was folded at the end of the bed over my legs, tucking me in. He brushes the hair away from my face, and I can tell he's just standing there. He leans down to place a soft kiss to my temple. I take the chance and open my eyes.

"Hey, you," I whisper, not wanting to startle him.

"Hey. I didn't want to wake you, but you end up with a stiff neck when you fall asleep on the couch. Sorry for waking you up."

"No, it's okay. Thank you for that. I didn't mean to fall asleep out there."

He smiles at me softly. This is the Carter that I've missed. This is *my* Carter.

"How was the book?" He sits on the bed next to me, and I do an internal happy dance at his closeness.

"It was so good. I cried way more than I thought was possible for a dark romantasy. And it ended on literally the worst cliffhanger. I've already downloaded the second book, so I can jump right in tomorrow."

"I'm glad you found something you love. Can you send me the link so I can grab it, too? Maybe I can listen to it while I go to Chicago with Shaun next week." I instantly am excited that he wants to read something with me, but then I register his words. I sit up and readjust myself so I'm facing him.

"Yeah, I can send it to you. But Chicago? Is this a last-minute thing? I don't remember you telling me about this. What's it for?"

"Well, aren't you a curious little kitten tonight?" He chuckles the question at me. That entire question and the look he's giving me makes it seem like a six-year-old girl asking why I don't have a pony and not a fully-grown woman wanting to know about her boyfriend's life. I don't say anything in response; I just wait.

He shakes his head and rests his hand on my blanket-covered

knee before he answers me, "It's not a new thing. We've had it scheduled since Thanksgiving. It's a restaurant and bar owner expo event in Chicago. Meeting with vendors, farmers, industry leaders, suppliers—the whole thing. It's a big deal that I get to go. I want you to be excited for me. It's just four days. Plus, the travel days. You won't even miss me." He pats my knee and stands to head to the closet.

"So, you leave Tuesday then?"

"Yeah, and we'll be back Monday. There shouldn't be anything too crazy at the restaurant while we are away. It's before the new semester starts, and no one else is on vacation. Don't have too much fun while I'm away," he jokes. Well, I guess he's trying to joke with me. I don't think it's very funny.

"Do you think maybe we can talk when you get back? Or go away just the two of us for a night or two? I miss you." I know I sound needy, and I hate it. But I don't want to push too much for this. I know this season is busy for him, and it's important for him to go to these things. Maybe one day he'll have his own place to run. Is that even something he wants now?

"Yeah, we can talk about it. I need to go through stuff real quick to see if I need to go shopping before the trip. Go back to sleep. Get your rest."

"Okay, let me know. Do you need me to go get you anything beforehand?" He stops for a moment to consider my offer.

"I'll check. I should be good. I may need just some of the travel toiletry bottles." I nod in acknowledgment and am just about to suggest he check under the sink because I may already have what he needs when his phone rings. He chuckles down at the phone before answering it.

"Hey, yeah, I'm just checking to see if I have everything I need or if I need to go shopping before the trip." He's quiet for a minute, listening to the other person talking. I get off the bed and head to the bathroom. I'll just take a quick look to see if there are any little containers already in here so we don't have to buy new things. I quickly find the deodorant, toothpaste, and lotion that he likes to use, along with a small brush, razor, and hair gel. No shopping trip needed. He's just wrapping up the call when I spot the open condom box under the sink. It's been months since we've had sex. I'm feeling hopeful tonight. He's in a good mood.

I set a packet next to the toiletries on the counter. Once he finishes the call, I'm sitting back on the bed. "I think everything you need on is the counter. Let me know if you still need anything, I can get it for you tomorrow before my shift."

"Thanks, Ky," he calls over his shoulder as he walks back into the small room. I wait for him to find the condom, curious to see what his reaction is going to be. Is he going to be playful and ask if I'm dropping hints? Is he going to pretend he didn't see it and then come out here and take charge? Is he going to decide we don't need to use it and he's ready to just be inside me again?

Apparently, it's option D: Throw it into the toiletry bag with everything else and then leave the vanity mirror open and all the bathroom lights on before saying goodnight and heads to the main room—to sleep on the couch again. Well, every action has an equal or opposite reaction, and I am done being quiet and waiting. I'm too tired to confront him, though, so I just go into the bathroom to close everything—and remove the condom and his toothpaste from the toiletry bag.

"Have a good trip, babe," I whisper angrily at the bag. And that's the first moment I start thinking that Carter may not be in love with me anymore.

Kylie

Chapter Thirteen

KYLIE

CHOCOLATE CHERRY LATTE

Social Post: There is seriously nothing worse than not knowing how to dress for an event or a night out. I'm looking at you @sashaloveslipstick! In all love though, I'm excited for tonight with my girls. #birthdaygirl #gettingready #girlsnightout

Image Description: Sneakers, sandals, and high heels lined up next to my bed because I have no clue how to dress for tonight.

When I was in college, I always saw the last year of my twenties as a time of adventure, discovery, contentment, and maybe even motherhood. I never expected to be celebrating my birthday this year as a girl's night out because my boyfriend (not fiancé, not husband) is on another trip for work. At least I can enjoy dressing up and going out to celebrate with the girls—Sasha, Ashley, and Tilly. The girls have become my sisters over the last several months. And getting to see the three of them pour their love and passion into Pink Every Day brings me incredible joy. I've been able to help with some of the marketing campaigns—picking colors, themes, and backdrops. It's nothing major, but it's fun. And it keeps me busy outside of the restaurant and at night, wondering how Carter is doing.

"So, where are we going tonight?" I ask for probably the fifth time since I was given a slinky black dress and a command to get ready an hour ago. All four of us are dressed nicely—cute cocktail-style dresses, hair and makeup done, and none of the guys in sight. Carter is in Chicago *again* with Shaun, Matt is going to some sort of craft faire with his friends, and Tilly and Ashley are both currently going solo. We'll see how long that lasts, though.

Ashley went through it a few months ago and has been home for the most part. After being kidnapped and banged up pretty badly, she's been home most of this semester. The three of us have gone over at least once a week to spend time with her as she recovers. So, this may be my birthday celebration, but we are all glad that Ashley is out of the house and seems to be doing a bit better.

"I'm surprised you don't have your shadow again tonight," I hear Tilly tease Ashley as we get in the car and make our way to wherever we are going.

"He's not my shadow. He's a professor, and there's nothing going on. I'm helping him with TA stuff like I'm supposed to be doing, and he is making sure I don't go crazy being at home all day, every day. He's not my babysitter." I glance at Sasha to see her looking right back. It's pretty obvious that they both have feelings for each other outside of their professional and academic relationship, but it's tricky. We'll have to see what happens once the semester wraps up.

"And on that note, like I've already said multiple times, it's a surprise. But I think you'll like it," Sasha adds, giving Ashley a break from the questioning. Tilly takes the hint to change the subject and starts chatting about the next Pink Every Day campaign that they are working on for the summer season. Lilacs and butterflies— the combination has created some really stunning flay lays, and I can't wait to see the final edits once Matt has a chance to play with them. I'm starting to find my creative spark, apparently. Going with Sasha to find florals and backdrop pieces over the last few weeks has been really enjoyable. I'm surprised at how well things have come together for this campaign. I don't think I want to go into marketing necessarily, but this is fun. And I think I deserve to have a little fun right now.

Speaking of fun, what the heck is this? I audibly gasp when we pull up outside a dance studio. "Please tell me we aren't going to do a ballroom dancing class or something else equally crazy. You know I can't dance," I aggressively whisper to Sasha as she parks the car directly outside the front door.

"No, we aren't taking a ballroom dancing class. It's an exhibition night for a local group. They are going to be performing in several styles tonight. It's a fun night out, and we get to watch people who know what they are doing for a bit. Plus, there might be a coffee and cupcake bar sponsoring the event that I've been wanting to try out."

"Look at you being all creative with your outings." I laugh at Sasha. I love that she is having fun with her new business owner role. She is having such a good time, and although she still deals with anxiety, it is nowhere near as debilitating as it used to be. I think having a steady partner in Matt, as well as the daily support of Ashley, really helps. It's so much more than makeup to her. And it shows.

"Okay, fine, let's go watch people not completely embarrass themselves." I grab my clutch and head inside with my sisters. I love these girls. I couldn't imagine doing life without them now that they are here in my circle.

Walking into the studio feels like excitement on Christmas morning and a perfect cup of coffee all in one. The space has a full wall of windows in the front that I'm sure allows for natural lighting during the day. One wall has mirrors with a barre along the length of it to allow for barre classes and ballet. The back of the large room is set up with seating for others to watch—I'm guessing that's where we will be heading. To the left is a hallway that probably has offices and other meeting spaces, and the coffee bar.

Sasha literally squeals when she sees it, and we head over there right away. We are given a program along with our choice of coffee and cupcake. There are so many choices that I just tell the barista to make me something yummy. Tilly ends up doing the same but asks for a tea or non-coffee option. No surprise that Sasha orders an iced lavender latte and Ashley gets a raspberry mocha. I'm given a chocolate cherry mocha, and I think I have a new favorite drink because it is amazing. After milling about the area and looking at some photos of past performances on the wall, we head to our seats. There are four sections of the evening, ranging from younger kids doing a mini showcase to adults preparing for competitions in the coming months. Kids' Ballet, Adult Line Dancing, Adult Ballet, and Adult West Coast Swing are on the agenda for tonight and I am excited about each of them.

I look over to the others, who are just as enthralled. The first group of kids comes out, and it is the cutest little performance. They do a series of dances from the Nutcracker and Swan Lake to show off what they have learned. My ovaries hurt at the sight. I end up watching a few of the moms across from me as they watch their little ones enjoy the music and movement. One day, that's going to be me. It has to be. As that section finishes, I find myself relieved that I don't have to act okay for the next few groups. I don't have to pretend now. I can just enjoy the music and dances and not stress about the lack of baby—or lack of supportive partner—at the moment.

Country and line dancing have always been a favorite for me to watch, and I am not disappointed by this group. I clap along to the music and the others watching the group of sixteen adults. They go through a series of classic songs and newer pop songs. I didn't know you could line-dance to Ed Sheeran, but here we are. I don't even realize that I've been smiling so much until the song stops and I go to close my mouth.

"Good surprise?" Sasha whispers to me as the group switches out for the next one.

"The best."

I get up to look around during the second half of the ballet set. I needed some air and a break from the noise for a few minutes. There's a slight chill in the air outside as I pass those standing by the doors. There are a lot of people here tonight, and I can see why. Between parents and grandparents watching their kids perform to friends supporting those they know, to a few groups like ours just enjoying a night out. I take a quick look at my phone to see if Carter has texted me. I don't know why I expect anything. It's been weeks since we've had more than a civil conversation. I don't know what I'm doing anymore. I'm surprised to see an unanswered text from him and try not to get my hopes up when I go to open it.

Carter: Happy birthday, beautiful.

Carter: Have fun tonight.

Carter: Not too much. ;)

Despite everything, I smile. Carter has been my closest friend for years, other than Sasha, anyway. I can't imagine not having him in my life. Just as I'm about to respond, my phone rings with a call from him. He must have seen that I saw the messages and figured I'd be available to chat. The next set isn't supposed to start for a few minutes, so I walk away from the door to answer without any background noise.

"Hello." I smile into the phone, even though I know he can't see me.

All I hear on the other end is talking, not to me, but it's like he pocket-dialed me. Who does that with the way phones lock now? Should I hang up? I'm just about to when I hear a familiar voice—Shaun.

"Dude, I know you've been traveling a lot, but not being there for her birthday had to be a hard one for her to take." The sound of glass connecting with a counter is clear, they must be out to dinner or something. Wait, it's ten in Chicago right now. Where are they?

"Truthfully, I don't even know if I told her I'd be gone. Things have been weird recently. I'm focusing on work and helping you, and she doesn't seem to get that. I'm not sure what is happening." He falls silent for a moment, and I cover my mouth, trying to hold back the sobs starting in my throat. I really should hang up. But I can't. Not yet. I'm both glad and devastated that I don't a moment later when the conversation continues.

"Now that, that is happening." He trails off for a brief second, but it feels like hours while I pray that he sees a couple holding hands across the room and not what I know in my gut he is going to say.

"Hey, beautiful, you look like you could use some company tonight."

It wasn't Shaun who said that. I hang up and take a deep breath before texting Sasha.

> Me: I stepped outside for a minute and got sick. I am going to call an Uber and head home. Thank you again for tonight. I'm bummed I'm going to miss the last set. You and the girls mean so much to me. I'll see you at the apartment.

After calling an Uber, I let myself look up at the stars and whisper a prayer to the heavens.

"Happy birthday to me."

Kylie

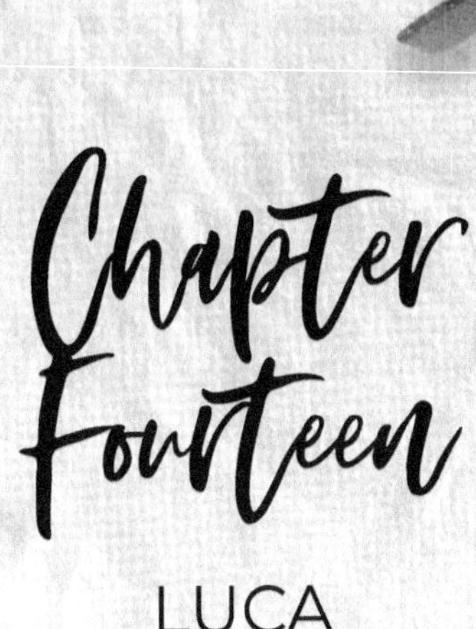

Chapter Fourteen

LUCA

PEACH GREEN TEA LEMONADE WITH EXTRA PEACH JUICE AND VANILLA COLD FOAM.

Social Post: My first exhibition night is here and I am terrified. Dance is an entirely different medium of art than woodworking is. I've learned a lot over these last few months and I'm excited to have a good time tonight. #westcoastswing #coloradonights

Image Description: A rare full mirror selfie. I'm wearing a pair of black pants and a loose-fitting blue shirt.

Seeing her heart break in front of my eyes is not how I thought tonight was going to go. It's my first event that I get to participate in with the West Coast Swing group. I had a song planned with my partner who I usually am paired, and then I was going to do a random song as part of the exhibition. It's the most fun part of our classes now that I kind of know what I'm doing. I'm not an expert and definitely not ready for competitions, but I am having so much fun. I'm able to turn my brain off for a little while when I'm dancing. And I get to experience my own version of joy and contentment.

I arrive the studio and am talking to my partner, Marie, outside when I saw Kylie come outside. She's gorgeous. Wearing a black dress that complements her figure perfectly and a light curl to her hair that shows she got to spend time pampering herself today before coming out tonight, she is hard not to notice. She must be out with her boyfriend tonight. I was supposed to be at the craft faire with Matt and Jonathan tonight, but this popped up, and we worked out a way for me to do both. Hence, I show up right before we take the floor instead of earlier like everyone else.

I wrap up my conversation with Marie, who lets me know where everyone is, and turn to say "hello" to Kylie, but notice that she's on the phone. I argue with myself about whether I should wait around or go inside. I have a few minutes, so I wait. I'm out of earshot of the conversation, so I won't be intruding on anything, but I'm close enough to see her face. It goes from happy to confused to absolutely devastated. My heart starts to race when she covers her mouth with her hand. What the heck is going on? Whatever it is, I want to fix it. Is someone hurt? I'm about to walk over to see if she needs anything when Marie pops her head out the front door.

"We are on in ten minutes; we need you inside, Luca," she says in a no-nonsense way. Marie is very particular about how she likes things to be done, which is honestly very beneficial while I'm still learning the basics of this dance method.

"Coming, I just need to touch base with a friend real fast, and then I'll be right there." She gives me a look that says she is not amused with my plan. I turn around to say something to Kylie only to see her walking away, her eyes on the stars, and a slump to her shoulders that says her day has been completely ruined, if not something bigger than that.

After wrapping up the entire event, I meet up with my troupe at the back of the studio. Tonight was such a good time. No pressures from competitions that some of the others will be doing next month, no judges, and no corrections. Just a fun night. We were able to get some new interest in the classes in the future, too. We had passed out a few free class coupons a few months ago, and tonight was a great chance for community members to see what we actually do. Apparently, Tilly and Kylie attended a class not too long ago when I was delivering a few finished pieces to a studio in Estes. I wonder if she enjoyed it.

"I knew you danced, but I didn't realize you had gotten this good!" I recognize Sasha's voice before I see her. I spin around to see her along with Ashley and Tilly—all dressed up, enjoying a night out. Minus Kylie now.

"I'm going to take that compliment and ignore the doubting-me part of your statement. What are you guys doing here?" I give Ashley a quick side-hug and give an awkward wave to the other two. They didn't initiate any physical contact, and I don't want to be the weird guy who hugs everyone—especially after dancing for close to an hour. I'm sweaty and gross. I desperately need a shower.

"We came out to celebrate Kylie's birthday. She got to come to that class with Tilly, but we haven't had the chance to come and watch. She loves watching this kind of stuff. She wasn't feeling well, so she left, but we wanted to stay until your part was done," Ashley offers the information. I don't think Kylie was sick, but if that's what she told them, I wasn't going to offer any additional commentary.

"Okay, well, I'm glad you guys came out. I think we have an open dance night at the end of the month. You should see about coming." I throw the small towel I had been holding over my shoulder. I really need to head home.

"We may just have to do that. Can you picture Matt coming to one of those with me?" Sasha is obviously pretty tickled by the idea from the blush on her cheeks. The other two immediately start laughing at the idea.

"Matt is an amazing guy, but I don't see him doing this. Maybe he'll come watch, though." I chuckle out my response. "Get home safe tonight, and I'll see you soon." After a quick check-in with Marie to verify practice times next week, I get my things and head home. My house feels quiet tonight. The adrenaline and excitement from the performance are wearing down, and I find my thoughts going back to Kylie. I hope she's okay.

After a quick shower and now wearing a pair of clean sweats, I shoot Matt a message.

> Me: I have those bookends I made for Kylie that I'd like to get to her without it being weird. Do you think Sasha could give it to her?

> Matt: Yeah, probably.

> Me: Can I bring them over tomorrow when I get to the faire?

> Matt: So, you're assuming I'm helping again tomorrow?

> Me: I can go back and find the texts where you said you would if that would make you feel better. ;)

> Matt: Not necessary. LOL. Yeah that should be fine.

> Matt: How did everything go tonight?

Me: It was a lot of fun. Sasha wants you to do a class with her.

There are several minutes before I get a reply, and I just know he's debating if he is willing to do that with her. The man is so gone for that girl.

Matt: If it is really important to her, I'll make it happen. But I'd much rather take her hiking or just go to your first competition with her.

Me: Who says I'm going to compete?

Matt: Because you don't do things halfway. And you are loving this. Don't force it if it's not going to happen. But I think you would really enjoy seeing what could happen with competing.

Me: I'll think about it. Goodnight, Matt. See you tomorrow.

Matt: Night.

Going to sleep takes longer than it should given how tired my body is supposed to be. My thoughts drift from dance steps to projects on my schedule for next week to the tiny honeybees that have started taking up residence in my workshop because I can't get a certain laugh out of my head.

Chapter Fifteen

KYLIE

HOT SPICED CITRUS TEA MOCKTAIL

Social Post: Lilacs and butterflies are such a pretty combination. Here's a behind the scenes look of what I've been helping @sashaloveslipstick with this month. #lilacsandbutterflies #pinkeveryday #socialmediacampaign #prettythings

Image Description: Lilac florals in different shades up against a soft wood background along with a new blush launch from a Colorado makeup brand.

I'm sitting on the couch when he gets home. I didn't bother with makeup today because I'll just cry it off. But I did put on my favorite oversized green sweater and a pair of light-wash denim jeans. I feel beautiful in this outfit. Even without my makeup done and my eyes puffy and red from crying for the last two days. It takes him a few moments to realize I am home. His eyes are on his cell phone, smiling at something as he finishes a text message. His gaze come up to meet mine across the room, and his smile falls.

"You good?" he asks. Seriously? I take a few deep breaths as he comes into the apartment, setting his bag on the ground next to the couch as he stands in front of me.

"I take it you don't realize you called me on my birthday?" I try to keep my tone even, not accusatory, just asking a question.

"I didn't call you."

"You did—go ahead and check." I give him a minute so he can see what time he called me and the fact that the call connected for a whole ninety-two seconds. That's all it took for me to get confirmation that he is done with this relationship. Whether or not I am. He scrolls on his phone for a moment, ignoring the vibration of at least one incoming text message.

"I don't know what you're trying to imply here, but I really don't need this the second I get home. It's been a long few days, and I just want to shower the plane off me." The actual audacity of this man.

"Carter, I heard you. You were out with Shaun at ten p.m.—I don't know why or what the heck you were doing. But you were out, drinking. Again, fine. It's a work trip. I know you have to check out other places on those meetings. But you were talking about me. About how I was distracting you from what you want to accomplish in your life. And then you started talking to someone else—asking if she wanted company for the night. Carter, what are you doing? Are you done with me? Because if you are, just tell me. Don't play these games with me. Please." I try so hard to stay strong through my conversation with him, but halfway through, his gaze hardens, and my will broke. The tears are streaming down my face again as he rolls his eyes. Yes, literally, rolls his eyes at me.

"Kylie, you're being a little dramatic. Nothing happened. I flirted a bit with one of the bartenders. It's part of what we do when we go out. I know things have been busy, but I'm not doing anything besides work when we are out. As for the other part of the conversation, I don't even remember what we were talking about. Whatever you think you heard didn't happen. And it hurts that you come at me with accusations and arguments as soon as I get home.

I'm going to go shower and calm down before I say something I will regret. Go read a book or something." He dismisses me with a wave of his hand to the book stack next to my chair.

So, I grab a book and curl up under my favorite blanket. And struggle to see the words through the tears that just won't stop coming.

The next week, I get hit with one of the worst cycles I've had in years. The pain is unbearable on the first day. It gets so bad that I can't manage the pain at home with what I have over the counter. Carter is at work, and Sasha is at a brand meeting, so I end up calling an Uber to take me to the Emergency Room. I sent Carter three texts asking if he could get home soon to take me. But they went unanswered. Seen but unanswered. Sasha at least texted me back that she was on her way back, but she was at least an hour out. And I didn't think I could wait that long.

Being in the ER by yourself as an adult sucks. Luckily, I'm taken back to a room quickly and given some pain meds while they get me set up with an ultrasound to see what's happening.

Nope, not pregnant. Kind of need to have sex for that one to happen. No, no longer on birth control. Yes, my periods are always awful. Yes, I'm aware I'm overweight, thank you very much. Yes, I am here by myself. Yes, I have someone coming to take me home. Yes, I would like stronger pain medications. Yes, please turn off the lights so I can try to rest before the doctor comes in to talk to me.

I know I probably was a little short with my responses, and I hate that I couldn't tune out the pain enough to respond appropriately. I always have been able to table my own feelings to put others first. I just can't block it out tonight. I must have dozed off because I wake up to a light knocking on the door.

"Hey, lady, can I come in?" Sasha is at the door, dressed in a pair of black dress slacks and a cute pink floral top. I nod at her and can feel the tears already coming again. Now that I'm awake, I recognize the pain again.

"Yeah, the doctor should be here soon to tell me what's going on and hopefully give me some more meds. I'm so sorry I pulled you from the meeting, but Carter wasn't answering, and I didn't know who else to call. I just didn't want to be alone." Sasha comes to sit next to me and puts her hand on the side of the bed, waiting for me to initiate any physical contact. I rest my hand on hers and squeeze gently. I need her here.

"We were almost done when you texted me. That's so weird that Carter didn't dip out to come with you. But I haven't seen him much recently. What happened?"

"I woke up from a nap and couldn't move. This is so much worse than normal cramps. I finally made it to the door and down the stairs to wait for the car. It took me a good fifteen minutes to do that. I don't know what's happening, but this is the worst pain that I have ever been in. I'm not bleeding much, so I don't know what's happening."

"Knock, knock, well that's where I come in." We look up at the door to see a female doctor holding a clipboard and a small paper cup—hopefully filled with more pills for me. "I'm Dr. Sharon Lowe. I know these aren't ideal circumstances to meet, but I took a look at your ultrasound images and the bloodwork we took when you got it. I also went through your history from the OBGYN office you go to, showing some history that might provide some insight on what is happening tonight. Am I good to share things with your friend here?" She comes to stand next to the bed on the opposite side of Sasha. She seems like who you would picture your favorite aunt being. She's probably in her late forties, average height, and the most gorgeous straight red hair pulled back in a headband from her freckled face. She is definitely rocking the no-makeup look, and it works for her.

"If she is good with it, I am." I look at Sasha for confirmation, and she nods. "What's going on?" I ask Dr. Lowe, adjusting my legs a bit to try to alleviate some of the pressure on my lower back.

"It looks like you had an ovarian cyst rupture, based on the fluid in your pelvic area. Have you had one of those before?"

"I don't think so. What does that mean? What do we need to

do now?"

"Most of the time, they resolve on their own. They either rupture or deflate. Rarely, they twist on themselves or even on an ovary, and that's when surgery is required. Unfortunately, you're going to have to ride this one out. The pain will be the worst tonight, but then it will fade tomorrow."

"So, why is this happening now?" Sasha asks. And I'm thankful to have a more competent adult with me to help ask the questions I need to ask.

"After looking through your bloodwork from your last few OBGYN visits, it looks like you have a few abnormal hormone levels. I want you to schedule an appointment with your gynecologist next week to follow up, but it looks like you may have PCOS. It's poly-cystic ovarian syndrome. Basically, your body is making too much testosterone, and your ovaries don't know what to do with it. So, it creates cysts. Sometimes, the cysts just hang out and don't cause any issues. Other times, like tonight, they rupture, causing a Friday night out at your local Emergency Room There are other side effects and implications, but that's the big one you need to know about tonight."

I take a moment to take it all in as Dr. Lowe waits to see if I have other questions. "Is there anything I can do to prevent this from happening again?"

"There are really two options for someone your age—go back on birth control or get pregnant. But to be completely up front with you, women with PCOS struggle to conceive. I won't say it's impossible, because it's not. But it sometimes takes a while. And most of the time, medical intervention is necessary." I blow out a breath, and Sasha grips my hand in silent support.

"Okay, thank you. Do you have some resources that I can read through later when my body isn't trying to kill me?" I do what I can to even out my response. I need to not cry over this. The pain is enough to keep me centered. I can't worry about that hope of becoming a mom getting even farther out of reach.

It's okay. I'll be okay. I'm fine.

Everything is just, fine.

Chapter Sixteen

KYLIE

GREEN TEA MOCKTAIL

Social Post: There is nothing better than a good book and a cozy blanket. #callmebasic #painrecoveryday #cozyday #cozyreads

Image Description: My view out my window from my reading chair, the trees are in bloom at the park area across the street and the spring season is officially here.

Carter: I am going to stay with Shaun this weekend. I think we need some time to breathe, apart from each other. Let me know if you need anything.

I wake up to the text from him the next morning. Yes, the morning after I was in the Emergency Room No sign that he saw the messages I sent him last night or acknowledgment that he even knew I had to go get checked out. Waking up to a good cry seems like the perfect start to a Saturday morning. I send a text to the other manager—not Shaun—and let her know that I won't be in today since I can still barely move. I'll try again on Sunday, hopefully. After being in bed for what feels like hours, I hear a soft knock on the door.

"It's open," I mumble and turn so I can see who it is, already knowing it's Sasha.

"How you doin', babe? Can I get you anything?" She stands in the doorway, and I finally give voice to the fear behind my tears this morning.

"I think Carter is seeing someone else."

Sunday at the restaurant is slow. And I'm thankful for it, because I am emotionally and physically exhausted. I was able to get a message to my doctor and have an appointment scheduled for two weeks from now. Hopefully, we will get some more concrete answers then. Because just waiting to see if I will be in debilitating pain every time I ovulate does not sound like my idea of fun. At least being aware means I can come up with a game plan for it. Carter shows up at the restaurant around two, looking about as good as I feel. Serves him right. I hate that I think that, but that's where I am right now. He hurt me.

"How are you feeling?" He comes up to me while I'm waiting on an order in the kitchen.

"Are you actually going to pretend you care about me today?" I snap at him and immediately cringe. Where did that come from? I am not this person.

"I probably deserved that. I'm sorry about the other night. I had been drinking and didn't see your messages until the next morning.

Not an excuse, but I needed to let you know." He looks at his feet and looks genuinely sorry for how he acted.

"I don't know what is going on, Carter. One minute you seem like you don't care that I am anywhere near you, and the next, you are the man I fell in love with. What do you want? Because I can't keep playing tiptoeing around you and rolling a dice to see how you are going to react. I got some not great news at the hospital, and there are some doctor's appointments coming up to find out the next steps. I need to know if you are with me for that." I try so hard to hold the tears back. We aren't alone here, but if he is finally ready to talk to me, I need to take advantage of the time he's giving me.

"I want you, Kylie. I messed up, and I own that. I don't want to do life without you." He rests his hand on my waist, and I stiffen. I'm not ready to be back in his arms, not right now anyway.

"Okay. Can we maybe do lunch together tomorrow? I'd like to talk somewhere other than at work. I think we both could use a night to rest and get our heads on straight before we talk through this." He smiles softly at my request, and I can't help but return one back at him. He really does have a really beautiful smile, dimples and all. I don't see the dimples now, though, which is totally fine with the sadness still visible in his eyes.

"I'd love that. Noon at the bistro downtown?"

"Perfect." His lips pull up again and he places a gentle kiss on my forehead.

I may regret this, but I can't walk away from him at our first big hurdle. He's been my everything for years. He's my person. I owe him this much.

The next morning, I take my time getting ready. I slip on a favorite sundress and an oversized cardigan because there is still a little nip in the air. It might be June, but Colorado weather is super finicky—I like to say that it's hormonal. Not as hormonal as

I've been recently, but it's all over the place. Nude wedge sandals, a high ponytail, and a subtle makeup look finish my prep at home. Last minute, I grab a bright pink lipstick. With the softer colors on my face, this shade is going to make my eyes pop. It is the perfect match to the florals on the dress. Looking at myself in the bathroom mirror, I'm happy with what I see. Yeah, my eyes still look a little sad and puffy from all the crying, and my coloring isn't great—I've spent a lot of days inside my bedroom recently. I really need to find something to do that gets me outside, or at least outside of the apartment more often.

"Hey, hon, I'm heading out to have lunch with Carter. What are you up to today?" I ask Sasha as I grab my keys and purse off the island in the kitchen.

"You okay with that? I know things are a little weird right now. You don't have to put up with him if he's just going to keep hurting you." Sasha is concerned, and I totally get that. I really hope this whole fiasco was a one-time thing and he's ready to make a commitment to me and to our life together.

"I know. And I won't keep letting him hurt me. I think he saw how badly he messed up. There are probably things I could have done differently too. But I have to hear him out. We've been together over six years. I can't just walk away the first time we have a problem."

"It's not just a problem, though, Kylie. He cheated on you. He hurt you. That's a big deal. I'm not telling you to kick him to the curb, but just think about it. I don't want to see you hurting. And I'm on your side no matter what happens, okay?" She gets up to give me a hug.

"I get that, Sasha. I totally do. And I don't have proof that he was cheating, just a really big clue and a gut feeling. We'll see what happens today and go from there. Love you, girlie."

"Love you, too. Text me if I need to come rescue you."

I hope it won't come to that. The drive to the bistro is quiet and easy. I absolutely love living here. It's busy enough that it doesn't feel like you're isolated, but it's still quiet on a weekday morning that you start to recognize some faces. The place where I'm meeting Carter is a town favorite. The food is good, the atmosphere is welcoming, and it's been our go-to date spot for years. There's something about the comfort of predictability, and I think we both need that today.

I quickly find a parking spot and head inside. It's a few minutes before noon, so I'm not sure if Carter is already here or will be soon. He sent me a good morning text this morning, and I didn't realize how much I needed that. It put me in a great mood as I got ready. I'm genuinely excited to share a meal with him today. I have missed him so much. The waitress brings me to a table by the window, and I sit so I can see the front door.

Me: I'm here. In one of the tables by the corner window. Do you want me to order you a drink or wait until you get here?

I barely get my phone back in my purse when I see him walk in. He's in dark-wash jeans and a short-sleeve light blue T-shirt. The color is one of my favorites, and I smile when I realize he remembered how much I liked it. He looks good. I feel my cheeks heat a little. Why am I nervous and acting like this is a first date? This isn't new.

"Hey, beautiful. Is that a new dress?" He asks after giving my forehead a kiss and sitting across from me.

"Not new, just haven't worn it much. I'm trying to go through the things in my wardrobe rather than sticking with the same things every day. I forgot how much I like getting dressed up and ready." I smile at him for a moment. "Thanks for doing this with me today. I've missed you."

"I've missed you, too. Again, I am so sorry for how things have been. I've been stressed at work, and I took that out on you and our relationship, and that wasn't okay. I know what you heard on the phone the other day. I need you to know, I flirted, I pretended a bit, but I never crossed that line, Kylie. I haven't slept with anyone else. You're it for me. I hate that I put you in the position to doubt that. I still will have travel to do, but I want to figure out a way to reassure you that I'm not with other women when I'm gone. I love you. And I need you to know that." My hands are folded tightly in my lap as I try to ground myself and hear what he is saying. I came into this conversation with so many questions and things I needed to talk through. And right now, I can't remember any of them. I'm more frustrated with myself than with him.

"I appreciate that, Carter. I want to trust you. I want that so badly. I think I just felt left behind. And ignored. There have been a lot of things the last few months that made me think that I was an afterthought for you. And that can't happen." I glance at the ceiling for a moment, trying to stave off the tears threatening to spill over.

Carter reaches over and rests his hand on the table in front of me. I give him my hand to hold, knowing what he is wordlessly asking for. "I'm here now, babe. You aren't an afterthought. You are my everything. Maybe we need to find you something to do when I'm gone so that you aren't sitting around the house stressing and imagining scenarios. What about that dance class you did with Tilly a few months ago? You always loved watching it; maybe that would be a good thing to look into." He smiles at me, and I go back to the night when I was supposed to watch the local troupe's exhibition. He's not wrong. I had such a good time at that class. I was awful, but I had so much fun.

"You know what, I like that idea. I'll see what options there are for beginner classes and what may work for my shift pattern. Thanks, hon."

"We can definitely talk about the schedule stuff too. If you want to back off on how many hours you are doing to have a better balance and give your body time to rest while we go through the next steps with your doctor, I totally get that. I make enough that you can pull back on your hours." I go to interrupt him to tell him that isn't necessary, but he knows where I'm going with things before I even start. "It is no problem, Kylie. You are more important than the restaurant. Financially, we are doing well. You can cut your hours, especially with the new employees we are bringing in for the summer. Now, tell me about this doctor's appointment and what I need to know."

This is the Carter I fell in love with. I squeeze his hand as a silent thank you and try to stop spiraling about what else I may want to do outside of dance. Maybe I can start thinking about something on the creativity side of things, too. Sasha, Ashley, and Tilly have Pink Every Day: What could I do? The next hour goes by quickly and smoothly. We have such a good conversation, and I feel like I have my Carter back. I've missed this. He walks me to my car and pulls a small box out of his back pocket before I get in.

"I got this for you the last time I was in Chicago. I hope you like it." Inside the box is a metal pin. Of a fish. Yeah, it's a fish. I try to school my expression so it looks like I like it. I'm supposed to like it, right?

"Um, thank you. Is there a story behind it?" I laugh a little as I take it out to get a better look.

"Honestly, I don't remember." He laughs as he peeks over the box to look at it again. "As I said, I was drinking a bit on the trip. I remember going into a jewelry store to get you something, and apparently, that's what I picked out for you. There might have been a story that I associated the fish with, or it might have just caught my eye. But I still wanted to give it to you. Maybe as a reminder to keep you as a priority, even when I'm gone."

"So, do you want to wear it then, as a reminder?" I really do hate it. At least he isn't expecting me to jump up and down in giddiness about how amazing it is. Because it definitely isn't.

"Would that help you forgive me for how big of a dick I was over the last few weeks?"

"You mean months?" I prod a bit, and he nods in agreement. "Then, yes, I think you need to wear the fish pin every time you go out of town for the next six months as a way to apologize to me." He laughs and pulls the pin out of the box. After attaching it to his shirt, he leans in for a chaste kiss. It's perfect and sweet and exactly what I need.

"Done. Can I come back to the apartment tonight? Not asking for anything to happen; I know I haven't earned that yet. But I want to be home with you."

"Wear that thing for the rest of the day, and you can come home tonight."

"Done."

Chapter Seventeen

KYLIE

PASSION FRUIT LEMONADE

Social Post: OOTD for a lunch date. It's been a while since I got dressed up to go out and I am starting to wonder why I ever stopped. #ootd #sundressweather #feelingpretty

Image Description: Full mirror selfie of my date outfit today, sundress, cardigan, and a pretty bold lipstick to tie it together.

I don't know why I'm nervous. Carter and I have slept together for literally years. It's been months since he has wanted to be close to me. Longer than that since we've been intimate. I don't know if he doesn't find me attractive any longer or if he was seeing someone else so didn't want to sleep with me too. But he told me there wasn't anyone else when we talked yesterday, and again today. So maybe it was just the stress of things that kept him from initiating intimacy with me. Getting home from the bistro,

I immediately start doing a bedroom reset. Clean sheets, fluff the pillows, fill the oil diffuser, and vacuum. Then a nice bath so I can soak and shave and enjoy the rest of my quiet time.

I'm on the couch, scrolling through West Coast Swing classes in the area when Sasha gets home.

"Hey, hon, how was lunch with Carter?" She sets her bag down and comes to sit next to me.

"It went really well. We got to chat, and I brought up the things that were bothering me. He addressed them and apologized, and I'm making him wear a horrid fish pin for the rest of the day."

"Fish pin?" She's just as confused as I was, well, am.

"Yeah. He drunk-bought it for me in Chicago, so I'm making him wear it. He's going to come back over tonight. I think he may actually sleep in bed with me. No clue if more is going to happen, but I miss being in his arms while we sleep."

"Are you ready for him to come back home?"

I take a moment to stare at the lonely bookshelf on the wall by the TV. "Yeah. I'm ready for him to be back. I miss him."

Sasha pats my leg, then gets up. "Sounds good, Kylie. Please be careful. I hate that he hurt you. You've got people on your side. Don't forget that, okay?"

"I won't. Thank you so much for being here for me. I really appreciate it." I start putting my laptop away. I need to chat with work before I book a class. I want to make a commitment to a full semester, and that means I need an adjusted work schedule first.

"Oh, I keep forgetting to give you these." She pulls out a tote bag next to the couch, one that's been there for a few days, if I remember correctly.

She hands over two stunning pieces of wood—a honeybee and a honeycomb. I think they're supposed to be bookends. "Sasha, these are gorgeous. Where did they come from?"

"Luca made them for you. He stained them with tea rather than coffee or traditional stain. He saw you were drinking tea for Halloween and figured that was your drink of choice. Apparently, tea staining has to be done over time, so it took a while to get these done." I look down at the pieces again; they are stunning. They have the lightest stain to them, and I can't help but smell them. There's a faint scent of what I think is Earl Grey, and maybe something else. The wood still comes through, too. It smells like the best kind of home.

"These are stunning. I'll have to take a picture for him once the bookshelf is set up. Now to decide how to rearrange my shelf to fit these in." Sasha smiles as I smell the bookends again.

"At least I know you won't get high off paint fumes, but probably don't smell them too much. People are going to start thinking things," she whispers conspiratorially, and I can't help but laugh at her. Now, time to fix these bookshelves.

Over the next few weeks, we fall into a new routine. Carter starts bringing food home again. It's a lot later when he comes home, but he brings things that can go in the fridge, so Sasha and I have things to choose from for lunch the next day. I have fewer shifts at the restaurant, only working four days for lunch and two for dinner. I'm home by nine every night, which means I have time for a soak in the tub, reading my latest arrival from my weekly bookshop adventures, and doing yoga in the living room to get ready to start dance classes.

I know I'm probably not going to be any sort of professional, but I want to set myself up for success. I start classes in the middle of August, so I have the whole summer to get ready. I have also been playing around with a sketchbook over the last few weeks. Building different reading corners, craft spaces, and even makeup setups. Magazine cut-outs, artsy quotes, fabric swatches, color palettes, and product ideas. It's so much fun. I haven't shown anyone else yet, but I've done ten projects like this. I wish I had my own space to do this in, but for now, it's in my sketchbook and secret Pinterest boards.

I've also started taking new aesthetic pictures for my social media. Mixed media and textures are inspirations behind my designs, weekly yoga stretches, reminders to drink water, and some of the quotes I've found that have resonated with me during research for my practice rooms. I don't want to monetize my content like the girls do, but I'm having fun with it. I took a really cool picture last week with Luca's bookends. I found a bunch of books that had yellow or pink in them, so they mimicked honey and flowers. Adding a few fake floral stems and a little bee pin to the shelf made a perfect photo. I took a chance and tagged him in it; that way, he could see it. And that I love them! He messaged me on Instagram to ask if I had any more pictures I could willing to share so he could post them too. And then asked if I had more shelf photos because he really liked them. Huh. Okay, maybe it was a good picture.

I'm in the middle of taking photos for a new content series, playing with lighting and some lilac fabric I picked up this week when Carter gets home. It's only noon so I wasn't expecting him. I shriek a little in surprise and then laugh when I see it's just him.

"Sorry, you scared me. How was work? You're home early." He sets his keys down, a little louder than necessary, and then walks over to where I am—in the middle of my lighting, too. "Do you mind taking a half step that way? I have the light hitting this just right from the window," I nudge softly. He didn't mean to get in the way.

"Do you not like having me home early, Kylie?" he asks in a teasing way, bending down where I'm working. He brushes the hair off my shoulder so my neck is bare on the side closest to him.

"No, I like it when you're home. I just wasn't expecting you, is all. I had a mini photo spread planned out and was just trying to get the last few shots before I work on editing and then getting them posted." He hums in acknowledgment before laying kisses on my neck and shoulder, his hands coming to rest on my legs, stroking them lightly over the linen pants I'm wearing.

"You're distracting me," I tease back, adjusting some of the items on my board so I can get new angles and variations.

"Is that a bad thing? This can wait until later, can't it? It's not like you're trying to hit a deadline for a paid project like Sasha does. I miss you." His head adjusts again next to mine, so I can get a small hint of his breath.

"Have you been drinking?" I'm quiet with my question. It's noon on a Thursday. Why on earth does he already smell this strongly of alcohol?

"Maybe a bit. Had a work brunch with Shaun and a few other restaurant owners in town. They started talking about going out last night, and I just had to come home to you." He reaches forward and takes my phone out of my hands and sets it on the ground. "You can work on this later." He pushes my work aside, knocking over the cup of tea that was at the corner of the setup, spilling it all over the book I had open on the edge of the fabric.

"Oh, Carter!" I can't help but yell. I jump up to pick up the cup and try to save the book. I know it's ruined, but this was my signed, special edition of my favorite romantasy. I can't replace this. The tears start falling harder when I realize that my sketchbook also didn't miss the lavender-and-honey-scented tea.

"Kylie, you need to settle down. It's a book. I'll buy you a new one. Can you pick this up and then come to bed with me?" He stands and starts heading to the bedroom, completely unfazed.

"No, Carter. It's not just a book. This is out of print. It can't be replaced. And my sketchbook..." I trail off, not ready to talk about it. I don't even want to open it, to see the destruction inside, the colors that inevitably have all bled together.

He turns around to face me, and his eyes have gone from lust to anger. "Kylie, I suggested you get a hobby, not something you are going to cry over. It's a book. Get over it. Either clean it up and try again or get your ass over here. You've been asking for kids. The doctor said you are good to start trying again, and I'm here and ready. Your choice." He walks away, and I wince at the slam of doors. I am ovulating at the moment. And we only have a few months left to try this naturally. My doctor has recommended medication soon if I don't get pregnant. I am just so very infrequently in the mood, and he hardly ever is. And there have only been two times when my ovulation dates lined up.

Who knows the next time he'll be in the mood? But is this really how I want a baby to be conceived? I stare out the window and let the tears fall for a moment before I make my decision. And start cleaning up the mess left behind by a man-sized temper tantrum.

Chapter Eighteen

LUCA

COCONUT LIME REFRESHER

Social Post: It's days like today where I wish I could work outside more.
#summerdays #woodworking #coloradomorning
Image Description: Blooming flowers outside of my garage workshop.

Someone needs to take my phone away from me. Or at least tell me to stop checking her page twenty times a day. She posts three times a week, maybe four. Me looking multiple times every day is just asinine. But it's a post day for her so she should have some new ones up this afternoon. And she usually sends me a couple that didn't quite "make the cut." Sometimes, it's a bookshelf photo, and sometimes, it's a random mix of other stuff. It's Thursday, so it's probably something book-related if I have to guess. She posted a new tea to her stories yesterday, so there's a chance that will have a feature in the photos too.

My bookends have shown up in a lot of her photos, and it makes me smile every time I see them. I need to make her something new, but those bookshelves are pretty basic. I wonder if I can make her some floating shelves. Can she put those up in the apartment? I'll have to ask her. Or should I ask Matt? That way I can surprise her with them. But that would be weird. Right?

This girl has me questioning every single thing I want to do, and I don't like it. I'm normally very even-keeled. I know what I want to do, and I do it. With Kylie, though, I keep going back to what I had thought to do. Probably because she's in a relationship, dingbat. My internal voice isn't always nice to me, but he's not wrong. She's practically married, without the ring or the title. What is that guy even waiting for? I haven't seen her in person since the night of the dance exhibition. But she posts bits and pieces on her feed. Mostly in her stories. Her feed is a beautiful aesthetic that matches her personality perfectly. She finds beauty in the simplest things, and you can tell which things bring her joy. And I like to think that the random honeybee things that occasionally pop up are her reminders that it's okay to laugh because someone will always smile at the sound.

The next morning comes, and there still isn't a new post up on her feed. I don't know why, but I'm worried. She's been consistent with her content all summer. She even had hinted in her stories recently that she's been working on a passion project she hoped to start sharing. I want to know what it is. I debate with myself for probably a good hour before I finally send her a message on Instagram.

@stainedbyluca: Hey Kylie. Hope you're doing well. I was thinking of making some floating bookshelves that coordinate with the bookends. Do you know if you can attach those to the walls in your apartment?

A few minutes go by before she sees the message, and then the bubbles appear and disappear several times. I finally set my phone down to go shower and get ready for the day. I'm driving myself crazy, wondering what she's going to say.

@kylieljames29: Thanks Luca. I don't think I can attach things like that to the walls. Thank you though. I still love the bookends you made for me. Any special projects this weekend?

I smile before responding. I'll keep it short. I can be just a friend, right?

@stainedbyluca: I have those floating bookshelves I want to play with. I want to do a mix of raw edge and finished sides. I think they'll do well as we start getting into cooler months.

@kylieljames29: LOL. You do know that it's the first week of August, right?

@stainedbyluca: I'm aware. But it takes time to work on these. And this way, I should have them available for purchase by early October.

@kylieljames29: I can't wait to see them.

@stainedbyluca: What about you? How's that secret project coming?

I see her open the message, and then her status changes to "offline." I hope I didn't overstep. Did I push too much? Or maybe she has to get ready for work. I try not to read too much into it. Time for a new project layout, though. I pull out my sketchbook and refill my cup of coffee before sitting down to map out the material needed and vision for these bookshelves. I may be able to do some standing pieces, too. I want to give her something, even if she can't hang it on the wall.

Two weeks later, it's the first dance class of the new season. I wasn't able to do much over the summer since most of the class have kids, which means vacations and lack of childcare. But now that school is back in session, schedules are becoming better managed. I've missed this. If nothing else, it's a night out with others who are looking to have fun and learn something new. It's time when I don't have to stress about orders to fulfill or stains to try out or how many more bees I can put in my workshop without it turning into some sort of an obsession. It may already be an obsession. I can't get Kylie or her sweet laughter out of my head. Sometimes, I think I can actually hear it.

Wait.

I did hear it.

I spin around in the studio to see Stacey talking to a woman about the same height as her. Thick, straight brown hair hangs to her mid-shoulders, and it's a beautiful contrast to the baby-pink T-shirt and black leggings she is wearing. I'm bordering on leering, but she is beautiful. She has just the perfect amount of curves, and I can tell she's been working out by the way her muscles are defined in her calves. There's no way. But then she laughs again, and I get confirmation of what I already knew. Kylie is in the dance studio, and she's dressed to do more than watch this time.

Luca

Chapter Nineteen

KYLIE

ICED MATCHA LATTE WITH LAVENDER COLD FOAM
Social Post: I may regret this in the morning, but here we go. #westcoastswing #somethingnew #adulting #newhobbies
Image Description: Flier from the West Coast Swing class I am taking tonight.

I spent way too much time in my car leading up to this class. It's a beginners' class. I can do this. I signed up for the whole semester—twelve weeks of classes, twice a week. Monday and Wednesday nights. Two hours. Sixteen people in the class, plus at least one instructor, maybe more for some classes.

I can do this. I want to do this. I'm doing this for me. Especially being back to square one with my design sketchbook, I need to do this tonight. Class doesn't start for another fifteen minutes, but I don't want to be the last one in. One more deep breath and I grab my bag and head inside the studio.

I've been here once before, and it feels like the best kind of coming home. It's just missing an oversized chair and a stack of books in the corner. There are a few other dancers already here, some chatting, some stretching, some finishing up phone calls. I go to the desk in the corner to meet Stacey. She's the dance instructor for this class, and she said she'd meet me here. At least I have a clear starting point of where to go. Soft jazz music is playing in the background and it really is settling my nerves about giving this a try.

"You must be Kylie. You're my only new student for this semester. Are you ready?" Stacey jumps into conversation as soon as I make it to the desk. I smile at her excitement. Her platinum-blonde hair is pulled back in a ponytail, and she has a full face of makeup, complete with Barbie-pink lipstick. I'm gonna like this girl.

"I'm super nervous, but I'm excited for this. I took one class last spring, but I want to do something a little more regular. I absolutely cannot dance. My boyfriend jokes that he can only take me out dancing if we are watching and not participating, but I love watching this style. And I figured, I'm going to be thirty next year, it's time I find a hobby that I enjoy, you know?" Why did I just give this woman, practically a stranger, so much information about myself? Internal face-palm, good one, Kylie.

"Everyone is a dancer, Kylie. I'm excited to have you join us. Now, have you done any dancing outside of that one class—maybe when you were in school or any type of barre classes?" I know she's trying to decipher what my baseline is, but the thought of me doing barre classes is legitimately funny. I don't even try to stifle the laugh at that. She smiles back at me as I find actual words.

"No, I haven't done any structured classes for anything dance-related. I've done some yoga—mostly at home. But nothing else. I haven't even thought about taking any dance classes before. I always thought I wasn't coordinated enough to even attempt them. But I made the commitment for this full semester, so I'm excited to see where it goes."

"I love that. And you're going to do great. I'm going to partner you up with someone who's been with the troupe for a few months. He's still learning, too, but he will be able to help you get the feel of things. And he's a couple of inches taller than you, which always helps when pairing people up. Let me call him over to introduce you." She motions to someone behind me, and I spin around to see who she is looking for. Turns out, I won't need an introduction. Because she's calling over Matt's friend, the one who still hasn't told me why I remind him of honeybees. Luca.

"What are you doing here?" he asks as we go to the back wall to start stretching and so he can give me a rundown of how things work.

"I figured I'd attempt to do some dancing. You?" I smile as I set my bag down and plop myself on the floor. I need to change my shoes and start stretching my legs. They're so tight after this morning's yoga practice.

"Same. I didn't know this was something you were interested in or that you would be here." He smiles before sitting next to me to do the same.

"Surprise," I say back. I honestly don't know what else to say, and he doesn't push it. "I'm a little nervous about this, but it's been a really long time since I've done something for me just because it's something I might enjoy. I wanted to give this a shot. I have no clue how it'll go and I may quit after my first class, but I'm here." Decision made; I can do this. I stand and start stretching out my calves, watching the rest of the dancers come in and get settled in their pairs.

"So, how does it work with the pairs? Are we stuck together for the full semester?" I switch to stretch out my other leg, swishing my hair to the side so I can actually see him while I talk.

"Um, yeah, for the most part. We do switch it up most classes so that way you are ready to adjust to any dancer if you decide to do any of the random or improv nights. But the core couples stay together so you can learn the basics. The higher-level classes are where it changes more often." He's quiet for a moment before it seems like something clicks. "Wait, stuck with me? Do I need to be offended by that?" I laugh at his feigned insult.

"No offense. I was just playing. I'm glad to have a familiar face here. Just don't get any splinters in my hands."

"My hands are splinter-free, I promise."

Stacey claps, and the music stops. And it's time for my first class to start.

Class is a whirlwind of laughter, stepped on toes, spins, and figuring out the basics. It's only weird for the first few minutes to have someone else's hands on me. I'm able to follow Luca's lead so easily, and we quickly fall into a sync together. It just... works. By the end of class, I am filled with so much joy and ease. For a few hours, I don't worry about ruined projects or absent boyfriends. I can just be. And it was amazing. It seems like Luca needed it just as much as I did, because he's visibly less stressed than he was at the beginning of class.

"So, what did you think?" he asks as I switch out my shoes and throw a hoodie over my T-shirt. I'm going to be freezing when I go outside. It's dark now, and I'm covered in sweat. I desperately need a shower and probably an unscheduled hair wash, too.

"I really enjoyed that. I was a total mess for half of it, but that was so much fun. It's the right amount of structure that I feel like I can learn and get better without stressing over being perfect right. You know?"

"That makes sense. It's why I love these classes. Can I walk you to your car?" He holds out his hand to help me up, and I don't hesitate to take it.

"If you want, I'm right outside the door under a light. So, I think I'm okay. See you next class?"

"See you next class. And I'm going to be watching for that secret project of yours, Kylie." I immediately feel like twenty pounds just got added to my shoes, and I have to force myself to keep moving toward the doors.

"It's, it's probably going to be a bit before that happens. The sketchbook I was working out of got ruined last week, and I didn't scan the images. I have some things saved on Pinterest, but I'll be starting it over if I decide to give it a go again."

"What happened?" He's genuinely concerned as he holds the door open for me.

"Carter, my boyfriend, accidentally knocked a cup of tea onto it. I had it all laid out on the floor for pictures, so it was my fault for having it in the way. I was careless, and it happened. It was an accident. It's okay."

"Are you convincing yourself or me of that, honeybee?" I place my hand on my car to steady myself and take a deep breath. That question hit a lot harder than he probably meant it to. I need to deflect, or I'm going to start crying and I didn't just put in all that work in that studio tonight to have it undone by a few questions.

"Are you going to tell me about the bee thing yet?" He smiles back at me as I throw my bag into the back seat of the car.

"Not yet. Drive safe, Kylie."

"Thanks, Luca. See you on Wednesday." He waits until my doors are locked and my engine is running before he heads back inside. I think over what he asked me the whole way back to the apartment. The empty apartment. And my empty bed.

Chapter Twenty

LUCA

BLACKBERRY LEMONADE

Social Post: Sometimes you just need a lunch with the guys who have been with you since day one. #localrestaurant #coloradorestaurant

Image Description: Tabletop at a local bar/restaurant with a mix of drinks and appetizers.

I did not expect to have her in my arms tonight. And I did not expect to love it so much. I have to remind myself the whole way home that she is taken. She's not available. She's not mine and can't be mine. I need to make sure I'm not putting myself in a position where I start having feelings for her. Because that can't happen. I decide that I need to schedule another guys' lunch and text Matt and Jonathan once I get home.

Me: What is everyone up to tomorrow around lunch time?

Matt: Nothing scheduled right now, what's up?

Jonathan: I'm free. Unless you want to move more heavy crap. I don't have the energy for that tomorrow.

Me: Did you actually have to work today? LOL

Jonathan: I take offense to that.

Jonathan: I do work.

Jonathan: Just because some of my work is in an office and not fully in the garage anymore, doesn't mean I don't work.

Jonathan: But yes, I had to do physical work today. I'm sore.

Matt: Aren't you the boss? Do you need to hire more guys?

Jonathan: I'm in charge of this location, yes. But I enjoy getting my hands dirty. I don't want to get out of practice with things.

Me: So, back to tomorrow…

Matt: What did you want to do?

Me: Figured we could get a casual lunch, without the girls.

Matt: You do realize I'm the only one with a girl, right?

Jonathan: Yes, but she usually has an entourage with her.

Matt: One of whom is my sister.

Jonathan: And her pain in the neck "bestie"

Me: Am I picking up some tension here?

Jonathan: No tension, none at all. Lunch is fine. Where do you want to go?

Me: The bar/restaurant near the studio. They have a good lunch menu, and their seasonal apps are pretty incredible. I want to get the caprese skewers one more time before they switch to the fall menu.

Matt: Sounds good. But are you turning into a foodie on us? First, dancing, now food. I can only keep up with so many hobbies.

I meet the guys outside the restaurant, and we all head in together. It's slow, so there's no one at the host's stand, just a sign that asks us to seat ourselves. We end up finding a table close to the bar and catch the eye of the blonde bartender working. I'm not sure if she's working the tables too, but she seems more than excited that a group of guys around her age just came in. Great. She walks over with a tray of water glasses and some menus before introducing herself.

"Hey, guys. Welcome in. I'm Chelsea, and I'll be helping out today. I'm normally just behind the bar, so let me know if there's something special you want. What brings you in today?" She positions herself between myself and Matt. I'm not sure about him, but she keeps lightly brushing up against me. It's a little weird. I subtly shift my seat so I can angle toward her and talk to her without her touching me.

"Can we start with two orders of the caprese skewers? And then I'll take the blackberry lemonade for my drink." The guys order something similar, and Chelsea sashays her way back to the bar to put in our orders.

"She is trying way too hard," Jonathan mumbles behind his menu once she's out of earshot.

"Okay, so it wasn't just me?" I try to keep my voice down, but being blatantly hit on is not something I'm used to. I'm not a bad-looking guy, but I tend to keep to myself. And when you spend most of your day locked up in a workshop, there's not a lot of opportunity to meet people.

"This is just another reason why I'm ready to get married—I need a ring on my hand so people leave me alone," Matt mumbles from his side of the table, and we both drop our menus to stare at him. He finally notices and continues, "Oh yeah, I think I'm going to propose to Sasha this fall. Do you want to see the ring?"

"You went ring shopping?" Jonathan is anything but quiet in his response, and I don't blame him.

"I can't believe you didn't tell us. We would have gone with you, Matt," I add as Matt pulls out his phone and presses an unholy number of buttons. He must have it hidden inside five different folders so Sasha can't find it.

He finally passes the phone over so we can take a look. It's a stunning marquis piece. A solitaire diamond is the center of the design, bracketed by smaller pink stones, all set in a white gold band.

"That's beautiful. She's going to love that. Sapphires or diamonds for the pink stones?" I ask as I pass the phone over to Jonathan to look.

"Diamonds. I got her a tennis bracelet to match, too. I'm thinking of proposing on one of our fall hikes. It's such a special thing for us, and she loves the mountains."

"I'm happy for you. She is a perfect fit for you. Just don't screw it up again."

"I'm going to do my best."

An hour later, I feel so much better. Getting to spend time with the guys is something I never take for granted. We've been friends since high school, and with jobs and relationships, things are changing. I don't want to lose what we have. I'm filling out the receipt when I notice the blonde behind the bar again. She is not quiet, so it's not hard to overhear her.

"Yeah, her hours got cut a bit. She thinks it was her choice, but it was going to happen either way. You know, she's getting a little older and isn't bringing in as much for tips anymore. And working with your boyfriend is bad luck. She ought to know that." I don't turn, but I hear another voice, probably a guy at the bar.

"Her boyfriend is in management here, isn't he? How is he doing not having her around as often?" There's a pause, and I make eye contact with Matt, trying to piece together what is being said. I'm almost one hundred percent positive that this is the place where

Kylie works. Is she talking about her?

"Honestly," she starts and then drops her voice, but I'm close enough to hear it. "He's a lot happier with how things have been between them recently. Now that she isn't here all the time, he's able to have a little fun without her being all clingy. They've been together forever. Maybe he's ready to try something new." She giggles, and it grates on me. I go to stand and motion for the guys to do the same. I'm really regretting leaving her a tip right now, but I'm not going to cross it off.

"Something or someone?" The suggestive voice at the bar just spurs me on.

Once outside, I look at Matt. "Please tell me that's not what I think it was. Kylie works here, doesn't she?"

Matt looks at the name of the restaurant and then pulls out his phone. After pulling something up, he nods. "Yeah. I really hope that girl wasn't talking about her and Carter, though. That would be devastating. I'll see if I can bring it up to Sasha and ask how things are going. I don't want to overstep, especially if she was talking about someone else."

"I get that. I just don't want to see her get hurt." I start walking to my car, mind running in a thousand different directions while I try to piece together what was said.

"She's in a relationship, Luca. Don't do something to hurt that. She's been with him for a long time." Matt is the voice of reason, and in this moment, I kind of hate him for it.

"I know she's in a relationship. I am fully aware. I had to dance with her last night and keep reminding myself of that fact. I just. I can't stop thinking about her. Now we have class together, I get to hold her and see her smile. The way she lit up last night was incredible. And it guts me to think that her boyfriend is throwing that away." I stop talking and look up at my friends. Both are staring at me, and I realize I just way overshared.

"Oh, you got it bad, dude." Jonathan doubles over laughing, and I give him a death glare, if I could do a death glare. I try anyway.

"Just be careful, Luca. I didn't know she was taking dance classes with you."

"Yeah, last night was her first class. I'll be careful." We say our goodbyes, and I head home. I have a new project to start working on for my honeybee. And I don't bother to correct myself when my thoughts call her that this time.

Chapter Twenty-One

KYLIE

RASPBERRY HIBISCUS TEA

Social Post: My view for sketching today. Thankful for weather changes and moments of calm in a busy season. #workview #myowncoffeedate #windsorco

Image Description: Black iron table outside the coffee shop, open sketchbook, colored pencils, and a mug of something warm and yummy.

The fall season is here, and I am loving the cooler weather. With my changing work schedule, I actually have time and energy to take walks in the mornings. My doctor said that me getting in shape and staying active will increase my chances of getting pregnant, so I'm trying to do what I can. The dance classes should help, too. The nip in the air is the right amount of chilly as I start my audiobook and begin walking to the coffee shop. It's a little over a mile and the perfect distance for what I need. Plus, the shop has become my place of inspiration.

I've started drawing again. I think this second round of spaces I've created is better than what I had in my first sketchbook. Different reading corners, hobby spaces, and a mix of elaborate and cozy spaces bring me more joy than I thought would be possible. I never thought I was necessarily good at any one thing. My friends had these big dreams while we were in high school and college, and I was content to go with the flow. I got to cheer on other people and support their dreams. And that was enough for me.

I think once I realized Carter was finding his dreams, and I was being left behind, that I allowed myself to begin finding my own passion. Will this ever turn into anything? I have no idea. But I'm having fun. And I think I'm doing a pretty good job. Once I make it to the coffee shop, I send Carter a quick text, telling him I made it okay. I rarely get a response, but I feel better when someone knows where I am.

> Me: I'm at the coffee shop. I'll probably be here until it's time for me to get ready for dance tonight.

> Carter: Okay. Have fun.

> Me: Do you think we can do lunch tomorrow? I have a doctor's appointment in the morning, and I know it'll be early, so you may not be able to come with me, but I'd like to spend some time with you.

> Carter: IDK Kylie. We have the menu switching over and there's things I need to do here. Let me know how it goes. And I'll see what I can do.

> Me: Okay. I am on track to be
> ovulating this weekend…

I'm not surprised when he doesn't respond. We have had sex four times this year. Yep, year. No exaggeration. Part of me is seriously questioning taking the step into parenthood with him. But another part of me realizes that I'm almost thirty. Do I really have the time to have a whole other relationship and life with someone before my chances of being able to conceive and carry a pregnancy decrease even more? I feel stuck, which is an awful thing to think. Carter has been more attentive in recent weeks. He even moved some things around in our bedroom so I could have a reading corner. I can't decorate since we are still in an apartment, but it's something.

I'm finishing up a raspberry hibiscus tea when one of the baristas comes over to clean the table next to me.

"What beautiful things are you whipping together today?" she asks as she looks over my shoulder at my sketchbook. I make a note of her name tag before I answer her to make sure I remember her name. I smile at myself when I realize I did remember that it was Charity. Yay me!

"It's definitely not a 'whip together' project. I've been coming back to this one a lot and think it's almost done. It's a reading corner for one of my friends. Her boyfriend, well, not technically her boyfriend, they had to pause that for a bit, but anyway… it's a reading corner for her. She's got an autoimmune disease that always makes her cold, so there are a lot of extra fabrics here to make it feel like a cozy space. The lavender décor complements her favorite pink that I have on the wall and pillows. Her boyfriend is in publishing, so I have the concept for a book wall here." I point out the features on the sketchbook and smile at the almost finished project. I don't know if I'll ever be able to build this for Ashley. But I needed to do this for her.

"What if you added some floating shelves with the book art? That way, it breaks up the texture and depth a little, and she has some flexibility to change it out. Since the paper art doesn't look like it would be easily moved," Charity suggests, and I take another look at the page.

"That would actually work out really well. I have a friend who does wood working; his shelves would look great here." I quickly make a note of the shelves and look at the finished piece. "I'm really happy with this." I smile at it. It's all done. And it's perfect.

"Are you working with an agency to start working on spaces like this?" she asks as she picks up my empty glass.

"No, I'm just fooling around. I don't think I could do this professionally." I close my book so I can start walking home. It's early, but I'm debating trying to chat with Luca about those shelves before the inspiration leaves me.

"Well, I'm graduating soon with a degree in interior design. There's a market for what you are doing. It doesn't have to be anything crazy, but you have a good eye. Just think about it."

"Thanks, Charity. I will." I smile at her and start heading home. Maybe I can start by creating some spaces for my friends. I don't have to launch a full-blown business. But I would love to see my drawings become a reality.

"I'm home! I had such a good work sesh at the coffee shop. Do you want to see what I finished?" I drop my keys and call into the apartment when I see Carter's keys are here. I thought he was at work, but I must have been mistaken. I'm home earlier than usual, so maybe he just popped home to get changed. He isn't in the main space, so I start making my way down the hall to our room. The door is cracked open, and I hear his voice on the other side. Maybe he's on the phone. I raise my hand to begin pushing it open when I hear another voice in there with him. And I freeze, unable to move as my world completely shatters on the other side of the door.

"I could spend the rest of my life right here, baby. You feel so good around me." Carter's voice is unmistakable; the exertion behind his words tells me what I would see if I were to open the door. I need to know who he's with, though. I have to know.

"Carter, don't stop. Please. She'll be home soon, and I need you." She gasps, and I cover my mouth with my hand to stifle the sobs quickly building. I know that voice. I knew. I knew he was seeing someone else, but I convinced myself that it was all in my head.

"I'm going to come inside of you, Chelsea. I'm going to give you what I never give her."

And with the sounds of his betrayal and her screams of pleasure still ringing in my ears, I grab my keys and head outside.

Chapter Twenty-Two

LUCA

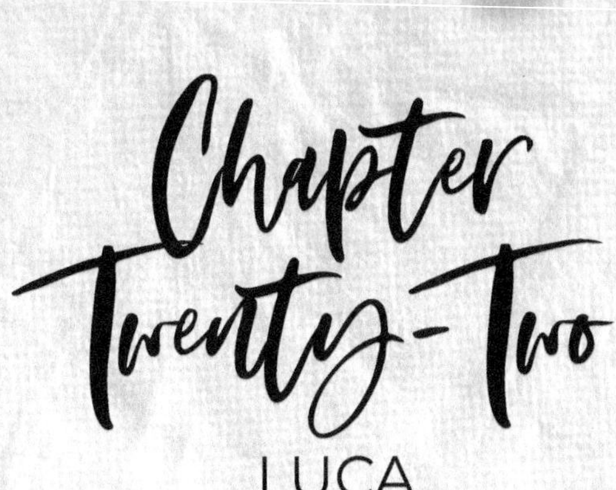

CARAMEL APPLE CIDER

Social Post: Updated WIP photo from some items I'm preparing for the holidays. I know it's early still, but gifting season never truly stops. What do you think? #holidaygifts #ornaments #somethingsimple

Image Description: First batch of finished Christmas ornaments before I stain them and prepare them for listing.

I'm getting ready to leave for the studio when my phone notifies me that someone has messaged me on Instagram. I get messages all day long because of the work I do, so I usually only check in the morning during my office hours. Otherwise, I would get nothing else done. I pull it out to put the app back on Do Not Disturb when I see that it's Kylie messaging me.

@kylieljames29: I'm sorry but I don't think I'll make it to class tonight.

@stainedbyluca: Is everything okay?

The bubbles pop up on my phone and disappear—over and over again. So, I send her another one.

@stainedbyluca: Are you okay?

@kylieljames29: Honestly, no. I'm not okay and things are not okay. I don't even know where I am right now. I just started driving and just realized that class starts in half an hour, and idk where I am.

@stainedbyluca: Can I come get you? Or meet you somewhere? Are you safe?

@kylieljames29: I don't think I should be driving. But I can't take you away from class. It's fine. I'll get an Uber or something.

@stainedbyluca: Send me your location. I'm coming to get you. Please let me do this.

There's another pause in her messages while I wait. I don't want to push her, but I need to know that she's okay.

@kylieljames29: Okay. Can I text it to you? I'm just in a parking lot with a coffee shop and a few other businesses. I'll wait in the coffee shop if that's okay.

I quickly send her my number and a moment later, her location drops into my messages.

> Me: I'm on my way. Get something yummy and sit tight. I'll let Stacey know we won't make it tonight.

> Honeybee: Okay. Thank you, Luca.

Forty minutes later, the Uber drops me at a coffee shop in north Denver. She seriously drove for quite a while if she ended up here. It's a smaller town, but she's not far from the craziness of those going into the city after work or to a midweek show. I recognize her car from the classes she's attended and make my way into the coffee shop. My eyes connect with hers as soon as I walk in the doors. The puffy eyes and tear stains on her cheeks tell me that her world has completely shattered. I send up a silent prayer that she will let me help her pick up the pieces.

I sit with her for a little while. She hasn't said anything, and I don't think I should push her. I sent a text to Matt, letting him know where I am and that Kylie is here and upset. Matt said he would talk to Sasha, but at least we know she is safe, and she doesn't appear to be physically hurt. I got a chai for each of us about twenty minutes ago, and she finally started sipping it once she saw me do the same.

"Do you want me to bring you home, or do you want to sit here for a little while longer?" I finally ask her. I don't want to push her too much, but it is getting late, and I don't know what she needs. This is the first time I've seen her outside of dance class since the Halloween party last year. She doesn't make eye contact with me, but she braces herself like she's going to tell me what happened.

"I got home earlier. About a year ago, I had a feeling that he might be seeing someone. But then he denied it and things were fine. We were going to try for a baby. But then he went back on that. There's been so much back and forth. He was supposed to be my everything. It's been seven stupid years. I'm almost thirty. I'm out of time, Luca. And he just threw it all away. And for what? A younger blonde model from the restaurant. His employee. How freakin' typical. I just… Why wasn't I good enough for him? Why am I not good enough? I have my fertility appointment tomorrow, and I needed him. But he obviously doesn't need me anymore. I don't know what I did wrong." She takes a deep breath, and I have to fight to stay still and listen. She isn't done, and she needs to get this out.

"What did I do wrong, Luca?" She looks at me, and the sadness in her eyes would have brought me to my knees if I weren't already sitting. I ball my hands into fists to avoid touching her or pulling her into the hug she so desperately needs right now.

"You didn't do anything wrong, honeybee. He messed up. He threw away the best thing in his life. He did this. Not you. He didn't see the treasure he had. You were good enough. You still are good enough. I am so sorry he didn't see it." I don't catch myself in time and reach up to brush a strand of her hair back from her face. I hate seeing her hurt like this.

"Do you want me to call Matt and see if you can stay with Sasha and him tonight? What do you need?" I ask her, trying to shift my body so I'm facing her a little better. Her phone dings at that moment, and she pulls it out, shaking her head when she sees what it is.

"What is it?" I ask her.

"Guess who's calling." She laughs derisively and goes to decline the call.

"Can I?" I ask her, holding out my hand.

"What are you going to do?" She is apprehensive, and I don't blame her. I don't think I've ever been angrier at any point in my life like I am now.

"I'm just going to tell him he messed up and I hope his dick falls off from sleeping around instead of taking care of what he had in front of him." She chuckles and ignores the call before putting the device back in her purse.

"Maybe later. I'm not ready to have a conversation with him. I don't think that would help anything. Can you take me home? We can call Sasha and Matt on the way and see what we can figure out for tonight. I have my appointment first thing in the morning, and I need to be rested for that. They're running the next round of tests to see what my levels are. And I guess I could probably cancel that since there won't be any baby-making practice in the next who knows how long." She pauses and gasps, causing me to jump a little.

"What? Are you okay?" Is she hurt? What just happened?

She stares straight ahead out the big windows in the front of the coffee shop. The tears fall silently now, and I wait for her to speak. When she finally does, I can't help but reach for her hand, giving her some stability in the midst of everything that has happened.

"Carter did want a baby. He just didn't want one with me."

Luca

Work has become my peace. Where I have been able to let myself be free. Don't get me wrong; I love Kylie. But our relationship has started feeling restrictive more than something to revel in. And the pressure to be parents, I don't know if I'm ready for that.

At least, I wasn't ready for that.

Until Chelsea.

This girl makes me feel things Kylie never did. She lets me take charge both in the restaurant and the bedroom. She provides support during work meetings and has brought so much to the restaurant. I don't know where I would be without her. I almost chuckle thinking back to when Kylie asked if she could be involved in the event planning. After seeing the little drawings in her books, I'm glad I told her 'no.' Could you imagine a girlie reading corner in the bar? I do chuckle at that.

I'm just finishing up going over inventory on the floor when I get a notification on my phone.

Reminder: Fertility appt today at ten.

Shit. I missed it. Did she really expect me at another one of these things, though? It's been bloodwork and specialist visits and medication. They had started talking about shots at the last visit and how I would probably need to help her. No, thank you. I'm debating sending her a text to see how it went when I look at the time. It's three in the afternoon. Why haven't I heard from her?

"Hey, baby. Are you staying with me tonight?" Chelsea presses her body into mine, and I immediately lose the tension in my shoulders at her closeness. She smells like vanilla and bourbon, and I love it. I love that my pillow at home smells like her, and I laugh at the thought that Kylie is so oblivious that she hasn't noticed.

"That's the plan. I'll be off before you, so I need to pop back to my place to get a change of clothes, and then I'll be over." I place a kiss to her forehead, inhaling her shampoo, and then head back to my apartment. If I time this right, Kylie should be working at the coffee shop again on her coloring pages or whatever she is doing and I won't run into her. She's always really moody after these appointments.

KYLIE

THAT MORNING

I didn't want to do this appointment alone, but Sasha had a meeting she couldn't move, and Ashley and Tilly both had classes. I spent the night at Sasha and Matt's last night, but I'll need to go back to my place tonight. If for nothing else than to pack a bag and get a hotel or something. I can't stay with Carter. I had gotten another round of bloodwork done on Monday, so today is to go over the results and see if we are any closer to getting to a place where I can conceive and carry. I get changed and settled on the uncomfortable table while I wait for my doctor. I have begun dreading this place. Seeing all the expecting moms in the waiting room, the newborn cries for first postpartum visits, and the baby announcements on the walls. When is it going to be my turn?

"Hey, Kylie. So sorry to keep you waiting." My doctor comes in with a soft smile on her face. She sits on the swivel chair and takes a moment to look over the papers in her hands.

"Have you and Carter discussed what you want to do about alternative parenting options?" she asks as soon as she has finished perusing the papers. What did she say?

"I'm sorry? What do you mean?" My hands are shaking, and my heart races as I wait for her to explain. I'm sitting here, wearing a paper gown, and if she just said what I think she did, I may honestly pass out.

"Did they not go over your bloodwork results when you first came in?" I shake my head, begging the tears not to fall yet. I need to hear her.

"Well, they don't look good, Kylie. With your age, the increase of cystic activity, and the levels you are currently showing, I don't believe you will be able to conceive naturally. I recommend we do an exploratory surgery to see the extent of scarring from the cysts. But if it's as bad as you say it has been, I don't think carrying a child would be a smart decision. It would put you or the baby at risk." She says the words as if they are from a script. No emotion. No sympathy. Just—oh, you wanted a baby? Sucks to be you. Not really, but that's how her words felt.

"Is Carter here with you today?" she asks, and I realize I must have zoned out at some point during her mini speech.

"Um, no. He had to work." I'm numb. Just completely numb.

"Okay. Go ahead and get dressed. I have some brochures here for you on IVF, surrogacy, and adoption and fostering options. There's more than one way for you to become a mom, Kylie. Natural conception isn't an option for you. Have a good day."

And then she's gone. I must zone out again because the next thing I know, I feel a hand on my shoulder. I turn to see Sasha. Why is she here?

"Why are you at my doctor's office?" I whisper to her.

"They called me. I'm still listed as your alternate contact in case they can't get in touch with Carter. Are you ready to go, babe? Let's get you dressed." I guess that means that Carter didn't answer. I go through the motions of getting dressed and walking to the car. I am vaguely aware of Matt's voice and someone else—it sounds like Luca—but I don't register anything.

"I'm going to take you to the apartment so we can pack a bag for you. You are going to come stay with us for a few days, okay?" Sasha's words are quiet, and all I can do is nod in acknowledgment.

"Are the guys coming, too?" I finally whisper. My throat hurts, and the words feel funny coming out. I don't even feel connected to my body right now.

"Yeah. Is that okay? I need to grab some things from my room, and we weren't sure how much you wanted." I nod again. Before I know it, we are home. Luca opens my car door and offers his hand to help me out. I take it for that moment but quickly drop it. I don't want to be touched right now. It feels weird. No, it felt good, but my body doesn't get to feel good right now. It doesn't work properly. Maybe that's why Carter didn't want me.

"How'd the appointment go?" I hear a familiar voice say seconds before a loud smack and then a thud as Carter's body hits the ground.

Kylie

Chapter Twenty-Four

LUCA

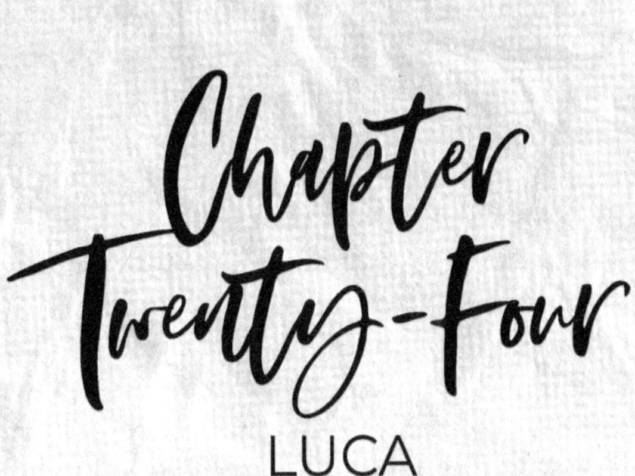

BROWN SUGAR PUMPKIN SPICE SHAKEN ESPRESSO

Social Post: Another perk of Colorado is all the sunshine. I'm able to leave wood out on the back deck to dry, cure, stain, and not worry about it getting rained on. Most of the time anyway. #projectprep #coloradowoodworking

Image Description: Various projects laid out on my back deck enjoying the sunshine.

I have never in my life hit another person. But the second we walked into that apartment, I saw that he was holding an overnight bag, his eyes still glued to his phone. He didn't realize we were standing there and his girlfriend was absolutely broken. And something snapped in me. One moment, I was entering the room, the next, I was standing over Carter with a sore hand and a bloody nose for him.

"What the hell, man? Who do you think you are?" Carter starts standing and then looks at the rest of the people in his apartment. "Kylie, what happened?" She just shakes her head and goes down the hall with Sasha. Matt stays next to me. I'm glad I have him here with me. I may have kept hitting Carter if I were here by myself.

"Why weren't you at that appointment today?" I take a breath and start with the most logical questions. I don't know if he even knows that Kylie knows he's been cheating. If I weren't so angry at this guy, I would be chuckling over the Friends similarities.

"I had to work. These appointments are all the same; I didn't need to be there. But I have to get back to work, so if you are done assaulting me in my own home." He goes to push past me, but Matt puts his hand on his shoulder to stop him.

"I think you need to sit for a minute." Matt motions to the couch.

"And if I don't?" The audacity of this man.

"I have no problem hitting you again. You messed up. Badly. And that incredible woman who you claim to love has had her world shatter in more than one way over the last twenty-four hours. You will not add to that by brushing it off." I hear a noise behind me and see Kylie. She's changed and is now in a pair of black leggings and an oversized green sweater. Her hair is in a messy bun, and she's taken off her makeup.

"Kylie, what is going on?" Carter attempts to sound interested and possibly even hurt. I shake my head and cross my arms, just waiting for a reason to hit him again.

"I walked in on you and Chelsea yesterday." She lets the words sink in, and Carter must know he's caught because the color drains from his face.

"It's not what you think, babe."

"It's not what I think? Are you serious right now? What does she have that I don't? Because I don't get it, Carter. We were supposed to be trying to get pregnant. Instead, I find out that you are busy filling her every chance you get. I have done my best to support you and be there for you. I was fine being in the shadows because I was looking forward to the days that I would get to be home with a baby. Our baby, Carter. And now that is gone. So, congratulations. You got your wish. You will never have that with me. You blew it. Get your stuff and get out. I'm not running away because you didn't have the decency to tell me you wanted to get your dick wet elsewhere." I have to fight back a smile at how proud I am of her strength.

Carter stands and starts walking toward her, but I am the one to put my hand on his shoulder this time. "You can talk to her from over here."

"I never meant for it to get like this, Kylie."

"You should have made that decision before you started cheating on me, Carter. Go get your stuff. I'm done."

"You can't kick me out."

"What?" I look at Kylie and see she is just as flabbergasted as I am. Sasha is, too, and I'm sure Matt is wearing a matching expression behind me.

"My name is on the lease. I'm not leaving. You can have Sasha's room, and I will stay in the other one until you can find another place." He's gone from remorseful to cold, and Kylie is visibly shaken at the switch. Sasha rests her hand on her friend's shoulder to steady her.

"But I will let you have a few days. I'll be at Chelsea's. Have your stuff moved to the other room by the time I get back on Monday. Oh, and you're fired. You've missed too many days without a doctor's note."

Over the next few days, I don't leave my workshop much. I text Kylie in the mornings to see how she's doing and if she needs anything. I get basic responses of she's okay and she's resting and she's taking her time, but nothing more. I don't want to push, though. Sasha has been staying at the apartment with her, so Matt has been on edge not having her with him. They got engaged a few weeks ago and are fully in wedding-planning mode. That has taken a back seat now so they can focus on Kylie. I don't think she realizes how much everyone around her loves her and would do anything for her. How long has Carter been treating her like trash? Because she seems to be surprised every time I check on her.

On Monday morning, I send her another good morning text. This time, with a picture attached. I finished a new project this weekend—being in the workshop for sixty hours will do that. It's a tea box. She may be a coffee drinker, but she loves tea. I stained it with the same tea that I made her honeybee bookends with. On the top of the box is a carving of a honeybee and a few lilac flowers.

> Me: Good morning. Can I pick you up for dance class tonight?

> Me: <Image Attached>

> Honeybee: That is so beautiful, Luca. What is it for?

> Me: You didn't answer my question...

> Honeybee: I'm not sure I'm up for class tonight.

> Me: Can I come get you and we will take it easy? We can just watch if that's all you want to do, but I think it would be good for you to come.

> Honeybee: Why?

> Me: Because the music makes you happy.

> Me: And you make me happy.

Honeybee: You can't say stuff like that, Luca.

Me: Why not?

Honeybee: Because I know we dance together, but I literally just got out of a pretty big relationship. I have had a horrible last few days. I know you think you're being sweet, but you're coming across as flirting. And I can't handle mixed signals or reading into things right now. So just, please, behave.

Me: What if I was trying to come across as flirting?

Honeybee: I don't know how to respond to that.

Me: I can wait until you're ready.

Me: And it's a tea box. For you. I'll give it to you when I pick you up tonight.

Honeybee: Luca

Me: I'll pick you up at six and I'll have a smoothie for you so you can eat something before class. Make sure you stretch, just in case you decide to dance.

Honeybee: We'll see

Chapter Twenty-Five

KYLIE

AUTUMN HARVEST PUNCH MOCKTAIL

Social Post: Grieving over someone who never actually existed is a sadness I wasn't expecting to ever feel, but the hurt is deep and I don't know how to handle it. Not ready to share the full story, but got the official infertility diagnosis last week. I've wanted to be a mom for forever, and having that dream gone is beyond devastating. #infertility #thisisgrief

Image Description: A baby book that I had purchased several years ago and have held onto, waiting for the chance to use it. The only things on the pages now are my tears and the latest round of lab results.

I don't remember much from the last few days. I've woken up, drank some water, gone to the bathroom, eaten whatever was easily grabbed, and gone back to bed. I've existed. I've cried. No, that's not right. I've been in mourning. Mourning the relationship I thought I had. The future that was in front of us.

Mourning the love and the time I gave him, and to have him throw it away so easily. How long has he been seeing her? Was it just her? How long did he say no for? Was he the one to initiate? Do I even want to know?

I've also been mourning the fact that at this rate, with my circumstances, I probably won't ever get to see those two pink lines on a pregnancy test. I won't get to take maternity pictures or plan a first birthday party. I won't be able to design the nursery in my sketchbook. The one covered in lilacs and honeybees. One of the few from my first sketchbook that wasn't ruined. I unfold the paper and stare at it again as I lie in bed. Luca's text woke me up, but I haven't gotten up yet. I barely had it in me to roll over to my nightstand—Sasha's nightstand—to get the paper. I was so proud of this design. I was even debating posting it on my socials. I'll never have the chance to create it now.

I press the paper to my chest and fall asleep again. It's the only time that everything doesn't hurt. In this moment, I can't handle all the feelings. I just need it to stop.

I don't know how long I've slept for, but I'm woken up when I hear voices in outside the bedroom door. Great, Carter is back. I can't deal with him right now. I'm about to pull the covers over my head when I hear a giggle—a female giggle. Did he seriously bring her back here? You have got to be kidding me. I peer at my phone and see that it's four in the afternoon. Luca will be here in two hours. I know it's only been a few days, but Carter doesn't get to see how much he's broken me. Time to get my ass in the shower and get ready to go dancing.

At 5:45, I get a text that Luca is outside. I'm just finishing adding a few curls to my ponytail and applying a bit of makeup. I know I'll sweat most of it off, but I need to feel put together and ready to face the night ahead. I even pulled out my favorite red lipstick. If Carter isn't going to be giving me grief over bright lipstick anymore, I

might as well own what I love. I text Luca to say that I'll be right down as I grab my gym bag and take one more quick look in the mirror. I'm in a sheer black skirt over green leggings tonight. I paired it with my favorite white strappy tank and black dance sweater. I look good. Inside, I may be completely broken, but on the outside, I like what I see.

I take one more deep breath and head out to the main space to find Chelsea sitting on the couch, drinking out of my mug. Seriously?

"So, we aren't going to pretend that you didn't know he was with me?" I can't help but ask her. She is definitely not a girl's girl.

"Kylie, jealousy and cattiness is not a good look on you, honey. Have fun at ballet or wherever you're going." I shake my head and start walking to the door. I hear Carter's footsteps, and I hope he lets me leave without comment. I'm not that lucky.

"So, you're already heading out to try to bag a new man then?" I spin around and look at him, hopefully conveying my utter disgust on my face when I make eye contact.

"Excuse me?"

"You heard me. At least you dressed age-appropriately when you didn't know about Chelsea. Now you think it's okay to dress like a whore to leave the house—red lipstick and all. I'm sure your 'dance partner' is going to appreciate that." The quotes around dance partner have my blood boiling.

"For your information, Luca is an incredible friend. Absolutely nothing has happened. He has never tried anything, and I do not seen him that way. You were my everything, Carter. And I'm sorry that I felt it necessary to conform to your wishes for how I should look and act when you were more concerned with sleeping with the entire bar staff. I like how I look. I'm nearly thirty, not sixty-five. I'm going dancing, not to seduce a man who is in a committed relationship. I would have to stoop to her level to do that." I know my words are coming out angry, and I don't care.

"I definitely liked you better when you knew how to act appropriately. This loud, obnoxious woman is not who I fell in love with." He goes to sit on the couch, immediately pulling Chelsea's legs over his own.

"It may not be who you fell in love with, but it's who I need to be right now. And since you are done telling me how to act and talk and dress and, yes, even dance, I'm ready to find out who twenty-nine-year-old Kylie is. Bright red lipstick and all." With that, I head out the door and walk right into Luca, who was apparently waiting at the door, ready to come save the day if I needed him.

"Can I please go hit him again?" he practically begs once I lock the door behind me.

"I don't think your clients would appreciate that. Isn't it hard to hold your tools when your knuckles are cracked and bloody?" He takes my bag, and we make our way down the stairs and to his car.

"It would be worth it, though. I do not like that guy. I still can't believe he did that to you."

"Me either. I'm still in shock over everything."

"I'm sure. Do you want to vent, talk it out, or just turn the music up and listen to something fun on the way to the studio?" He opens the door for me and waits until I'm settled before he closes the door and walks over to his side.

"Music, please. I'm not ready to talk about it. I should probably start looking for a therapist or something. I just want to zone out a bit tonight. Is that okay?" I glance over at him and see he's already looking at me, waiting for my response.

He nods and offers a soft smile. "Whatever you want is okay, honeybee. Let's get to class. Oh, that is for you." He motions to the cup in the holder. I forgot he was going to bring me this. I haven't had an actual meal since Wednesday, and it's Monday. Tonight is not going to be fun if I attempt to dance.

"Thanks, Luca. Are you ready to tell me about the whole honeybee thing yet? Not that I don't love it; I think it's cute. I just want to know where it came from." He chuckles quietly, and I have to smile in response.

"When I was little, I used to get stung by bees every summer. At least once, sometimes more often than that. I remember being so frustrated that I would always get stung and my friends didn't. It was almost like I attracted them. I was probably around ten and I was inside the house with my mom. I had been stung for like the third time that summer, and I was angry that it surprised me, and

I cried in front of my friends. I was a big ten-year-old, and crying over getting hurt was just not cool. My mom was icing the spot and checking to make sure the stinger was out when she told me the reason I always got stung was because I was so sweet." I chuckle at the statement, and he does, too, but then he keeps going.

"I had a similar reaction. I was not impressed by that, but she had more to say, which I still remember vividly. Honeybees are attracted to what they see as beautiful. What they want a part of. The things that draw them in and attract them enough to say, 'I need some of this because it's amazing.' That day at Matt's house, when I saw how sad you were, and then you laughed. I don't even remember why, but you laughed. And that was my first thought— she is absolutely beautiful. If I were a honeybee, I would do my best to pick up some of that beauty and happiness and essence of what makes her, her and would carry it with me, showing the other flowers the most beautiful thing I had found. All I wanted to do was see what I needed to do to remind you of your beauty. Because it is immense, Kylie." He takes a breath, and I realize I'm crying again. I stay quiet, not wanting to interrupt his thoughts.

"I don't know when that man started taking you for granted and seeing you as a flower that had lost its scent and beauty. But I need you to know—I see it. And I think you still have some blooming to do. I will sit here and remind you of that every single day. Maybe one day, you will believe that. But for now, I'm happy with being able to dance with you and call you my honeybee." He parks in front of the studio, looks over at me, and smiles.

Then I do something probably incredibly stupid. But I'm not second-guessing myself anymore. I reach over and hold his hand and give it a little squeeze.

"Thank you, Luca. I think I'm ready to remember what it feels like to be beautiful. To own my beauty and that it's okay if others see it too." I take a deep breath and look at the studio. "Would you like to come dance with me?"

"You never have to ask."

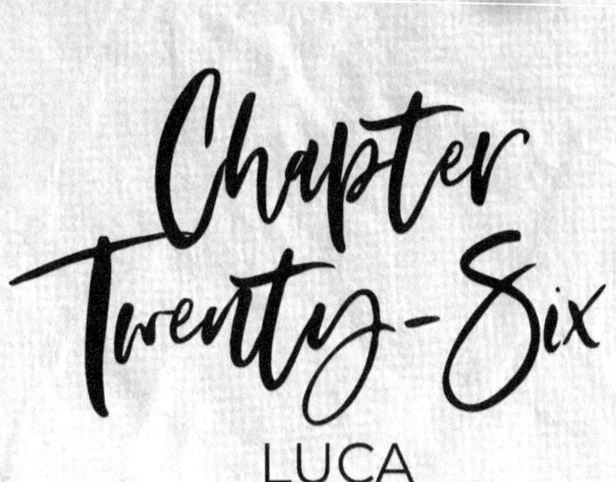

Chapter Twenty-Six

LUCA

LAVENDER & DULCE LECHE ICED CHAI

Social Post: Two places feel like home to me right now, my workshop and the dance studio. #ifeelbetterwhenimdancing #westcoastswing

Image Description: The dance floor at our local West Coast Swing Studio.

Dancing with Kylie tonight is a completely new experience. It's almost as if she has given herself permission to enjoy it now. Like, fully enjoy it. She jumps right in with everything that Stacey shows us tonight and goes with the flow when we switch partners for one of the songs. We're starting to work on the improv pieces and what it may look like if we ever enter any competitions.

My partner and I got "Shivers" by Ed Sheeran, and we both had already danced to this one before, so we really got to enjoy it and fall into some familiar territory. I'm excited to see what Kylie and her partner got for their random song. The giggles that started when the intro played and she recognized the song were contagious. Their song was "Mamma Mia" by Abba. And while their dance is far from perfect, as the girlies say, "the vibes were immaculate." She laughs through the whole thing. Really laughs. And I can't help but smile.

"How long have you two been dating?" Laura, the woman I had danced with, leans over and asks me as Kylie and Jason finish their song.

"Oh, we aren't dating. Just friends." I clap with everyone else and wait for Kylie to come back over to me once they finish up.

"Keep telling yourself that." Laura laughs and walks back to her partner. I barely register the words—I am too busy watching my girl fall in love with herself.

The next several weeks are sweet. Not in the "oh cool" way, but in the soft, gentle, easy way. Because that is exactly what it is. I get to pick Kylie up for dance classes, sometimes taking her out for a light dinner before or a hot cocoa afterward. I text her in the morning to see how she is doing. I send her pictures of finished projects, and she starts suggesting some functional décor pieces that I may like to make—and that she would like to see completed. She still won't show me what her secret project is. But I have the feeling she was working on it again. Sometimes, when I pick her up, I come up to the apartment when Carter wasn't there, and her sketchbook and design magazines would still be out on the table where she had been working. I don't want to push her, but I am curious about what she was working on.

From what I have gathered, she hasn't found another place yet but has started looking. And there are lots of hours spent talking about Matt and Sasha's wedding. They will be getting married next fall, so that way, it's after Ashley graduates. Tilly would still be in school, but schedules would work for everyone to attend and have some time off around the wedding.

The last class of the semester comes too soon. Christmas was coming fast, and that means a few weeks off from dancing. At least the structured classes, anyway. I have to stop myself from drooling when Kylie took off her coat in the studio. It was obvious that she isn't criticizing her body and its "failings" anymore. At least not as much as before. She is in a pair of black leggings that showed off her curves beautifully, along with a cropped white tank top and a hunter-green button-down linen shirt, left open to show off more of those delicious curves and a whole section of skin that I so desperately want to touch.

"What? Do I have something on my shirt?" She is so oblivious sometimes, and I just have to chuckle at her questions.

"No. You look amazing, Kylie. You may have to pinch me to make sure I'm paying attention to Stacey tonight." The blush on her cheeks does something to me, and I want to see if I can make that happen again tonight.

"Thanks, Luca. You ready for tonight?"

"Yeah. A few weeks off will be nice, but I love doing this with you. Maybe we can see the class schedule for spring and see if there's something we want to do. What do you think?"

"Maybe. I need to start looking for a job, though. The time off has been nice, and the rest has been needed. But I need to get out of that apartment. I need to start doing something on my own."

"What about the mystery sketchbook?"

She pauses for a moment, like she's actually thinking about it. "Maybe. Can I show you something next week and see if you think it's any good? And then maybe I can see if there's other interest. I have only shown one of the baristas at the coffee shop, so it may just be something she says to get tips out of me." Kylie laughs, but it's not the self-deprecating laugh that I used to hear. This is one where she is thinking about something that brings her joy.

"We can definitely do that."

Two hours later, we are all tired and sweaty but feeling good. I think it's pretty much impossible to leave a West Coast Swing class in a bad mood. So much of it is about following the music and enjoying the flow with your partner. We are getting ready to head out when Stacey comes over to the two of us.

"I had something I wanted to talk to you both about if you have a quick minute."

"Sure, what's up?" Kylie asks as she uses her towel to dry off the back of her neck, and the front of her neck, and her chest… I need to not be staring at her right now.

"There's an opening with the competition group. I want you two to join us. And before you say no, it would be one competition a quarter. It's smaller groups, mostly local. And everyone is pretty much at the same level you are right now. The two of you dance so beautifully together. Just think about it. Here are the class times and when we would meet. The first competition isn't until April, but I want you to be there." She hands papers over to us and then walks off, leaving no room for argument.

"I guess our lunch date next week just had another item added to the agenda." I open the door, and we make our way outside. The temperature has dropped, and it almost smells like snow.

"I'm so ready for snow only because that means spring is next." Kylie laughs as she shivers visibly. I need to get her a scarf or something. My nana showed me how to knit when I was little. I wonder if I still know how to do that…My thoughts are interrupted when we get to my car. "What are you off in la-la land about over there?" Kylie chuckles while she waits for me to unlock the car.

"Knitting."

Luca

Chapter Twenty-Seven

KYLIE

RED VELVET FRAPPE

Social Post: I think I'm almost ready to share what's inside of my sketchbook. Almost. Until then, hope you're taking time for something you love today. #myjoy #sketches #justforme

Image Description: Closed sketchbook with doodles of lilacs and honeybees on the cover.

"I've given you months, Kylie. You need to move out. I can't keep doing this with you."

"By 'this' you mean being civil for the five minutes we see each other twice a week?"

"Chelsea is moving in when she gets back from her parents for Christmas. I would like you gone by then." Carter sets his coffee mug in the sink and turns to face me again. I'm at the table, sketching and enjoying looking over my new design magazines that I bought for myself—it is Christmas after all.

"I can probably find something, but I won't be able to take my furniture for a little while. Can I trust you to leave it alone if I need to keep it here for a while?" My voice is steady. I have to almost distance myself from the conversation when I have to actually talk to him. Otherwise, it's too easy to see the man I fell in love with and not the man who broke my heart.

"That's fine. No later than Valentine's Day, Kylie. I need you sleeping somewhere else by then."

"Oh, goodie," I mumble under my breath. "So, you remember the special things for her then? Good for you."

"Don't give me that, Kylie. I did all of that with you for years. But you always wanted more. More that I didn't want."

"You mean a baby. Well, newsflash, that was never going to happen. I can't get pregnant. So, you would have gotten your way anyway." My voice catches at the end. I don't think I ever told him how that appointment went. He never asked.

"What?" His voice drops, and he looks at me like he actually cares about what I'm going to say.

"That was the appointment you missed. The doctor told me I can't get pregnant, Carter. It's not going to happen naturally for me. So, you got your wish. You wouldn't have ever had to worry about being a dad, about parenting alongside me. It wasn't going to happen. No matter how badly I wanted it or how often I told you that it was what we needed, I don't get that chance." I don't stop the tears. This is the first time I've said those words out loud outside therapy. And it hurts because now it's all too real.

"Kylie, I'm sorry. I know how much you wanted to be a mom. Are you okay?" He starts walking to me, and I immediately put my hand up to stop him.

"You don't get to be sorry now. You gave up that right when you slept with someone else. No, when you start thinking about someone else. You messed up. You lost the privilege of making me feel better. Go enjoy your chosen child-free life with someone else. Just leave me alone, please, Carter." He starts to say something else but must realize I'm done listening because he walks down the hall to his bedroom. The one he now shares with Chelsea.

"Do you really think I can do this?" I look over the design book in front of me as Luca flips through it. It's mid-January, and I've finally gotten to see his workshop. This place smells like my new favorite thing. Now I know why he always smells so good. It's a mix of wood shavings, oil from the machine parts, and something else that is just Luca. I just want to bottle it up and take the smell home with me. Okay, that thought came out of nowhere.

"These are really good, Kylie. You could easily package these as pre-made, and people could buy material lists, or you could do one-on-one consultations. I love how you incorporated some of my pieces in these." He winks at me, and I can't help but laugh.

"Functional décor is important, especially for these small places. I so desperately wanted a book corner like this, but it didn't work out in the size of our apartment. But if the décor was built so it looked attractive and served a purpose, it's an easier purchase. From the investment side of things and the space side, too. Do you think you can make one of these shelves for me so I can do a mockup?" I know it's a big ask, but I really want to see if this is even possible.

"Sure, do you want to pick out a wood and a stain?" He motions to his wall of shades. There are so many. It's like the paint wall at Home Depot, only with squares of wood and stain options. It's beautiful.

"I think I need to see where I can build this mini space first. Which means I need to find a place. Ugh." I cover my face with my hands. I hate this. Every time I find somewhere that might work, it falls through at the last minute. And I can't justify spending over two grand a month on a place, especially without a job.

"What about building it out in my house? I have an office, a spare bedroom, and a decent-sized living room—you can pick whatever works best with lighting and wall space and build it here."

"I couldn't ask you to do that. The space I want to create is just lavender walls."

"It's paint, Kylie. It can be covered. Come on, grab your sketchbook, and let's go pick a space. Then I'll take you shopping."

"I don't want to take up more of your time. I should let you get back to it." I start to put my sketchbook away when Luca places his hand over mine.

"Kylie, you aren't taking up anything more than I want to give you. I want you here, in my space. I want you to create something you love in my home. And, if you are open to it, I want to offer you my spare bedroom. I know you need to find a place to live, and maybe this way, we can work together a little more easily."

"Can I think about it?"

"Of course, and there's an added perk too if you decide you want to try."

"What's that?"

"More dance practice time." He winks at me and then marches into his house with my sketchbook, leaving me to chase him inside to get it back. Well played, sir.

Kylie

Chapter Twenty-Eight

KYLIE

PEACH AND THYME GREEN TEA LEMONADE REFRESHER

Social Post: What do you think? Can we turn this corner into something cozy? #interiordesign #cozyspaces #functionaldecor

Image Description: A blank wall/corner inside a friend's house. He may be letting me have some fun with redoing it. We'll see.

Luca's house is exactly how I pictured it. The entryway is open and bright, featuring several pieces of furniture and décor that I immediately recognize as his style. The navy-blue and soft yellow accents provide just the right amount of color.

"Did you decorate this place or did you hire someone?" I ask after toeing off my shoes and following him into the kitchen. He's already at the stove, getting the kettle on to boil and pulling down a box that looks oddly familiar.

"Yes, I made one for me, too. Figured I should have some options for you here in case this ever happened." It even has the same carving on the top. "And yes, I did the décor in here. Picked out the furniture, fixtures, paint, and everything else. I am definitely not an expert when it comes to interior design, but I wanted to make this space feel like me. Especially living alone, I didn't want to feel like I was in a hotel or a furnished house. Maybe you can help with the rooms I haven't quite finished yet." He moves effortlessly through the naturally lit kitchen, pulling out honey and mugs, laying out the options on the island.

"You're talking like it's already a done deal that I'm moving in," I tease, sifting through the options in the tea box. Not surprisingly, there are all my favorites, plus a few more that I've not tried yet. I choose a spiced ginger chai, and Luca turns to grab the milk out of the fridge once he sees what I have picked.

"It's called manifesting." He smiles at me as he sets the milk in front of me. I can't help but laugh at his reaction.

"I don't think that's what that means."

"I can try."

We spend about twenty minutes sipping tea and going over his upcoming projects, trying to see when he will have space to create a few of my ideas. Once we finish our drinks, he offers to show me the rest of the house. The flow stays similar to the entryway and kitchen. It's a split level, so he shows me downstairs first. There's a large family room with a flat screen on one wall, complete with an entertainment center filled with board games and game systems. Definitely a guy space, but clean and organized.

The office is off the side of the family room and only has a small window, and a lower ceiling. There's one desk in here, but it features a full wall of bookshelves—half of them filled with DVDs and other tchotzkis, the other half is filled with books. There's a couch along the wall and a basic coffee table.

"This room feels like it hasn't gotten your full touch yet," I notice as I go over to the window to pull back the blue shades.

"Not quite. I spend more time in the workshop and the family room. I don't have much computer work to do, and I don't get to spend nearly as much time reading as I would like. Maybe this could be where you start your first project. The corner over there isn't being used, it would make for a good, cozy reading corner." He points to the area that is almost like an alcove inside the room.

The layout of this room definitely isn't great for a functional workspace. But I let myself imagine what it would look like as a split office and reading space. That corner is the perfect size for a hanging seat, especially with the lower ceiling. And the walls are a soft off-white; it should be pretty easy to add in a mural or some wall hangings. I'll be limited in my color choices since there isn't much natural light. But if we stick with lighter colored wood and add a mirror to the back of the wall, it might actually work.

I turn back to look at the shelves again and see if there's anything that I may be missing, only to see Luca leaning against them with a soft smirk on his face.

"What is that look for?"

"I like seeing you here, in my space. And I love seeing the wheels turning. Do you have any ideas about what you want to do?" I smile back at him because I think I do. And if I'm being honest with myself, seeing him so content just watching me does something to me. *He's too young for you, and he's just being nice. You cannot go there, Kylie.* My internal voice is loud today, and I need to listen to her. She's there for a reason.

"Okay, then, I'm gonna go grab my sketchbook. I have some ideas that I think will work."

Before we know it, hours have gone by. I have paint swatches from the back of my sketchbook taped to the wall, and Luca has brought a few raw pieces of wood in from the workshop so I could see the colors together. I picked out a light piece of oak and a complementary stain and then a light gray that has a blue undertone for the wall. I'm going to try to find some art prints, greenery, and a mirror to add some dimension to the corner, too.

"I think I'm ready to go shopping," I finally say after taking down a few more notes and measurements. "Where do we go first?"

"Always Home Depot." He laughs as he puts his notebook away. He doesn't have a full sketchbook like me, just a small one that fits in his back pocket. The back pocket of the jeans that fit him very, very well. I have got to stop looking at him like that.

"How often are you in there?" I force myself to continue the conversation.

"At least once a week. I saw Sasha in there several times before I knew who she was. They always have some wood scraps from cuttings, and depending on who's working, I get to bring some home. They're good for practicing new techniques and some of the smaller projects."

The next few hours are a blur of paint samples, comparing the grain of the wood to other pieces, and going to the décor store to browse the art pieces and a mirror. It's been such a fun day. It's been good to get to know Luca a little bit better, outside of dancing. He makes a few more flirtatious comments, which have me blushing and brushing them off. I still don't know how to react to that. He's made his interest clear, but I'm still broken when it comes to relationship things.

"When did Carter say you need to be out of the house?" Luca asks as we bring the last of our shopping into the house. Well, he's carrying the shopping bags; I'm carrying the takeout bags. It got late, and it was definitely time to eat.

"Valentine's Day. He said I could keep some stuff there if I needed to. But I have three weeks."

"Okay, that's plenty of time. Do you want to go see your room?"

"You're not going to drop this, are you?"

He looks at me with that mischievous look again. "Never."

Kylie

Chapter Twenty-Nine

LUCA

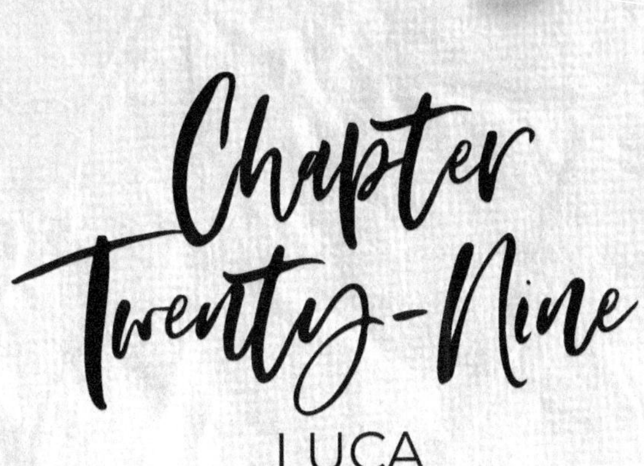

TOASTED WHITE CHOCOLATE MOCHA

Social Post: Time to transform something a little larger than some furniture. #movingday #newspaces #spareroomdecor

Image Description: The spare room of my house with a few boxes in the corner that I'm working on cleaning out.

A week later, I have Kylie's room cleaned out and ready for her. She decided to use the bed I already have here so she doesn't have to try to move the other one. Apparently, the dresser and a few other pieces are ones that she had prior to meeting Carter, so she wants to try to get those, but he hasn't been very helpful with scheduling a time to clear those out so we can get them. It's also time to decide what dance group we are going to join this semester.

I really hope Kylie will be up for the competition group. She's good enough for it, and I won't say no to more opportunities to show her off. Her confidence has grown drastically in the last few months, and I love that I've gotten to see it. She's coming over today to bring over some of her things and for us to put the finishing touches on her reading corner. We've done a few sneak peeks on her social media, and her followers can't wait to see what she's working on. They are excited to see the finished project, and I hope it turns into a few jobs for her. I think she will feel a lot more comfortable moving in here if she's bringing in some money of her own. She doesn't want to go back into waitressing, and honestly, I don't blame her.

The doorbell rings, and I make my way down the stairs and to the front door. I can see her through the glass panel on the door and immediately quicken my steps to help her.

"Why didn't you tell me you were on your way over? I would have come and helped you with this." I take the bag from her shoulder and hold the door open so she can step inside.

"I'm already taking over a room in your house. I don't want to take more of your time and energy than is absolutely necessary." She plops the other bag on the floor in front of her and then sits on the wood planks right beside it.

"You doing okay?" I ask, starting to get a little worried. She looks completely drained, more so than she normally is.

"This may be TMI, but I think I'm getting ready to start my cycle. I need to get things set so I can rest. Tomorrow is probably going to be a stay-in-bed day for me at this rate."

"Do you always get bad periods?" She seems almost surprised by my question, and I don't know why. I have no issue talking about stuff like this.

"Um, yeah, I have PCOS, and my cycles are irregular because of that. I also have cysts every once in a while that completely lay me out for a day or two. I'll be fine once my cycle actually starts and I have a full day to rest."

"Okay, how about you go chill on the couch downstairs with a book or a movie? I'll get the heating pad. You can rest while I bring everything upstairs and make your bed. Sound good?" She stares at me from the floor for a moment, like she's processing my offer.

"I don't want to give you more work, Luca. But I think that would probably be the best idea. I'm so drained. And yeah, the heating pad sounds nice." I help her stand and turn the TV on before giving her the remote. I pull a blanket off the back of the couch so she has it close and then run upstairs to grab the heating pad. I have to use it fairly frequently because of how much I'm bent over working on things. I may only be twenty-five, but my back feels like an eighty-year-old's sometimes.

It doesn't take me long to get everything inside and her bed made up so she can lie down if she wants to. I'm just about to make her a cup of tea to see if that will help at all when I notice that she's asleep. I dim the lights and make sure she's covered up before going to start something for dinner. I'm in the middle of watching a recent West Coast Swing competition on my phone and waiting for the food to be done when I hear Kylie stirring. She comes upstairs, looking sleepy and all kinds of gorgeous.

"How are you feeling?" I ask as I fill a glass with water and pass it over to her.

"Okay, for now. What are you up to?"

"Watching the WCS competition from last fall. There are a few couples that I follow on social media who post a lot of their dances. Do you want to watch?"

"Sure." She sits on the chair next to me, and we watch the dances. Some of these couples have been together for years, while others have just started competing together. But they all have one thing in common; they're having a great time.

"I think I want to try the competition group with you," Kylie says as she takes my phone from me when I get up to pull dinner out of the oven.

"Yeah?"

"Yeah. Let's do it. And I think I have an idea for one of the songs I want to try if you're open for a little bit of pettiness."

"I'm always open to pettiness."

Something really cool about West Coast Swing is that it combines several dance styles. And the music is just as eclectic as those who dance it. From theater favorites to trending pop hits, it's a dance medium that appeals to every age group. The songs can range from slow and seductive to fast and happy. The ways that the dancers interpret each song is unique as well. So, when Kylie gave me the green light to pick the song we would be working on together, I couldn't pass it up.

I've converted the family room into a practice space for us, moving the couch to the side and laying a temporary dance floor on the carpet. Kylie is feeling better today and wanted to try mapping out the dance together but wasn't ready to go to the studio. So, I brought the studio to her.

"What did you have in mind for this petty competition song?" she asks as she comes down the stairs, putting her hair up in a ponytail and drawing my attention to her neck and bare shoulders. I seriously love the flowy tank tops she wears around the house. She looks casual and comfortable but still effortlessly beautiful.

I have to make myself look at the music station on the entertainment center rather than stare at her as she starts stretching on the floor. This woman is going to kill me. I don't answer her, I just press play. Her responding laughter tells me that she recognizes it immediately.

"Does that mean you approve?"

"Absolutely, yes! But we should pick something that isn't as catty, just in case."

"Done. What do you think of this one?" I switch to the second song, one that I know she loves and something that I hope she can listen to and remember how absolutely incredible she is.

"It's perfect."

"Okay then, let's get practicing."

Luca

Chapter Thirty

KYLIE

OATMEAL COOKIE LATTE

Social Post: It's almost time to start dancing again. #wcs #westcoastswing #coloradodancer

Image Description: New shoes for this dance season.

I went back to the apartment on February 13 to grab the last of my things, only to find that the locks had been changed. I stared at the door for a few minutes, unsure of what to do next. Besides my furniture, the tea box from Luca and the shoes I've used for dancing are inside the apartment. I really want to get them. The furniture was going to have to wait anyway. Carter has not been very easy to coordinate with to get those things. And apparently, Chelsea is quite fond of my dresser. She may be borrowing it for the meantime, but that is mine, and I will have it back.

I finally head over to the restaurant. It's a few hours before I need to meet Luca for dance class, and I need to try to get into the apartment for those shoes. If Carter would actually answer his phone, I wouldn't have to do this. I've never been a confrontational person, but I think that's about to change.

Walking into the restaurant, it feels like I'm in a space I've never been in before, rather than the place that I used to spend hours in most days. The décor has been switched for the holidays, and I hate that it looks good in here. Max is behind the bar, so I walk over to see how he's doing. By the looks of things, he's cleaning glasses and getting ready for the next group of patrons to come in.

"Hey, Max. How are you doing?" I jump up onto a bar stool and pick up a menu. I might as well eat something while I'm here.

"Hey, you. It's been a while. And before I say anything else, I'm sorry for how everything went down. I honestly didn't know what was happening, or I would have said something. How have you been?" He places the bar towel over his shoulder to give me his full attention. And this is why he's one of the staple bartenders here. He's good at his job, and he enjoys it too.

"Doing okay. I'm actually getting ready to launch a micro interior design service at the end of the week, and Luca and I have our first dance competition together in April. It's been good. Do you know if Carter is here? He changed the locks on the apartment, and I need to get my shoes and tea box. I forgot them on the last run somehow, and I really need them." Max shakes his head.

"He's not. I'm sorry, Kylie. He's out of town with Shaun again. Chelsea should be back later today. She will have a key, but I don't know if you want to do that." I shake my head immediately. I do not like that girl and would prefer not to run into her. "Do you want me to let him know you stopped by?" he offers, and I debate it for a moment.

"No. I'll try again next week. I need to run to the store and try to find a different pair of shoes, though. You should come see our practice event before the competition if you're not working."

"I'd love that. Send me the info and I'll see what I can do." I make sure I still have his number and then head out. Sitting in my car, I decide that I don't want to wait until the end of the week to start sharing my interior design service. I pull up the website that Matt and Sasha helped me with last weekend and click publish. A few more clicks and I have a video posted on my Instagram, introducing the space I designed at Luca's house as well as some of the sketchbook pieces. I'm giving myself space for three consultations this month. Now, I just have to cross my fingers and see what happens.

By the time I find a pair of shoes that will work, I'm almost running late for practice. I have to book it to the studio. I'm glad I brought my bag with me so I can freshen up a bit and get changed in the dressing room. I've started doing my makeup specifically for dance nights. It helps me get into the headspace of a performer as well as a dancer. And it gives me a few moments to settle the nerves that come every single time I know I'll be in close proximity to Luca.

I'd be lying if I said there was no attraction there. He's made it obvious on more than one occasion that he's interested in me, but I've been nervous about it. He has seen me at my worst. He's seen me broken. He's seen me hurting. And he's seen me at my best now, too. He's seen me create and dance and smile and laugh. And I really think he loves me for it. I'm not ready to jump into anything, but I'm also not going to tell him to stop when he continues to flirt with me. Not gonna lie, it feels kind of good to be told that I'm beautiful on an almost daily basis again. And I think I'm starting to believe him when he says it, too.

I'm putting my hair up into a ponytail and walking into the studio when I see Luca walking in with Stacey. His eyes immediately find mine, and I don't miss the quick perusal his eyes take of my outfit. I'm wearing the sheer black skirt again with a pair of black leggings underneath. I don't know why, but it seems to be his favorite; at least, I think it is based on how he's looking at me. I don't try to hide my blush as his eyes connect with mine again.

"So, do you two want to show me what you've been working on?" Stacey asks as she sets her own bag down next to mine.

"Sure. It's definitely not ready for April, but it's a start. We have two songs we are working on," I tell Stacey, looking to Luca for acknowledgment, and he nods in agreement.

"You have the floor." She motions to the space in front of us, and Luca hands Stacey his phone before coming to meet me in the middle of the floor.

The first song begins to play once Stacey starts it, and I immediately fall into the familiarity of the dance. "SexyBack" is the first song that we've been having fun with, and I love the things we've incorporated in this one. The way I get to glide my hands along my own body, as well as Luca's, brings me alive. The heat in his eyes is unmistakable. I'm the one to lead the touches on this one. Luca wanted me to be the one to tell the story and show that I am sexy and wanted as I am. And that I can show that off in subtle ways on a dance floor. I love it.

When we finish and look at Stacey, she makes a show of fanning herself off. "You two are something else. I can't wait to see it once it's been rehearsed more, but that is going to be a showstopper in April! And in June, for our first major competition if you end up entering that one." We stop to take a quick drink and catch our breaths while Stacey gives us a few specific pointers from the dance.

"We have about ten minutes before the rest of the class gets here. Do you want to show me the next one?"

"Absolutely." Luca smirks and leads me back to the center of the floor.

By the time we get home from dance that night, I am in the best mood. My muscles are achy in a way that shows I worked hard, and I know I'll be deliciously sore in the morning. I should probably stretch downstairs before I shower and call it a night. Luca left the temporary dance floor out since I've moved in, and I've turned it into my yoga studio whenever I can. Now that the weather should hopefully start warming up, I may even take my mat outside some mornings. I'm just grabbing my mat to head downstairs when I hear Luca in the kitchen.

"Do you want some tea before you go stretch or save it for after?" he calls as I peek into the room.

"Um, after probably. Thank you. You can leave the box out."

"So, I saw that you posted about the design services today. How has the excitement been on that?" He walks over to me with a bottle of water, which I happily take before walking down the stairs, already knowing he will follow.

"Honestly, I haven't looked. I've stayed off my phone since I posted it. I'm not ready to hear any criticism, and I'm worried about how things would be taken." I set my mat down on the floor and take off my socks before sitting in the middle of the grey foam. Luca is sitting on the stairs so he can make eye contact with me while we talk while still giving me space to move around.

"Do you want me to look?" he offers. I take a moment to think it over.

"Yeah, actually. Do you mind? I think having a bit of a buffer would be a good idea. My laptop is on the table upstairs if you want to grab it. I published the website today so that people could submit for consultation or grab the digital lookbook I've been working on."

He jogs up the stairs to grab my laptop and then comes back down. I'm in the middle of a stretch of my lower back when I hear the first clicks of his fingers on the keyboard.

"Okay, so, you have a little over five hundred email subscribers, two hundred lookbook downloads, and fifty-seven inquiries for a consultation. I'd say not too bad for having everything up for less than twelve hours." He stops talking when he realizes I'm just standing there staring at him.

"Can you check that again, please? Because there's no way."

"That's what it says, Kylie. Oh, I'm sorry." He pauses for a second, and I let out a sigh. I knew it was too good to be true. "You just got another consultation inquiry, so that's fifty-eight."

I walk over to him on autopilot and hold out my hands so I

can see for myself. He hands over the laptop, and I take a look at the screen. It's all right there. The consultation inquiries are for everything, too. Book nooks, coffee corners, work areas, kid's rooms, a nursery, a work office breakroom, and even a few makeup setups. "How?" I breathe out the question. I can't even voice it.

"That's all you, honeybee. I told you that you could do this." He stands and takes the laptop from me, closing it and setting it aside before placing his hands gently on my shoulders. I gaze up into his eyes as he drifts his hands from my shoulders to my hands, interlocking our fingers.

"You are capable of such amazing things. And I love that others are getting to see the beauty that you create. You deserve every single bit of any success that comes to you. Don't forget that." He smiles at me before tucking a loose strand of hair behind my ear.

"Luca?" I start to ask a question but then second-guess myself.

"What do you need, Kylie?"

"Can you kiss me, please?"

Kylie

Chapter Thirty-One

LUCA

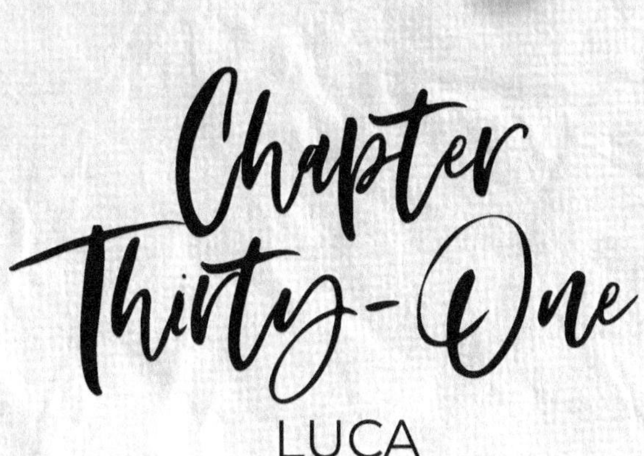

VANILLA ALMOND SNOWFLAKE LATTE

Social Post: Seeing her find her joy is the best feeling in the world. #myhoneybee

Image Description: Finished cozy reading corner in my house complete with wood shelves and honeycomb planter from the workshop.

"Can you kiss me, please?" The words are barely out of her mouth, and then my lips are on hers. My hands cup her face as I hold her steady. I've been waiting for her to ask for months. I don't hesitate to show her how much I've been wanting her and hope I can convey in a kiss how much I feel for her. The callouses on my hands contrast with the smoothness of her skin and neck, and I knew she would feel this good in my hands. I start gently, but still showing her that I want her. I'm not rough with my exploration of her lips, of her mouth, of her moans, but it's enough that I know I want more.

She must want it too because she takes half a step forward so her breasts are pressed against my chest. I stifle a groan as I tangle one hand in her hair and trail the other to her waist, anchoring her body to my own. I don't bother trying to shift my body so she doesn't feel my growing desire for her. I won't hide from her. I smile against her lips as she finally takes a breath and begins to draw away. I can see every color difference in her hazel eyes, even with her pupils blown wide.

I brush my thumb over her cheek, feeling the warmth of her blush. "You never have to ask, but I'm glad you did." She smiles back up at me and leans in to give me a hug. It's simple and quiet, but being able to hold her like this just became my new favorite thing. She's letting me show her affection and care and safety. And I couldn't ask for anything more.

"Do you have time to help me sort through all of those emails tomorrow?" she asks as she pulls away a bit. I know that she is going to want to roll up her yoga mat and get ready for a shower before bed.

"I can definitely do that. I have a project to work on, but I only have about two hours to go before it needs to sit in the stain solution for a few days. And then, would you let me take you to lunch?"

"I think that sounds like a really good idea. Thank you, Luca." She passes me to go up the stairs, and I don't even try to hold myself back this time. I give her ass a light tap and revel in the giggles she lets out as she runs up the stairs to her room.

Before the end of the week, Kylie has a full calendar of consultations through the end of April. The others received an email asking if they would like to be put on a waitlist to schedule once she's through the first group or if they would like to look elsewhere. Out of the fifty-seven inquiries she got in for consultations, twelve have calls scheduled, and thirty-nine asked to be put on the waitlist. She has two calls booked each week, and from there, hopefully, it will turn into projects. She is going to be offering virtual shopping visits and in-person design services for those who are close. And the best part? There has been zero pushback when she sent over the pricing guides for consultations. My girl is officially bringing in an income.

I sneak into the house after finishing another piece to grab a quick snack and hear her on the phone. I try to stay quiet, wanting to let her focus on her conversation. But I can't help standing in the doorway for a minute, watching her light up as she listens to the client on the other side of the screen talk about things that make them happy and what they envision for their home office. Kylie doesn't hesitate to start making suggestions, and it is incredibly obvious how much she loves this. She's a natural. She may not have a degree or license to back it up, but connecting people to the spaces that they will love is her superpower. I snap a quick picture on my phone and post it to my stories.

"Seeing her find her joy is perfection." I tag her account and then pocket my phone again. I glance up to see her smiling back at me. I blow her a kiss and stay long enough to see the blush creep up her cheeks.

A notification dings on my phone just as I get to the kitchen to start preparing lunch.

@cobartendercarter: You didn't take long at all did you?

It may be petty, but I have the time.

@stainedbyluca: Not that you deserve any sort of explanation, but absolutely nothing happened between the two of us until this week. And even then, it is her prerogative to do whatever the hell she wants to do. She's a grown woman who is perfectly capable of expressing her wants and desires.

@cobartendercarter: And you think she wants you?

@stainedbyluca: I know she does.

@cobartendercarter: Have fun getting that awful lipstick off your lips. I never got why she insisted on wearing it.

@stainedbyluca: Because it makes her happy. And I'll happily kiss it off her any time she lets me.

I debate blocking him. But I still need to play nice, at least a little bit, as long as she still has belongings in the apartment. We need to get them out of there. I hear Kylie coming down the stairs, so I grab the kettle to fill up in case she wants some tea.

"Hey, beautiful." I smile at her as soon as she rounds the corner. "How was the call?"

She comes over to me and wraps her arms around my neck, pulling me down for a quick kiss against her bright red lips. "I have my first paid project booked." I pick her up and swing her in a circle, reveling in the laugh she lets out.

"I knew you could do it, honeybee. I'm so proud of you. Do you need to do some shopping or some more sketches before you start working on it?" I place another gentle kiss against her lips. She seems to be thinking over the question a bit before reaching up to wipe my lips, probably trying to remove the signs of the color on her lips.

"You don't have to wipe it off. I like that your kiss leaves a mark on me." She giggles and blushes again. I love how much she blushes around me. It's kind of adorable.

"You know all of the right things to say to me, don't you?"

"You make it easy. Now, pick out your mug and tea and have a seat. We have a date tonight, and I want you to have some downtime before you have to get ready."

"This is the first you've told me about this, isn't it?" I can tell her mind is racing, and she is worried that she might have messed something up.

"Yes, it is. I was waiting to see if something was available, and I got the all-clear a little bit ago. How would you like to go on a horse-drawn carriage ride through Old Town Fort Collins and have dinner with me?"

"I thought they only did the carriage rides in December."

"It helps that I just finished a project for the guy who owns the horses." I wink at her, and she plants another kiss on my cheek.

Luca

Chapter Thirty-Two

KYLIE

NUTMEG CRANBERRY WHITE TEA

Social Post: Thank you to everyone who has already booked a consultation with me or downloaded the lookbook. Each one of you means so much to me! Looking ahead, what other projects would you like to see? #interiordesign #cozyspaces #cozydesign

Image Description: Design magazines stacked next to my sketchbook and a wooden tea box.

At 5:30 on the dot, there's a knock on my bedroom door. I have just finished setting my makeup when Luca walks up to the door. Oh, he's making this all kinds of official. Okay. I walk over to the door, already feeling the blush on my cheeks grow.

"Yes?" I call out, deciding to play along a little bit.

"Um, yes, I'm here for Miss Kylie James, interior designer and resident of this room."

"And what would you like to speak to her about?"

"I would love the opportunity to escort her out for an evening of carriage rides, dinner, and potentially a walk downtown if the weather isn't too atrocious." I decide to put him out of his misery and open the door.

"I think that sounds like a wonderful evening, Mr. Graham. Are you ready to head out?"

"I would love to head out, but there is just one problem."

"And what would that be?"

"I really want to kiss you, but you obviously spent time on your makeup, and I don't want to ruin it before we even leave the house." I chuckle at his admission. He really is adorable.

"Well, good thing it won't smudge then, isn't it?" He doesn't even ask me again, he just leans in to kiss me. I love that he doesn't hesitate. I know if I ever tell him no, he would stop immediately, but letting him take charge is such a good feeling.

He pulls away and looks at my lips for a long time before he speaks again. "Okay, whatever you did tonight is magic. How did you do that? It didn't smudge at all; it still looks great. Well, your lips always look great. It's just that the last time I kissed you when you were wearing that same shade, it smudged all over the place, which I loved, by the way." I go up on my tiptoes to plant another kiss on his lips to stop his rambling.

"I didn't set it earlier because I didn't know there was a reason to. Now, shall we go?" I hold out my arm so he can link his with mine, and then we are off to our evening together.

After an amazing ride through Old Town, he takes me to a little French restaurant that neither of us has been able to try yet. There are only about fifteen tables inside, and it's a good thing he got us reservations because several people have been turned away. I was able to check something off my bucket list tonight, though. Escargot, surprisingly isn't as scary as I was making it in my head.

"They taste like mushrooms," I tell Luca as I pick up another one with the tiny fork.

"Thanks for being a little adventurous with me tonight," he responds as he grabs his own.

"I'm having a really good time. Thank you again for setting this up."

"So, I hate to ask because we haven't talked about it yet, but your thirtieth is coming up soon. Is there anything special you want to do?" I think about it for a moment and then realize something.

"It's the same weekend as our first exhibition performance. So, I honestly didn't think we would be doing anything else."

"I love that you automatically thought that *we* were going to be doing something," he jokes, and I kind of wish he was closer so I could kiss the smirk off his face.

"You know what I mean, but yeah, I wasn't expecting anything. Maybe we can get a hotel downtown and take it easy after the competition. Maybe dinner here if we can make it work." I know I may be coming across a bit forward, but it's still over a month away. And I'm done denying my attraction to this man. Yes, he's a little younger than me, but the way he treats me is far and beyond how Carter ever treated me. I want to see where this goes.

"Would you be mad if I said I already booked a place for us for the night before and the night of the competition?" I laugh out loud, because of course he did, and then immediately have to cover my mouth. I forgot we were at a nice restaurant, and I was way too loud. Luca reaches over the table and gently pulls my hands away from my face.

"Don't ever feel like you need to do that. You get to be as loud as you need to be. Your laugh is one of the things I love about you." My jaw drops, and I stare at him. Did he really just say that?

"Yes, you heard that right. Now, finish your water, they're bringing out our entrees." He sends a wink across the table, and I pick up my water glass to try to hide how wide my grin is. It doesn't work, because he follows up his last comment with a "good girl."

I know it sounds weird, but I genuinely forget about Carter for the next few weeks. Luca and I fall into our new routine of dance, walking, yoga, dinner, and working. We both have flexibility because of our work, so we are able to make time for each other every day. Sometimes, it's only a cup of coffee in the mornings, other times we are able to sit at the table on our laptops side by side for hours. I've been able to keep a full calendar, and I am loving the mix between online content creation, the generic guides I make available on my website, and the personalized designs I make for each client.

Each project has also included an item from Luca. It can be a sign, or a floating shelf, or a tea box, but I've wanted something of him in every finished project. He's also started using some of my designed backdrops to display his completed pieces when he lists them on his website. The projects that aren't bought while he is still building them, that is. Ninety percent of what he does is commissioned work, and it's not hard to see why. So much love and care go into every piece. I hope I am showing each of my clients as much personalized attention with their projects, too.

It's not until I'm walking through Home Goods at the end of March that I realize how much I have forgotten about the man I used to love. I'm looking for something to go on a coffee cabinet that Luca is currently building for one of my clients. What I'm looking for, I don't know. I'll know it when I see it, though. I'm sorting through some ceramic figurines of mountain-scapes when I hear a familiar voice.

"Kylie, how are you doing?" I look up to see Carter holding a handbasket filled with greenery and other small vines with floral buds. He must be adding some new things to the bar or something.

"Um, hey. I'm doing all right. Working on a client project at the moment. What about you?" I motion to the basket, hoping to keep the conversation light and short. I really don't want to get into things with him right now.

"Very cool. I've been watching your posts on Instagram. I really liked the game room you finished last week. And yeah, I'm doing a reset for the bathrooms at the restaurant. Apparently, they're outdated and dark." I can't help but laugh at that.

"It's a bar bathroom—what are they wanting?" He laughs with me; at least we can agree on this.

"I have no clue. But I figured we'd start with a new coat of paint and see where it goes from there." He hesitates in the aisle, and I wait to see if he needs to say something else or if he just wants me to be the one to cut off the conversation.

"I miss you," are the words to come out of his mouth, which I was not prepared for. I don't respond. I don't know how to. "Do you think we could do lunch sometime? Talk?" Again, I just stare. Is he really asking me that right now?

"Carter, you cheated on me. More than once. For a long time. You lost the right to miss me. You don't get to ask me to lunch or anything like that. I was being civil with the conversation, but no, I don't want to get lunch with you." He has the audacity to look hurt by my words.

"I guess I deserved that."

"You guess? Are you serious? Carter, you systematically put me in a place where I had to rely on you for everything—my employment, my housing, my schedule, everything. When I started asking about things that we had previously agreed about, like having children, you basically told me it wasn't going to happen and to get over it. I went to so many appointments, to the hospital, by myself. You didn't care then. You don't get to care now. Have a good day." And with that, I walk away. I'll come back for what I need later. For now, I need to get away from him. And I hate that I go to my car and cry. How many more tears will I shed for this man?

Chapter Thirty-Three

LUCA

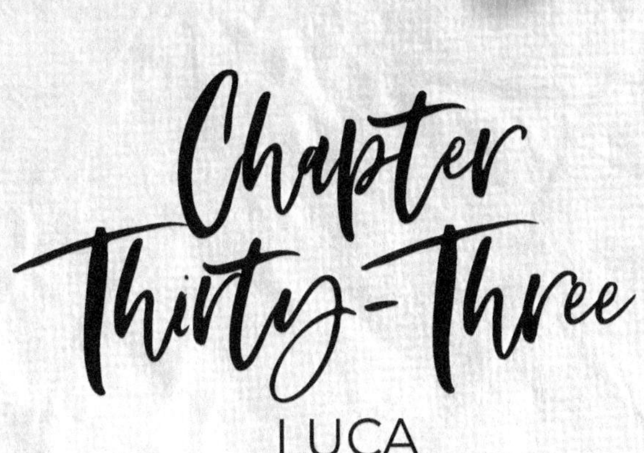

BLACKBERRY SAGE ICED TEA LATTE

Social Post: Newest at home addition: a tray under the sink that easily holds all of the bath essentials and can be pulled out for restocking or use in either bathroom. What else do I need to add to this? #bathroomcabinet #practicaldecor #functionaldecor #bathsupplies #forher

Image Description: Wooden tray with handles that holds a container of bath bombs, three jars of bath salts, a container of body scrub, and a variety of face masks and body lotions for after the bath.

Kylie came home tonight with her hair in her face, trying to hide from me. I knew something was off before she even came in the house. Seeing her red, blotchy eyes when she came in had my heart dropping.

"Honey, what happened? Are you hurt? What do you need?" I keep my hands on her shoulders, wanting to look into her eyes but also needing to keep myself steady.

"I'm fine. I ran into Carter, and, ugh, I cannot believe that man." She stops, and I give her a second to continue, but she doesn't.

"What did he say?" She takes a shuddering breath that tells me she's been crying hard, probably for a while.

"He misses me. And wants to get lunch or something. When I realized he was serious, I told him, not so politely, no. Does he really think we can be friends, or even civil, given how he treated me? I don't understand what he wants. I hate that I feel so out of control when I'm around him." She leans into me, and I hold her close while she cries.

After a while, she seems to settle, but my mind is still racing. He hasn't tried to contact me again since that first message. What is he trying to accomplish here?

"Why don't you go take a bath, and I'll work on dinner. And then we can cuddle on the couch and watch a movie," I suggest once she pulls away and wipes her eyes.

"I was going to cook tonight. I even went shopping yesterday so I could make chicken cutlets and spaghetti." I can tell she's bummed, but I think she needs to give herself permission to have a night off.

"You cooked last night, and the chicken will hold for another day. It's okay. I've got it. Carter took up emotional space he had no right to today. And you are set to start your cycle in a few days. Do some extra self-care tonight and let me take care of you. Please?" I smile down at her and brush another tear away with my thumb while I hold her face.

"Okay, since you said 'please.' And how do you know my cycle schedule better than I do?"

"It probably is not a normal thing for guys to know, but I want to take care of you. Knowing when you are going to need a little extra love or support means I can better take care of you. Taking care of you makes me happy. Is that okay?" She smiles back at me before turning toward the stairs so she can take a bath.

"That sounds very okay."

Me: So, who is coming to the exhibition event on Friday?

Matt: We will be there. Still planning to do Kylie's birthday dinner right after?

Me: That's the plan. I got us reservations at The Melting Pot for nine.

Jonathan: That's going to be a bit pricey for a dinner for a woman who isn't your girlfriend...

Me: We haven't labeled anything, but things are moving in that direction.

Jonathan: Does she know?

Me: Considering she was the one that suggested we get a hotel room for the night...

Matt: Okay, no more details please. Are Ashley and Tilly invited too?

Me: Yeah. No on the Professor still, right?

Matt: Yep. Just a few more weeks until graduation.

Me: Sounds good. See you guys on Friday.

Thursday ends up being busy for both of us. I have a few deliveries to make across town, and Kylie has a final meeting with a client for another reading corner. They are definitely her most popular installations. And even though everyone has been different based on the individual's tastes and reading habits, they are absolutely beautiful. The plan is for me to pick her up at the house, and then we will head to a quick dinner before heading to our hotel room. We haven't taken the physical side of our relationship very far yet, and I haven't pushed. I would be lying if I said I wasn't hoping to do more this weekend. Every time we have tried or she's hinted that she wants to do more, she has a bad flare up or unexpectedly starts her cycle. And while I've told her I'm totally okay with getting a little messy, she is not ready for that. Apparently, Carter wouldn't touch her at all if she was bleeding. He may be older than me, but that man is a child. And I've told her as much.

I get home with just enough time to shower and change before Kylie gets back. We need to leave the house by four in order to make our dinner reservations. I planned for an earlier evening so we can have some downtime at the hotel, especially since tomorrow will be a late night. I'm throwing the last few things in my duffel bag with a towel wrapped around me when I hear Kylie downstairs. It's only 3:30, so we have a little time. I hear her footsteps on the stairs and realize a second too late that my door didn't fully close when I came up here earlier.

I look up to see her standing in the doorway, holding her sketchbook, and her jaw is practically on the floor as she glances over my body—my wet, almost-naked body.

"See something you like, honeybee?" I know I'm messing with

her a bit right now, but I can't help it. Her eyes jump up to meet mine, and I wink at her, causing that blush to deepen even more.

"I, um, I'm sorry. I just got home and need to finish packing my bags; I'll let you get back to getting ready. Meet you downstairs in a bit, okay, yeah." She trips over her words as she turns to run to her room. I just chuckle in response. A moment later, I hear her voice behind me. I turn to see her in the doorway wearing a floral dress and holding a coordinating pink cardigan. She looks amazing.

"Can I help you with something?" I ask, wondering why she came back when I am still very much just in a towel.

"Um, I really want to wear this dress tonight for dinner, but I didn't realize I would need help with the zipper. Do you mind?" She pulls her hair over to one side and turns so I can see her back. I don't miss the fact that there isn't a bra strap. I run my fingers from the base of the zipper all the way to the top, along her skin. When I get to the nape of her neck, she visibly shivers.

"Do I have to zip it up?" I move in closer and whisper in her ear, my hand on her hip, holding her close. I wonder if she can feel the heat from my body on her own.

"Unless you want me walking outside like this." She adjusts her head a little to make eye contact with me. I comply, unwillingly, and zip up her dress. I go slowly, reveling in the way her breath quickens as she feels my gaze on her. Once I get to the top, I attach the hook and eye and then place a kiss at the top.

"You are so beautiful, Kylie. Happy early birthday." I turn her and lean in for a kiss. She accepts it willingly, and I forget for a moment that I'm only in a towel. She doesn't, though, because a moment later, I feel her hand at the center of the knot. "Are you trying to make us late?" I ask as she looks back up at me.

"Maybe. Do we have to make that dinner reservation?"

"Are you hungry?" I want to take care of her, but I will not turn down the chance to explore things with this amazing woman.

"I am…but maybe not for food quite yet." She has a mischievous look in her eyes, and I know exactly what she's thinking. I stop her before she gets too far on her journey to kneel in front of me.

"Baby, I would absolutely love to experience that with you. But the first time we do more than have a hot make-out session is not going to be you giving me a blow job on our way to your birthday dinner. Let me spoil you tonight. When we get to the hotel, we'll see where things go, okay?" I can tell she's a little disappointed, but I need to treat her like the queen she is. And that means I'll be getting on my knees for her first. Always, if she'll let me.

Luca

Chapter Thirty-Four

KYLIE

COCONUT LAVENDER LEMONADE

Social Post: We have our first performance tomorrow night and I am so excited and so incredibly nervous at the same time. Wish us luck! #wcs #westcoastswing #localdance

Image Description: Dance floor inside the studio where we will be performing tomorrow night.

I know he's right, but I really, really wanted to be on my knees for Luca back at the house. It's not ever been something I enjoyed or something I initiated, but in that moment, that's exactly what I wanted. I appreciate the fact that he told me 'no' though. It would have messed up my dress, my makeup, and probably my hair. I wonder if he would have held my head to keep me where he wanted me. I press my thighs together and shift in my seat at the restaurant thinking about it. I didn't think it was obvious, but Luca must have seen, because he starts chuckling into his water glass.

"What are you laughing at?" I ask him, trying to act like I have no idea.

"Just that you are probably as turned on as I am right now." He takes a sip of his drink, and I take a quick look around to make sure no one heard him.

"And what if I am?" I try to play coy, not sure if it's actually working. It's been so long since I've done this, and I don't want to come across as trying too hard. But I really do want this with Luca. I want him.

"Then I think you should decide whether you want to finish your dinner here or if we should ask for boxes and check into our room a little early."

"Would you be okay if I say I'd like to head to the room a little early?"

"I'd be okay with whatever you ask of me, honeybee. As long as I get to be with you."

"That was really cheesy, you know that, right?" I laugh as I start looking around for a waiter so I can get a box.

"But you loved it." And I absolutely did.

When Luca said he booked a hotel, I was not expecting one of the nicest places in Fort Collins. Fort Collins may be a college town, but it's also a perfect place for date nights and a staycation. This is my first time in the Armstrong Hotel, and I am not disappointed. Luca gets us checked in and then grabs our bags before walking to the elevators. We have a room on the fourth floor, and it is absolutely beautiful.

The dark grey paint on one of the walls makes the space feel homey, while the large window makes it feel more open. The textures of the wall hanging and the blanket on the bed add the right amount of depth to the space, too. "This is perfect, Luca." I turn toward him after taking in the room to see him placing the "Do not Disturb" placard on our door.

The click of the lock doesn't scare me, instead, it excites me. I don't know what to do with the anticipation in my body right now.

"Luca," I start, making eye contact with him as he walks over to me. He wore a button-down shirt and tie to dinner, and watching him loosen his tie should not be as hot as it is.

"Yes?" he asks, and I realize I stopped talking.

"I have only been with one other person before Carter, and it's been a really, really long time. I want you to make me feel good. I want you." He steps closer, brushing his lips over mine before trailing up my cheek and closer to my ear.

"Tell me what you need, Kylie. I'll give you whatever you want. But I need to know what you need. Name it and it's yours." His lips on my neck are distracting in the very best way, and I forget that he asked me something. It's not until he steps behind me, sweeping my hair to the side so he can kiss the spot above my zipper again, that I remember I need to say something.

"I need you, Luca. Please." The request is barely a breath as he slowly starts to unzip my dress. He doesn't go all the way down, though.

"Tell me what you need, Kylie. Use your words." Why was that so hot?

"I need you to finish taking off my dress, let me help you out of your clothes, and then I want you to show me all the things you've been dreaming about doing to me since I moved in with you." I don't know how it happened, but the next moment, my dress is on the ground, and I'm standing in front of Luca in only a pair of pink, lacy, cheeky panties. His eyes drift over my body, and his pupils dilate even further as he takes me in.

"And what if all I wanted to do was hold you in bed while we sleep?"

"I'd call you a liar."

"Why's that?" His self-control is much more than mine is as I can't help but reach for the buttons on his shirt, slowly undoing them.

"Because I imagine you've been thinking about the same things

I have been. Because I've been thinking of what it would feel like to have your hands play with my nipples, to have your teeth leave marks where you know they won't be seen, but I'll remember them. I've been thinking of having you fill me. Of bringing each other pleasure. I've been thinking of letting you take control, of giving myself to you. Because I know you would take care of me while you find your own pleasure. I want that. I want you, Luca." I finish with his shirt and push it off his shoulders, letting it fall to the floor. Then, I reach for his belt.

"Unless you want this over before I have a chance to thoroughly blow your mind, I would recommend you keep your hands above my belt for a little while longer." He captures my hands in his own, and then his lips are on mine. Our kisses before may have been passionate and full of words we didn't say, but this one is hungry. Luca doesn't just kiss; he consumes. I moan into his mouth as he wraps one arm around my back, pulling me into him so there's no room between my body and his.

My nipples are hard and feel even more sensation as they press against the dark hair on his chest. It's the right amount of friction, and I have to break away from the kiss to catch my breath. Luca takes the opportunity to begin trailing his lips down my neck, feeling his breath and his lips on my chest is an incredible sensation, and I never want him to stop. My fingers tangle in his hair as I press his head closer. I need more. Without having to say anything, he seems to know exactly what I need. His hand plays with one nipple while his mouth takes care of the other one. It takes everything in me to be quiet. He alternates between long, deep pulls and shorter ones, adding in just the right amount of teeth and finger pressure. And before I know it, I'm approaching my first climax.

"Please don't stop, Luca, please." I breathe out. I'm so close, and I will literally scream if he doesn't make me come right now.

"I wouldn't dream of it, honeybee." He pulls away just long enough to respond to me before continuing his efforts. This is one moment I am thankful that my breasts are so sensitive because it's only another few motions of his mouth on my skin before I hit that first peak. I practically collapse into Luca's arms. He guides me to the bed and lays me in the center. He kisses me gently, thoroughly, bringing me back down to the present.

"I'm going to need to see that again." He says as he smiles down at me.

"I won't argue with that."

Before I realize what's happening, he begins kissing down my neck, paying attention to my now slightly tender nipples along the way. His hands caress my curves and squeeze me in all the right places. I've never been a skinny girl, always having enough to grab on to, and Luca is taking advantage of that. I raise my head when he pauses his journey to make eye contact with him. "Why'd you stop?" I breathe out. I have to press my thighs together to try to relieve the ache between them.

"I want to make sure you're still with me. I'm going to take these off you." I nod in agreement and let my head fall back as he slowly peels my panties down my thighs. I don't even want to know how wet the fabric is; I can feel it by the sudden coolness between my legs. Did he just blow on me?

"What are you doing?"

"Seeing how responsive you are."

I don't know what comes over me, but there is zero hesitation in my reply, "How about you put your fingers or your mouth there and find out for yourself."

Luca seems surprised by my sudden assertiveness too because he smiles at me before he responds with a "Yes, ma'am."

The next thing I know, he's gently pushing my legs open, and then his mouth is on me. I wasn't prepared, and I practically scream his name as he starts devouring me. That's the only way I can describe it. His mouth is everywhere. Licking, sucking, biting, kissing. It's too much and not enough all at the same time.

"I… need… more… Luca… please," I breathe out. I want to close my legs to get him where I need him, but he continues to hold me open. I practically growl in frustration. Right when I'm about to try again, he moves his shoulder so it's holding my leg open, leaving his hand free. I realize why in the next moment when he plunges two fingers inside me. He wastes no time filling me while he continues to suck on my clit. Only a second later, he finds that spot inside me and applies the perfect amount of pressure. And I'm shattering for him a second time.

He slows his movements enough to see me through it and then slowly pulls out as I come back down. My breathing is heavy, and everything feels alive. I open my eyes to see Luca hovering over me. "I will never get tired of that," he pants out as he leans in to kiss me. Tasting myself on his tongue is better than I thought it would be. My need for him continues to grow, but I pull away long enough to ask.

"Get tired of what?"

"Tasting you, bringing you pleasure, making you come. You are incredible, Kylie." He smiles at me and places another kiss on my lips.

"Imagine what it will be like when you take off your pants and fill me with something else," I tease him, and he laughs before leaning in to consume my lips again.

Kylie

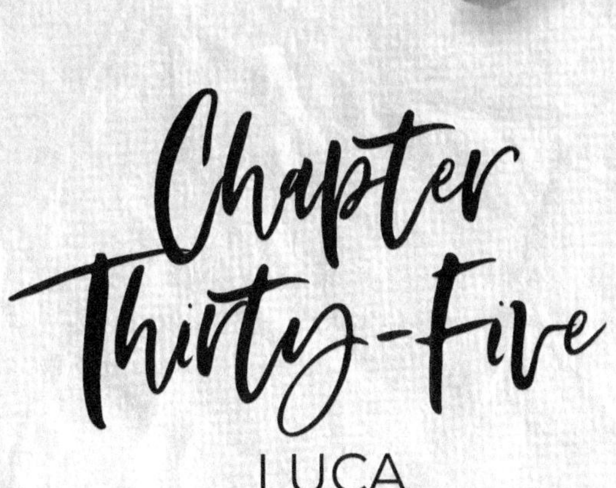

Chapter Thirty-Five

LUCA

HIBISCUS HONEY LATTE

Social post: Intentional rest time before a performance may become a requirement. We'll see how tomorrow goes before a final decision gets made. #wcs #westcoastswing #nocoevents #nococouples #couplesdancing

Image Description: View from the room at the Armstrong Hotel in downtown Fort Collins, Colorado.

Looking down at the woman underneath me, I am struck with just how stunning she is. Her body is covered with the blush from her arousal as well as the path my mouth and hands have already taken. Her breaths are heavy, as are mine, and the desire is evident in her eyes. She wants this. She wants me. And I love that I am finally in the space where I can give her everything she needs. I stand long enough to remove my belt, pants, and boxer briefs. I don't miss the way her eyes drink me in. My cock is so hard, the tip practically purple, already leaking for her. I grip my length, trying to alleviate some of the need while I pull a condom from my discarded pants.

"You sure you're good with this, Kylie?" I ask again before climbing on the bed in between her thighs. I want to make sure she still wants this before I lose my mind.

"Yes, but I need to tell you something first." I hold the condom and wait.

"This is going to sound so weird, but my last partner was a little on the small side." She pauses before glancing at my very not-small dick in my hand. "And I am honestly not sure how I'm going to handle, well, that." She motions to what I'm holding, and I grin at her.

"We'll take it slow. Trust me, you were made for me, honeybee. I'm going to make sure you feel amazing. Now, how about you let me see just how well I fit inside you," I glide the condom down my shaft and then run my fingers down her slit again. Spreading the wetness around her opening and then up to her clit, making sure that she is open and ready for me.

"Let me know if you need me to stop." I lean in and kiss her as I start slowly entering her. The grip along my shaft is exquisite. She is perfect, as I knew she would be. She arches her chest into me as I continue to slide into her. I take that as my cue to suck on her nipples again and am rewarded with another contraction of her walls around me. Finally, I am fully seated inside her. I give her a moment to adjust, to feel all of me, swirling my hips just enough to alleviate the pressure and to see if I can stimulate her clit this way.

With how she throws her head back when I do, I'd say she likes it. "I'm all the way in, honeybee. You're doing so good for me." I run my hands up and down her thighs, reveling in the way her skin feels underneath my grip. Her breathing is labored, just enough to tell me she is enjoying how I feel, but I want to give her more. "Am I good to start moving, or do you need another moment?" I ask as I lean in to kiss her ear and then start traveling down her neck, the way I know drives her crazy.

"Please, move. I need to feel you move. Please." Her plea on her lips has me coming undone, and I can't help but follow her request. I need to feel her come again, this time while I'm fully seated inside her. "Can you come just from this, Love?" I pant next to her ear. I need to know what she needs. I have to give it to her.

"I honestly don't know. I think this is the first real dick that's ever been inside of me," she laughs out, and I can't help but smile against her heated skin.

"I'm going to come back to that later. For now, let's see what you need to get there again."

"Please, Luca. Just touch me." I don't make her ask me twice. My mouth descends onto hers again while one hand holds her head steady and the other presses on her lower belly. I have a feeling this is just what she needs. It only takes a few strokes more, and she is finding her release around me, throwing her head back in pleasure. And I happily follow her over the edge.

Waking up with Kylie in my arms is going to become my new favorite thing. Her hair is spread on the blankets and pillows underneath her; the sun is coming in just enough that I can see the highlights throughout the strands. I don't think she colors her hair, but if she does, the end result is perfection. She put on one of my T-shirts to sleep in last night, and I was not prepared for what it would do to me. She may have just started thinking it to be true, but she is mine. My honeybee.

I let my fingers trace her arm from the sleeve of the shirt to the strands of her hair. I wonder if she'd let me brush it, take care of her even in the small things like doing her hair after she showers. I look down at her face and see that she is already staring at me.

"Good morning, beautiful." My voice is scratchy with sleep, and she hums in appreciation. "Happy birthday, Kylie." I lean down to kiss her, but she immediately covers her mouth.

"I need to go brush first!" she practically screeches and then jumps out of bed to run to the bathroom. I can't help but laugh in response. A few minutes later, she comes back out and slides into my arms.

"So, I'm thinking brunch and then wandering around downtown before we head to the venue for warm-ups. How does that sound?"

"Like a very perfect way to spend a birthday."

The day is spent taking our time perusing in and out of stores and exhibitions downtown. A bookstore that used to be a fire station, several vintage stores, and even a speakeasy all feature in our stroll. The speakeasy was closed since it was only noon, but we got to peek inside. We'll have to come back there at some point. I have a hard time not buying everything Kylie points out. I know she isn't asking for everything she touches, she's just admiring. But I so badly want to give her anything she wants. She deserves it all. It is her birthday, after all. The biggest thing holding me back is the fact that I'll have to carry it all around until we make our way back to my car. And I still have a performance tonight.

By four, we are ready to have a light pre-dinner and then head to the studio. Having a full meal before dancing is not a good idea, especially when we will have an audience. We find a vegan restaurant and each pick something that has enough protein to keep us going but not so many carbs that we will be ready for a nap. Maybe tomorrow.

We get to the studio, and there are people setting up already there. The others from our class are going to have one or two paired dances each, and then there's another adult class doing some Jazz after us. Most of the audience are friends, family, and the occasional couple out for a date night. As I head back to get changed, I see a familiar car parked right outside of the building. If he is going to try to come in here tonight, he's not going to recognize the one he let get away.

Luca

Chapter Thirty-Six

KYLIE

BLUEBERRY LEMON COLD BREW

Social Post: Here we go. Happy birthday to me and time to dance for our first public performance. #wcs #westcoastswing #birthdaygirl #thirty
Image Description: Selfie with Luca outside the studio we are dancing in tonight.

"I think I'm going to be sick. I can't believe I agreed to this," I tell Stacey as I'm finishing my makeup in the back. Luca and I are set to be the first couple to dance. We are going to open with "SexyBack" and then the other couples will do their dances. And then we have the big finish before the Jazz group comes out. Originally, we were doing the bookend performances so Stacey could introduce us as the newest to the troupe and encourage more adult dancers to give West Coast Swing a try. Now, minutes before we take to the floor, I'm second-guessing the decision.

"You and Luca are flawless in your performances. You're going to do great. This isn't a competition. It's just for fun. That's why you're doing this, right? To have fun?" I nod in agreement. I take a deep breath and apply my lipstick. It's become my signature shade—bright red. And I'm owning it again tonight.

"You really do rock that color, Kylie. I love it on you," one of the other dancers tells me as I snap a quick selfie to send to Luca. It's that moment that I decide I'm ready for a rebrand. Sasha and Ashley have both found their passions and how that ties into their social media presence. And I think I just found mine.

Before I can change my mind, I change my username and post on Instagram.

"Happy birthday to me—if I can do it, you can too. Spending the night dancing and celebrating with my friends. So thankful for each of you who has been a part of the launch of my cozy spaces! In case you needed the reminder like I've needed so much over the last year, it's okay to decide to do something for yourself. For me, that means I'm going to remind myself to wear whatever lipstick makes me happy. Bright, bold, and fun, yes, even at thirty. Own your lipstick, babe. Here's mine. #ownyourlipstick #rebrand #happybirthdaytome"

I never thought I would be the girl in the middle of the dance floor with a partner, our friends watching on. I definitely never imagined having fun doing it. But as Luca meets me at the edge of the hallway, I am filled with immense joy. I am doing something I love, and I have someone by my side cheering me on every step of the way. It may be too early to say that I love him, but I know that I care deeply for him. I am so thankful that our paths crossed to bring us here.

Luca takes my hand and leans in to brush a kiss on my cheek while we wait for things to start and for Stacey to introduce our group. The room is full of people. It's the same space I came to last year with the girls. But this time, I get to be the one dancing. And hopefully, there will be no crazy phone calls this time.

"You look beautiful, Kylie. Are you ready for this?" He whispers while Stacey begins to greet those that have come out tonight.

"As much as I can be. I'll be better once this first dance is done and I have a moment to breathe before the second one. I can't believe this is real life. But I'm ready. Just have the next hour to get through, and then we can enjoy watching the second group before dinner with our friends." I smile up at him and wait for the kiss I know he's going to give me. He keeps it pretty tame since we are in public, but I love that he doesn't shy away from reminding me he's thinking of me. Sometimes with a gentle squeeze of my hand or a kiss on the cheek or a smile from across the room. I know I'm never far from his mind.

A moment later, our music kicks up, and we walk to the center of the floor. Our friends cheer and others around them politely clap. I take a deep breath and focus on the man in front of me. And then I let my body feel the music and fall into step with Luca. We've practiced this so many times, the movements and touches are almost autopilot. I focus on him, not seeing anything around us. I don't want to be distracted, especially since there's a bit of touching involved in this performance. What did you expect with "SexyBack"?

By the time we hit the final pose, we are both laughing and breathing heavily. It's only a three-minute version of the song, but we don't stop moving throughout. We take our bows, and Luca pulls me in for a quick kiss. I smile against his lips, then look for our friends as we make our way to the edge of the floor to watch the rest of our group. My eyes don't find who I'm searching for. They do land on Carter, though. Sitting by himself and not looking happy at what he sees.

I excuse myself and tell Luca I need to grab a drink and make my way to the dressing room. I have about twenty minutes before we are on again, and I can't be watching Carter's glare the whole time. I find my water bottle, take a few sips, and close my eyes to re-center myself. Sasha and Ashley have both taught me some grounding techniques, and I use those now to bring myself back to calm and happy. It's my birthday, and today is going to be everything I need it to be. Carter showing up is not going to derail that plan.

I'm just about to head back to meet Luca when I run into Carter in the hallway. Literally. I take a step back and roll my shoulders, making eye contact with him. I clear my throat and glance around to see if anyone else is present. Of course, there isn't.

"What are you doing here, Carter?" I ask, and I know my tone is accusatory. I don't want him here. He shouldn't be here.

"I wanted to see you dance. And wish you a happy birthday. That's allowed, isn't it?" His tone isn't angry. It's flirty. I don't understand what he's hoping to accomplish here.

"You never came to any of my things when we were together. You actually didn't take any of this seriously at all. I'm pretty sure you were sleeping with someone else on my last birthday. So again, I ask, why are you here?" I cross my arms in front of me, and I hate that it draws his gaze to my chest.

"I messed up, Kylie. And I am so sorry it's taken me this long to realize that. I want you back. I want to try to fix us." He seems genuinely remorseful, which just makes me angrier.

"No, Carter."

"What do you mean, no? I came here to apologize. Do you think it was easy for me to show up here tonight? With all your friends and the guy you're living with. To see another man touch you. But I did. I showed up. I need you, Kylie. Don't throw away all those years because of a misunderstanding. I even kept the room just how you had it." He reaches for me, and I take a step back.

"Did you really think that you coming here and offering a little apology would be enough? Carter, you didn't just hurt me. You broke me. There isn't going to be a second chance. You had your second chance. Back when I asked you if you were seeing someone else and you told me that you weren't. Back when you had the chance to be there for me and support me. Back when you didn't have to lie to me or embarrass me in front of our friends and coworkers. You had your chance." I go to walk around him, but he grabs my wrist to stop me. Oh, that is so not going to happen.

"And what about Chelsea? Tired of her already?" He has the audacity to look hurt at my question.

"She's, um, she's back with her family for a few weeks." I laugh. Actually laugh out loud. There is a break in the music, so I know everyone in the building probably can hear me. But I don't have it in me to care.

"I will not be the other woman, Carter. I have a man out there who has already made me his everything. And I will not go back to being an afterthought." I start to walk away, to Luca. He's at the end of the hall, smiling. He must have been waiting there to see if I would need him. This time, I handled it okay on my own, though.

"Since you're here, you might as well stay for our last song. I think you'll appreciate it," Luca calls over my shoulder before turning to me. I jump onto my tiptoes to plant a kiss on his lips and then lead him back out to the dance floor.

The music starts, and I turn to face Carter, standing at the edge of the dance floor. His eyes are angry as he sees Luca's hands on my hips. But I don't care. With the opening lines from Meghan Trainor's "Whoops" playing, I start singing, making sure to point to him when I get to the chorus. He messed up. And now everyone else in the studio knows it.

Chapter Thirty-Seven

LUCA

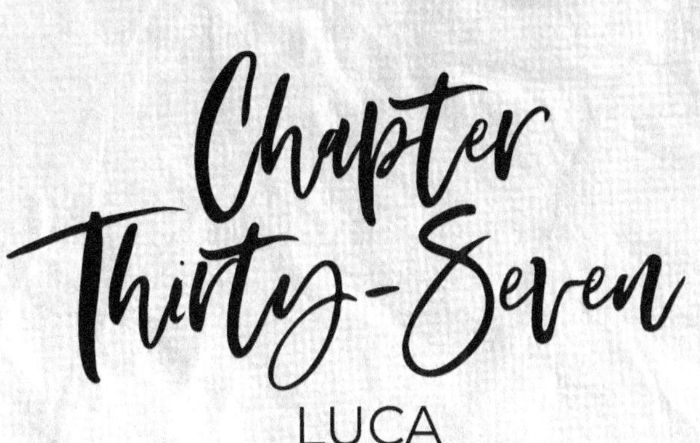

SALTED MAPLE CINNAMON COLD BREW

Social Post: Kylie and I are working on a few new projects together this fall, but not before one more out of state competition. If you are needing some spaces redone, make sure to get on the consultation list. We only have a few more spots this year. #withmyhoneybee #coloradowoodworker

Image Description: Weekly calendar and to do list spread of projects completed and ones we are working on together.

Our first showcase together for Kylie's birthday in April was just the start. After Carter walked out of the studio with every eye on him, we haven't heard from him. We have been able to enjoy our journey, dancing together a few nights a week, creating together in the workshop and office, and growing our relationship. By the time fall rolls around, the two of us have started traveling to competitions and classes across the country.

We aren't masters or professionals, but we have been able to be students in a few classes and workshops led by some of the best teachers in the States.

Since we both have the flexibility of working for ourselves, we decided traveling to an event once a quarter would be our goal, as long as it worked out financially. We have a special event to attend in North Carolina next week, but we are still up in the air about it. Kylie is set to start her cycle any day now, and she still has a rough time the first day or so. If she starts on time, we should be able to make it. But if she's late, we will stay home. That was not an easy conversation for her, but an important one for the two of us to have.

"I don't know if this is ever going to get better. I hate that this is what dictates our travel schedule. You should go, even if I can't." She buries her face in her hands and lets out a groan. I know this frustrates her, and it kills me that I can't fix it. I walk over to sit next to her on the couch and pull her close so I can hold her.

"Kylie, this is what life looks like for us. Not just you, but me, too. When I said I wanted a relationship with you, I knew this was part of it. Flare ups and bad pain days and doctor visits, I get it. I'm here for whatever that looks like. Travel insurance is an automatic add for every plane ticket and hotel reservation, just in case. And I will never resent you for having to change our plans. If we get to go, awesome. If we stay home, we have a few unplanned staycation days. Maybe we can go explore somewhere local if you're feeling better. Or we stay at home and read and try new concoctions to stain wood or something." She laughs at that, and I place a kiss on the top of her head, smelling her signature strawberry scent.

"I love you, Kylie. And I want to spend the rest of my life with you." She sits up quickly and stares at me, holding up a hand to stop me.

"We are not having the marriage and forever conversation yet, Luca. It's been less than a year. And there are some big things we need to discuss first."

"Like what?" I turn her so she's on my lap again. I need to hold her. I start kissing her neck while she thinks.

"Stop trying to distract me." She giggles out as I nip her ear, but I let her go so she can talk. "I can't have kids, Luca. Is that something you are going to be okay with in ten years? Or after Matt and Sasha get married and announce they're expecting? Or Ashley and Marcus? You may be okay with that now, but will you be okay with that when you realize what you missed? What I made you miss?" She is trying so hard to hold back the tears, and I rest my forehead on hers, needing to be as close to her as possible.

"Kylie, I know about your diagnosis. You told me when it happened that you wouldn't be able to conceive or carry a baby. I came to terms with that before I ever told you that I love you. And that hasn't changed. If you decide at some point that you want to adopt or foster, awesome. If you want it to just be the two of us for forever, I'm okay with that too. I just want to be the one who gets to choose the dance for you at every competition."

"Every competition?"

"Every single one."

Kylie ended up starting on time, so we had a few quiet days before we got ready to travel to North Carolina. It is our first time there, so we planned to have a few days to stay in one of the tourist towns after the event. We got to dance with each other and then did a random partner, random song dance during the last day of the event. I got to dance to another Abba song—it's becoming a running joke that I get Abba when it's time for a random match. I got to watch Kylie shine as she danced to "Me Too" by Meghan Trainor. She and her partner had such a good time with it, and I beamed, getting to watch my girl do something that she loves.

Getting to the downtown area that we are staying in, we check into the bed and breakfast and then head out to find somewhere to eat dinner. I already have reservations for the French restaurant by the water, but she doesn't know that. So, she is pleasantly surprised when we arrive at the restaurant with a line out the door and we get ushered inside to a table overlooking the ocean.

"Why do I have the feeling that you set this up before we got here?" she asks as the waiter brings over our drinks and appetizer shortly after we are seated.

"Why do you think I did that?"

"Because we haven't ordered anything. And the line was out the door."

"Well, it is a nice restaurant, so they do a pre-fix menu, so they were going to bring this out regardless." I smirk at her before passing her a small piece of bread so she can sample the escargot.

"Okay…" She trails off once she takes a bite of the food. This place is probably as good as the restaurant in Fort Collins. We haven't had a chance to go back there since our first time, but we talk about it often. I wanted to do something special to mark a year since she got the official diagnosis and started this new chapter. And hopefully to celebrate something else too.

After a meal that mirrored our first French meal back in Colorado, which she quickly picks up on, we walk outside to explore the beach and watch the tide going out before we head back to the bed and breakfast.

"This has been absolutely perfect, Luca. Thank you for making this happen." She turns to look at me, and I hold out my phone.

"Dance with me?"

"Do I get to pick the song this time?"

"You know what you agreed to. I get to pick the music when it's a dance for you." She smiles and concedes. I press play and take her in my arms. And we watch the sun approach the horizon as "Forever" by Chris Brown plays. It's one we've been practicing at home, and while it doesn't translate to the sand really well, the familiarity of the words and movement take over, and we just get to be in each other's arms. As the song finishes, I pull out the small box from my back pocket and get down on one knee in front of the girl of my dreams.

Her hands go to her mouth as she looks down at me. I'm kind of surprised she wasn't expecting this. "Kylie, I love you with everything I have. I want to continue loving you for the rest of my life. Will you let me pick the dances for the rest of our lives? Will you marry me?" I don't get an audible answer, but the squeals and jumps and then the kiss to my lips tell me it's probably in the affirmative. When she slides the marquise yellow diamond ring onto her finger, I couldn't be happier.

Chapter Thirty-Eight

KYLIE

MAPLE PECAN LATTE

Social Post: Dancing on the beach may not be as easy as the studio, but it is a moment I will never forget. I love you, Luca. #dancingtogether #hepicksthemusic #sunsetdances

Image Description: Seashells on the sand next to the tide coming in.

Part of me wanted to wait to announce our engagement until after Matt and Sasha's wedding next month. But Luca pointed out that as long as we don't announce it at their wedding, they would be upset if we didn't tell them right away. He really does make a lot of sense sometimes.

We are waiting on our luggage at the airport when my phone rings. I see that it's Carter, which is confusing. I haven't heard from him since the dance competition on my birthday.

I show the phone to Luca and then answer it.

"Hello?"

"Hey, Kylie. I know it's been a while, so please don't hang up, but I was thinking about you and..." I cut him off before he can say anything else.

"If you are seriously calling me to ask for me to come back again, you are out of your mind. It's not happening, Carter. I need you to stop doing this. I don't want to, but I will block you." He's quiet for a moment, and Luca holds out his hand for my phone. I give it to him because I really am done with Carter.

"Carter, I've been really patient with things, but I'm done with these games you are playing. I don't know what you are trying to do or if you're just lonely when someone isn't at your beck and call twenty-four-seven, but it ends now. I need you to leave a key under the mat. We will be at the apartment in two hours. You better not be there. We are getting the rest of Kylie's things, and then you will delete her number. Do you understand?"

I don't hear what Carter says, but it sounds like he isn't happy with the arrangement.

"We have given you time. We are done giving it. I am done giving it. You have two hours to clean out the dresser. Kylie's tea box better be sitting on the island in the kitchen. If that isn't the case, I will be going to the authorities. Your games have gone on long enough." He hits the end call button and slips the phone into my back pocket.

"Thank you," I whisper to him. "I need this chapter to be done so we can start our lives together."

"Let's go get your stuff, babe."

Walking into that apartment after being gone for six months is such a weird feeling. The space hasn't changed much, but enough to realize that this isn't my home anymore. And it hasn't been my home for a long time, even before I left. I take a moment to look around. This isn't my life anymore. And that's okay. Matt and

Marcus are at lunch with the girls, so we are going to attempt to move my dresser on our own. When I step into the bedroom, my heart drops.

My dresser, the one that had been given to me by my grandmother when I graduated from high school, is in pieces. It looks like he went at it with a sledgehammer. While it was full of rocks. There are shards of wood everywhere, and I can't stop the tears that fall. I walk over to the destroyed piece and pick up the biggest slab that I can find, running my hands over the wood. "My grandfather cut down the tree that was used to make this. It was on their property when he bought the land. This dresser was one of the pieces he made with it."

"You didn't mention that your grandfather was a woodworker." I hear Luca behind me and force myself to get the words out.

"I think it's one of those things that I thought I told you but apparently didn't. I remember trying to tell Carter the story of this piece, but he was never interested. So, I didn't think it was important. I guess he didn't think it was important. I'm sorry I didn't give you the chance to listen." Luca comes up beside me and starts picking up pieces of the destroyed dresser, placing them in a box. Where he found a box, I have no idea.

"What are you doing?"

"I may not be able to salvage all of this or fully recreate what your grandfather made, but I can do my best." I love this man so much. I lean down to kiss him and start picking up pieces of broken wood. This day just keeps getting better because I manage to give myself a massive splinter.

"Why don't you go try to clean that up, and I'll finish here. I'd like to get you home, run you a nice bath, and have a quiet night on the couch."

"That sounds perfect." I walk into the bathroom and open the medicine cabinet to find a pair of tweezers. I look a bit more in the cabinet to find a bottle of alcohol. I am not using this on my hand until it is fully sanitized. After getting the splinter out, I root around for a bandage and find one pretty easily. Of course, it's bright pink with martini glasses on it. Real classy, Chelsea. I turn to throw the wrapper in the trash, only to find a pregnancy test at the bottom of the canister. And it's positive.

Part of me hopes it was either Sasha's or Ashley's. Maybe they were the ones to come back to the apartment to get my stuff and used it. That could be a possibility, right? Luca sits next to me while I call the girls, willing it to be true. It has to be one of them. I don't know why, but the thought that Carter is going to be a dad, and it isn't going to be with me, hurt. Even after repeatedly telling him that I didn't want him back, part of me is still hurt that Chelsea is going to get to live what I thought my happily ever after was going to look like.

After a phone call with Ashley, it's confirmed that the test isn't theirs. "I don't know why I'm so upset by this." I lean my head on Luca's shoulder and let the tears fall.

"Even though you are confident in your decision not to be with him, you envisioned a life together. And he repeatedly told you he didn't want kids. It's okay that this hurts, Kylie. You're allowed to be upset or angry or whatever else you're feeling." He places a kiss on my forehead and turns so he can look in my eyes. "Can I take you home now, please?"

"Yes. I don't want to be here anymore."

The next day, I pull out a notebook that Sasha gave me last year when they launched Pink Every Day officially. We had gone for a lunch with Ashley and Tilly and had all written down ten things we wished for our future selves. Looking at that list now, I realize it's time to make a new one.

1. I wish I am content with the life I have lived over the last ten years
2. I wish I found something that brings me joy
3. I wish I found contentment in motherhood
4. I wish I found other mom friends to connect with
5. I wish I danced

6. I wish I traveled to the beach at least once
7. I wish I took a chance on something scary
8. I wish I have a space that is mine
9. I wish I take time to read just because
10. I wish I am happily married

As I look over the list, I let the tears fall, knowing that some of these aren't going to happen. I take a moment to cross off three and four and write something new.

3. I wish I create a space for joy for my friends and family
4. I wish I celebrate every success of those my friends and family

And I know in my heart that every single one of those wishes will come true.

Chapter Thirty-Nine

LUCA

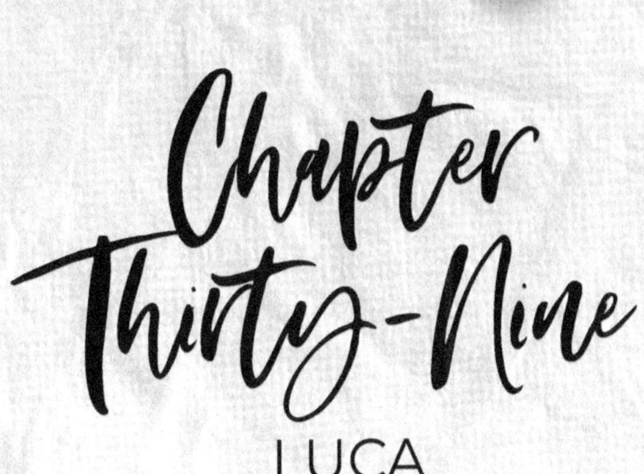

BROWN SUGAR CARDAMOM LATTE

Social Post: Back from our trip and I'm back in my workshop. Using pieces that were once a part of something else to create something new can be challenging. These boards and splinters used to be a dresser. Time to see what we can create for their new story. #coloradowoodworker #reclaimedwood #newproject

Image Description: Boards laid out on my workbench along with my sander.

Getting home from that trip was supposed to be bliss and settling into our own version of happily ever after. I shouldn't have been surprised over what Carter pulled though. That man has done everything in his power to hurt the woman he claimed to love. As I sit in my workshop, looking over the shattered boards and stripped hardware, I give myself a moment to be angry. Angry at the way he treated her. Angry at the fact that Chelsea and Carter are going to have a baby. Angry at the thought that Kylie thinks she wasn't enough, that she isn't enough. I was honest when I told her I don't need kids to be happy. And I know she believes that. But being told and being shown are two different things.

"Guess I'll have to show her." I mumble to myself as I pull out my sketchbook and start planning what this piece is going to be for my honeybee.

A week later, I'm setting up the new piece of furniture in the downstairs family room when I hear Kylie opening the front door.

"I'll be right up," I holler up the stairs before anchoring the last bolt in place. I make sure there are no nails on the ground and take a second to admire the piece in the room before I jog up the stores to see my girl. She's standing at the dining room table, fussing over a gift bag. A baby gift bag.

"What's all this?" I ask as I come closer to her and place a kiss on her cheek. She's been quiet since the Carolina trip. And I don't blame her, but I hope she is starting to come out of the dark place she's been in since the incident at the apartment.

"I'm ready to say goodbye." She whispers down at the bag, arranging the pretty pink tissue paper so it's picture perfect.

"Goodbye to what, Kylie?" I don't want to spook her with my questions, but I honestly don't know what she's getting at here.

"Goodbye to what might have been. To me being a mom. To that version of a happily ever after together. Goodbye to Carter and that chapter of my life. I don't think I can say I am fully content with where we are until I say goodbye. And this is the only way I know how to do that." She pushes the bag over to me so I can look inside.

In the bag is a bunch of products I recognize from a recent campaign for Pink Every Day. It's a maternity and pregnancy product bundle from a company out of Boulder. And a beautiful notebook too.

"It's for Chelsea. I just want to drop it off at the restaurant and be done with it. I know it sounds weird and 'why am I spending money on the girl that ruined what I had' but I need to do this." I place another kiss on her cheek as I put the tissue paper back in place.

"When do you want to go?"

KYLIE

I never wanted to be back in this place. But walking into the restaurant knowing that it's my last time feels right. I'm closing a chapter. And then I'll be able to fully step into this new phase of life with Luca, my partner, my fiancé, and soon to be, my husband. I hold the bag of butters and lotions and candles for Chelsea as I make my way into the space. It's quiet for a Thursday afternoon, but I quickly make eye contact with the blonde behind the bar. I take a deep breath and walk over to her, a pleasant smile on my face.

"I wanted to give this to you, and wish you both congratulations." I pass her the bag and she just stares at me.

"What is it?" Chelsea asks as she reaches for the bag.

"A few products that I thought you might enjoy. Sasha worked with this brand a few months ago and they get really good reviews. Sometimes the mom is forgotten when a new baby is on the way and I wanted you to know that you are important too. And I wish you well." Luca places his hand reassuringly on my hip, letting me get out what I need to say, and telling me with that gesture that he's here for me.

"Um, thank you. Did Carter tell you? We only just found out."

"I saw the test in the trash last week when I came to pick up the last of my things. I got a splinter trying to pick up the shattered wood and saw it. I promise I wasn't snooping."

"Why are you doing this? I mean, thank you, I appreciate it, but I don't understand." She takes the bag and sets it on the counter behind her, but not before taking a peek inside to see what's in there. Probably making sure it's actually what I said it was and not just garbage.

"My happily ever after doesn't look like what I imagined it to be when I graduated college or even when Carter and I moved in together. I'm learning to redefine what success looks like to me and how I find my contentment. I may not get to be a mom in the traditional sense, but I am loved, and I am adored. I am happy. And I wasn't happy when I was with Carter, not really, anyway. And looking back on things, I see that now. But I want you to find your happiness, with Carter, and with this new little one." I take a deep breath and glance to the ceiling for a moment, staving off the tears that threaten to fall down my face.

"I want to have a part in your happily ever after. And maybe that's this bag of things for you. But that's my part in your story. I don't want to be the one that you look back on in twenty years and have horrible thoughts about. That's not who I am." Chelsea nods at me and I return the gesture. Luca laces his fingers with mine and we head out the door.

I'm on autopilot the entire way home. I don't register anything that passes by or the music on the radio. I don't cry. I don't feel. I just am. Luca parks and comes around to open my door. The smile he gives me feels like home. And as he leads me inside, I know I did the right thing. She may turn around and throw the present away. But I'm happy with where life has led me.

"I know that was hard. I need you to know I am so proud of you." Luca leans in to kiss me once we are inside and I let myself settle into his arms, being held, being cared for. "Do you want to see what I made for you?"

"Always," I beam up at him and have to stop myself from hurrying him along. He's been in the workshop for the last week with the broken pieces from my dresser and I can't wait to see what he came up with. I'm not able to stop the tears from falling when I get downstairs.

There are three pieces completed along the wall. All of them have some of the original wood, but I also recognize colors in each of them that match the original bookends that Luca made me – his first project gifted to me. A combination of the old with the new.

The first is a chest, big enough for blankets and a sweater or two. It's up against the base of the couch, resting open to show the variety of fabrics inside. The second is a bookcase of sorts, but it looks like an oversized honeycomb. It's anchored to the wall and has a mix of planters, books, and a honeybee figurine in the open spots. And the last item is a shelf. It's empty, except for a photo of the two of us on the beach and a shell that we each took home to remember our dance together there.

"They're perfect, Luca." I turn in his arms and kiss him again. He always knows exactly what I need and he was right again with this.

"I wasn't going to be able to recreate what your grandfather made for you. But I wanted you to have things that reminded you of him and me, whenever you looked at them. Something to keep you cozy and safe, something to show off your latest project, and something to make you smile. You deserve every bit of happiness, Kylie. And I am honored that you allow me to have a piece of that alongside you."

"Thank you. So much." I look over the items again and then take my phone out of my pocket to rest on the honeycomb piece. "I have one more request for you tonight, though."

"Name it."

"Dance with me?"

The End

Epilogue One

KYLIE

There's something about weddings. Especially when it's to celebrate your best friend with the love of her life. As I watch Sasha and Matt enjoy their first dance, I can't help but tear up. I have gone through life with her for the last ten years, and now she gets to celebrate this brand-new chapter with the man who would do anything for her. The party is small, there are about fifty of us at the reception, and I think I know everyone here. The ceremony was beautiful, outside, with the changing colors of the aspen trees in the background.

As their song finishes, Jonathan, who's DJing, takes the mic. Instead of calling everyone to come join them like I thought was on the schedule, he asks for Luca and me to come up. Luca takes the mic and looks at the group here tonight.

"I promise I am not taking away from these two. Matt asked

we do this for you all. Many of you know that Kylie and I are part of the local West Coast Swing dance group. So we are opening up the invitation; if you want to learn some basics and enjoy a dance with us, you are welcome to do so. Jonathan, play something fun. Welcome to dance class, everyone."

The crowd laughs and claps, and many of them join us on the dance floor. The next twenty minutes are filled with so much fun. This is why I dance. And I love that this is what the rest of my life is going to look like.

Kylie

You are cordially invited
to the wedding of

Epilogue Two

TILLY

I love weddings. Sasha has become such a dear friend over the last few years, and I love that she gets to have her fairy tale moment with her best friend. I spend way too much time laughing on the dance floor with Ashley and finally bow out once I notice most of the group has called it a night. I sit at the table and slide my shoes off. My heels are super comfortable, but dancing in them for three hours probably was not the best choice.

I pull out my phone to see if there's anything that needs to be dealt with. Between my senior year at CSU and getting ready to go full-time with Pink Every Day in just a few months, life is busy. I know I'm technically not working right now, but social media never turns off. I manage the pages now that Sasha is doing CEO stuff like the boss babe she is. I post the approved wedding announcement from earlier and then slide my phone back into my purse. But not before a text comes through that I do not have the energy for tonight.

Sperm Donor: You and your mother have been gone long enough. It's time to come home. Jason is expecting you home for Christmas, and you have an engagement party to plan. We had an agreement, Tilly. Don't make me come get you.

Tilly: What are the chances that we can amend that agreement?

Sperm Donor: Unless you plan on getting married to someone of equal caliber before December, I expect you home and ready to comply by December 5th.

Tilly: Okay.

Now I just have two and a half months to find myself a husband.

TILLY'S STORY COMING
fall 2025

Subscribe to Nikki Grant's newsletter to be the first to learn about release dates and more.

Also, there may be an extended epilogue from Kylie and Luca coming soon too!

OTHER BOOKS BY NIKKI GRANT

MAKEUP AND MOCHAS

The Funnel to You
The Man for You
The Dance for You
The Ride for You (Fall 2025)
Holiday Novella (Winter 2025)

Our Journeys to Love (Winter 2025)

Check nikkigrantwrites.com for other updates on future projects.

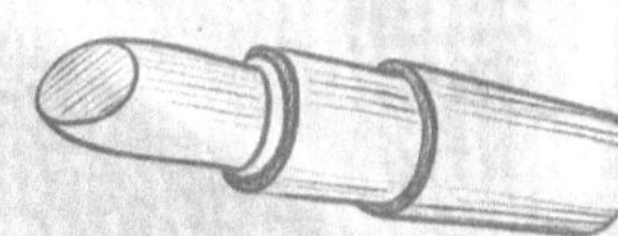

ACKNOWLEDGEMENTS 

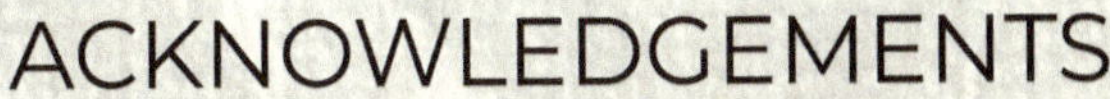

Writing The End for this book was more cathartic than I thought it would be. So much of my own story is woven in these pages and I hope that there may be some things inside that spoke to you as well.

To my husband, thank you for being by my side through the negative pregnancy tests, the tears, and the appointments. I am so thankful that we get to do life together, and that we have the opportunity to parent together too. I love that I get to be your honeybee.

Bookish Bubbly thank you for helping with promotion and being a sounding board with so many parts of this story.

Charly, you killed it with this cover as always!

Katie and Spice Me Up Editing - thank you for helping make this the best it could be!

Chris and Eric - I am so glad I got to work with you for the cover photo for this project. Eric, you were who I saw as Luca when I got to meet you last year, and I am so glad it worked to have you as the model!

Amy, Jamie, Bethany, John, Elizabeth, Alyssa, Teia, Teanna - thank you for your support and help in the editing stages. I appreciate each of you and can't wait to work on Tilly's story with you!

ARC readers, you all are amazing and I cannot thank you enough for the help in the early reviews and promotion of this book.

Jamie, this one's for you. OW drama, the fish pin, the Casper quote, and a few other little things in Kylie's story are my nods to you. Thank you for all of your help and inspiration in the writing process. I can't thank you enough for all of your help over the last year. Your books are some of my favorites, and I hope the little things I put in here to hint at your characters and books are done well.